STAR TREK
THE NEXT GENERATION ®

THE GORN CRISIS

Written by
Kevin J. Anderson and Rebecca Moesta

Painted by
Igor Kordey

Lettered by
Richard Starkings and Comicraft's
Albert Deschesne ™

Designed by
Alex Sinclair

Edited by
Jeff Mariotte

STAR TREK: THE NEXT GENERATION — THE GORN CRISIS. January, 2001. Published by WildStorm Productions,
an imprint of DC Comics under exclusive license from Paramount Pictures Corporation.
Editorial Offices: 7910 Ivanhoe St., #438, La Jolla, CA 92037. Copyright © 2001 Paramount Pictures. All Rights Reserved.
STAR TREK and all related marks are trademarks of Paramount Pictures. DC Comics authorized user.
Any similarities to persons living or dead are purely coincidental.
PRINTED IN CANADA. ISBN# 1-56389-754-7
DC Comics. A division of Warner Bros.—A Time Warner Entertainment Company

DEDICATIONS

This book is for Greg Smith and Randy Futor, two lost friends and Star Trek fans, who always enjoyed good times and good science fiction.
REBECCA MOESTA AND KEVIN J. ANDERSON

This one is for two Franks, Hampson and Bellamy, who created the best sf comic ever — *Dan Dare*, in the fifties and early sixties. Thanks to them I learned to draw, read, and write and decided to be a comic artist when I was four. Both of them were Brits, both of them artistic geniuses, and both of them died long ago.
IGOR KORDEY

ACKNOWLEDGMENTS

With special appreciation for Jeff Mariotte at WildStorm, for choosing us for this project and for his enthusiasm and confidence every step of the way, and Paula Block at Paramount for helping us navigate the waters of the approval process and helping us to remain true to the letter and the spirit of the Star Trek universe.
REBECCA MOESTA AND KEVIN J. ANDERSON

My greatest "thank you" to my girls Andrea, Rosa, Vilena and Rita for giving me their love and endless tolerance. Thanks to Kevin for letting me interfere — a very nice experience doing real teamwork with the big shot. Thanks to Jeff for being quite a peculiar editor — a man of few words who always answers the phone calls and always does what he promises to do.
IGOR KORDEY

JENETTE KAHN President & Editor-in-Chief PAUL LEVITZ Executive Vice President & Publisher
JIM LEE Editorial Director — WildStorm JOHN NEE VP & General Manager — WildStorm
SCOTT DUNBIER Group Editor JEFF MARIOTTE Editor RICHARD BRUNING VP - Creative Director
PATRICK CALDON VP — Finance & Operations DOROTHY CROUCH VP — Licensed Publishing
TERRI CUNNINGHAM VP — Managing Editor JOEL EHRLICH Senior VP — Advertising & Promotions
ALISON GILL Exec. Director — Manufacturing LILLIAN LASERSON VP & General Counsel
BOB WAYNE VP — Direct Sales

"ONE GENERATION AFTER ANOTHER, THE RULERS OF GORN HAVE BEEN NURTURED..."

"SECURE IN THEIR POWER... PAMPERED..."

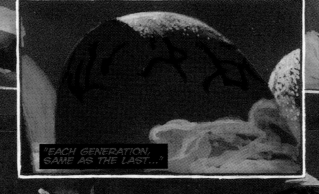

"EACH GENERATION, SAME AS THE LAST..."

"WEAK AS THE LAST!"

SPDLKKT

"THE FEDERATION DEFEATED US ONCE. WE HAVE ALLOWED THAT DEFEAT, LONG AGO, TO KEEP US SUBMISSIVE."

"BUT NO LONGER!"

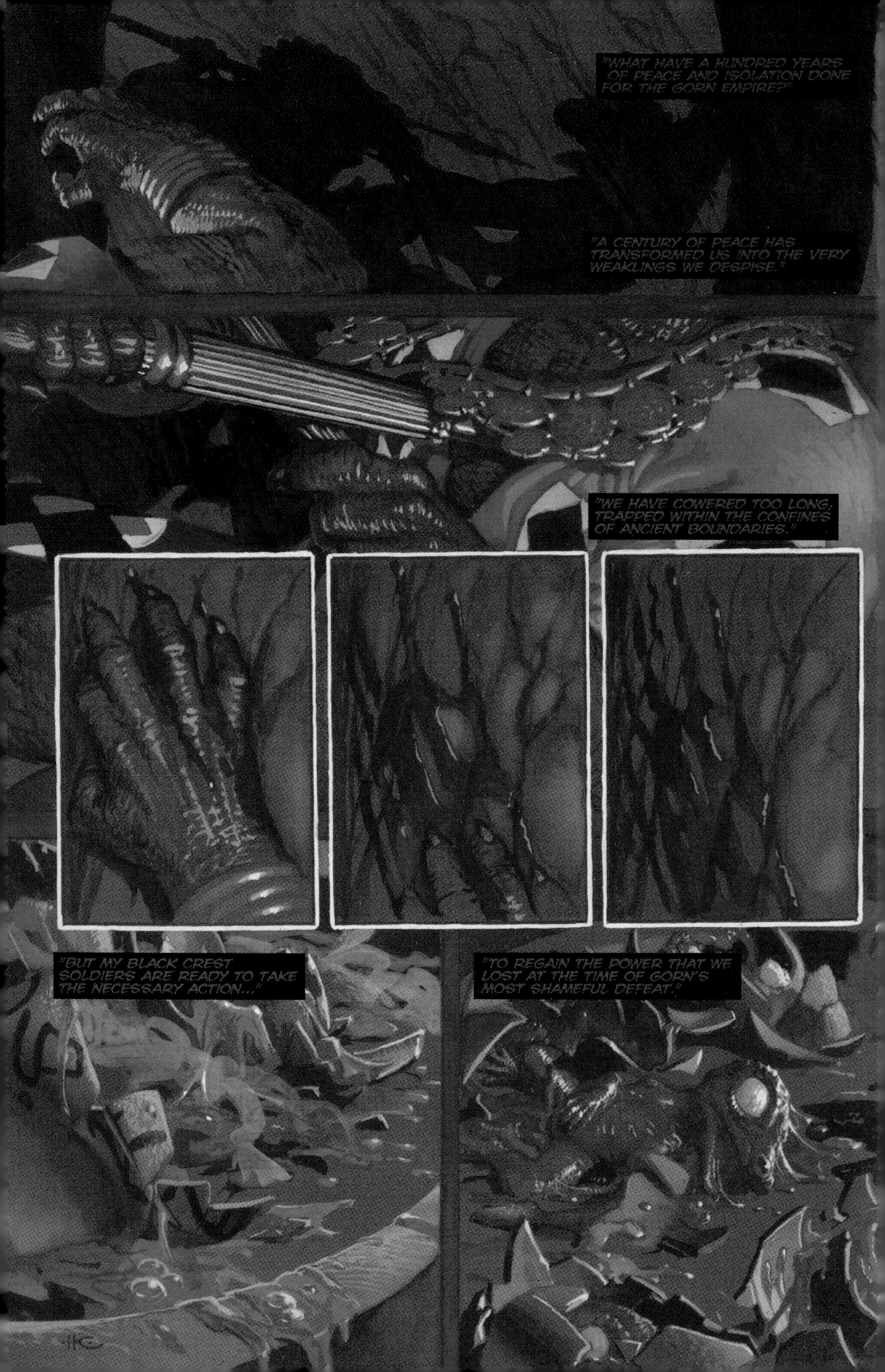
"WHAT HAVE A HUNDRED YEARS OF PEACE AND ISOLATION DONE FOR THE GORN EMPIRE?"
"A CENTURY OF PEACE HAS TRANSFORMED US INTO THE VERY WEAKLINGS WE DESPISE."
"WE HAVE COWERED TOO LONG, TRAPPED WITHIN THE CONFINES OF ANCIENT BOUNDARIES."
"BUT MY BLACK CREST SOLDIERS ARE READY TO TAKE THE NECESSARY ACTION..."
"TO REGAIN THE POWER THAT WE LOST AT THE TIME OF GORN'S MOST SHAMEFUL DEFEAT."

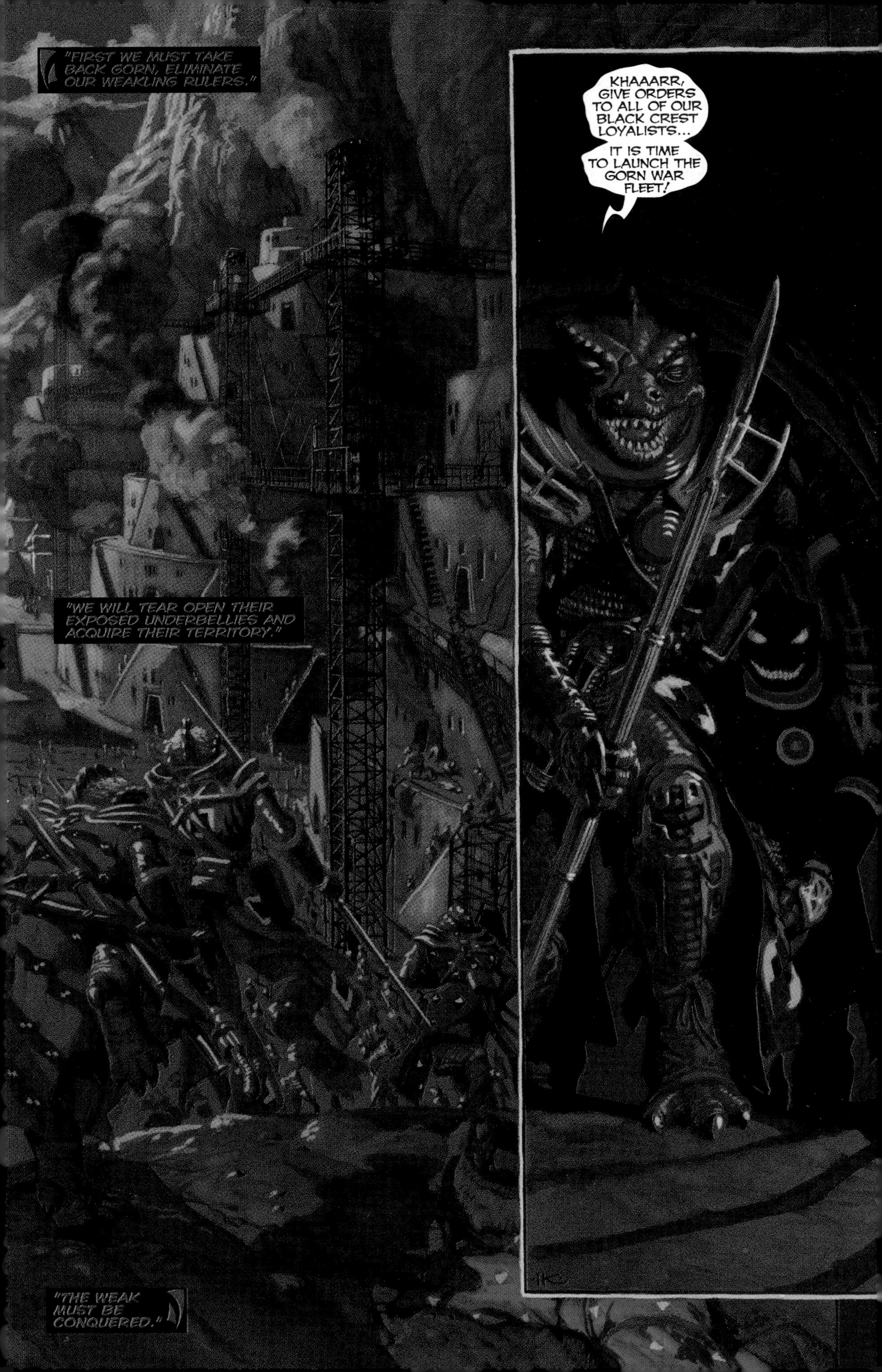
"FIRST WE MUST TAKE BACK GORN, ELIMINATE OUR WEAKLING RULERS."
KHAAARR, GIVE ORDERS TO ALL OF OUR BLACK CREST LOYALISTS...
IT IS TIME TO LAUNCH THE GORN WAR FLEET!
"WE WILL TEAR OPEN THEIR EXPOSED UNDERBELLIES AND ACQUIRE THEIR TERRITORY."
"THE WEAK MUST BE CONQUERED."

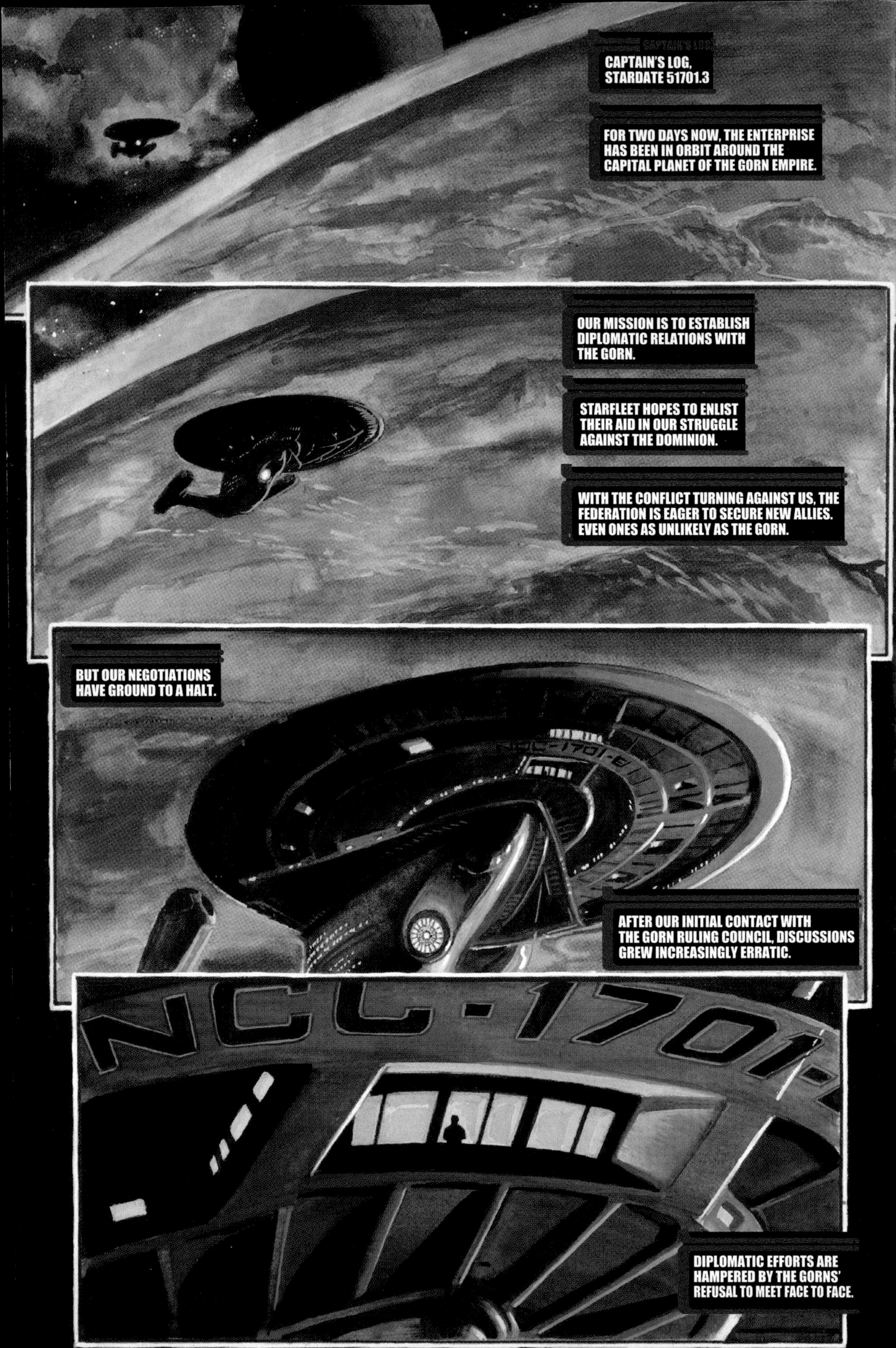
CAPTAIN'S LOG, STARDATE 51701.3
FOR TWO DAYS NOW, THE ENTERPRISE HAS BEEN IN ORBIT AROUND THE CAPITAL PLANET OF THE GORN EMPIRE.
OUR MISSION IS TO ESTABLISH DIPLOMATIC RELATIONS WITH THE GORN.
STARFLEET HOPES TO ENLIST THEIR AID IN OUR STRUGGLE AGAINST THE DOMINION.
WITH THE CONFLICT TURNING AGAINST US, THE FEDERATION IS EAGER TO SECURE NEW ALLIES. EVEN ONES AS UNLIKELY AS THE GORN.
BUT OUR NEGOTIATIONS HAVE GROUND TO A HALT.
AFTER OUR INITIAL CONTACT WITH THE GORN RULING COUNCIL, DISCUSSIONS GREW INCREASINGLY ERRATIC.
DIPLOMATIC EFFORTS ARE HAMPERED BY THE GORNS' REFUSAL TO MEET FACE TO FACE.

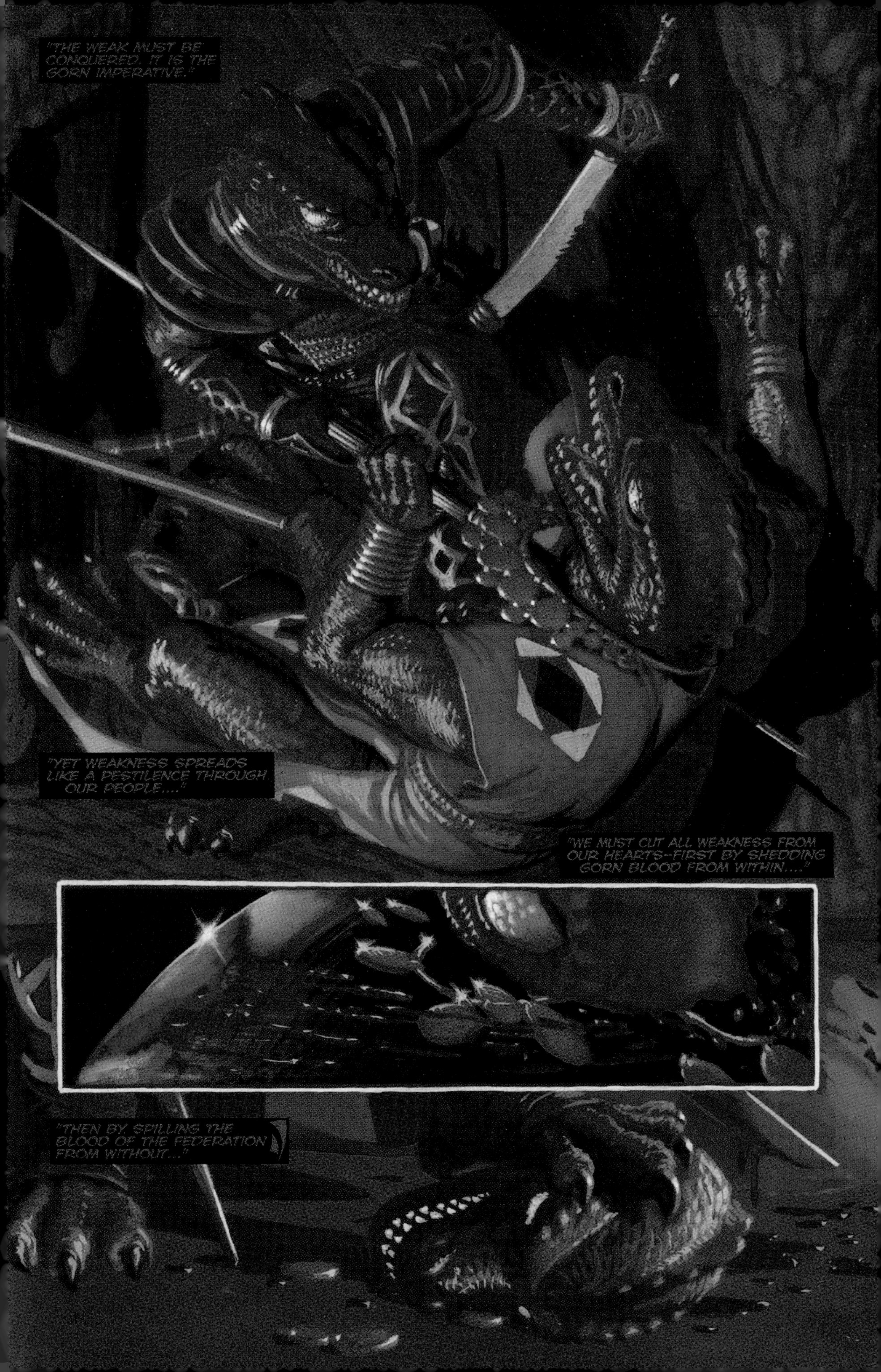
"THE WEAK MUST BE CONQUERED. IT IS THE GORN IMPERATIVE."
"YET WEAKNESS SPREADS LIKE A PESTILENCE THROUGH OUR PEOPLE...."
"WE MUST CUT ALL WEAKNESS FROM OUR HEARTS--FIRST BY SHEDDING GORN BLOOD FROM WITHIN...."
"THEN BY SPILLING THE BLOOD OF THE FEDERATION FROM WITHOUT..."

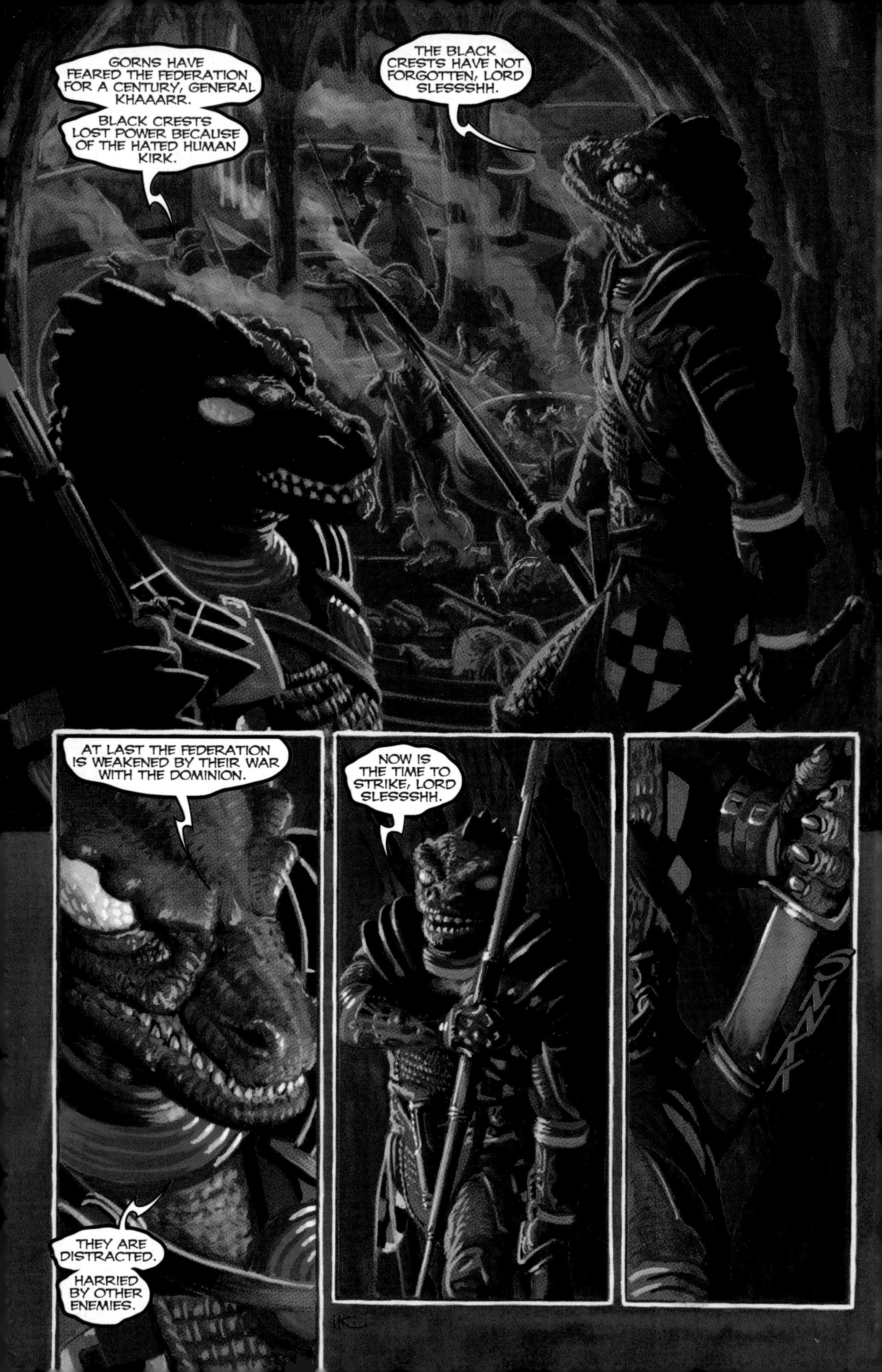
GORNS HAVE FEARED THE FEDERATION FOR A CENTURY, GENERAL KHAAARR.
BLACK CRESTS LOST POWER BECAUSE OF THE HATED HUMAN KIRK.
THE BLACK CRESTS HAVE NOT FORGOTTEN, LORD SLESSSHH.
AT LAST THE FEDERATION IS WEAKENED BY THEIR WAR WITH THE DOMINION.
THEY ARE DISTRACTED.
HARRIED BY OTHER ENEMIES.
NOW IS THE TIME TO STRIKE, LORD SLESSSHH.
SNIKK

MOST DISCONCERTING IS THAT, AS OF 0500 HOURS, WE LOST ALL CONTACT WITH THE RULING COUNCIL.

THE FEDERATION'S HISTORICAL EXPERIENCE WITH THE GORN HAS NEVER BEEN CHARACTERIZED AS FRIENDLY...

YET REPORTS FROM OUR OUTPOST ON CESTUS III, ATTACKED A CENTURY AGO, INDICATE THAT THE GORN HAVE CEASED ALL ATTEMPTS AT EXPANSION...

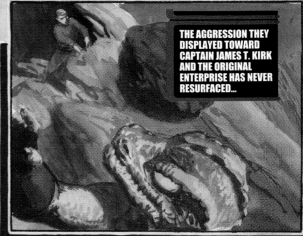

THE AGGRESSION THEY DISPLAYED TOWARD CAPTAIN JAMES T. KIRK AND THE ORIGINAL ENTERPRISE HAS NEVER RESURFACED...

THE FEDERATION BELIEVES THAT THIS DEMONSTRATES A READINESS ON THE PART OF THE GORN TO ACCEPT THEIR PLACE IN GALACTIC SOCIETY.

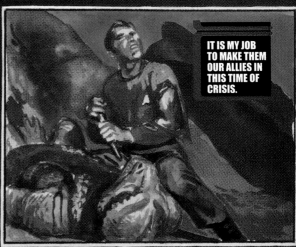

IT IS MY JOB TO MAKE THEM OUR ALLIES IN THIS TIME OF CRISIS.

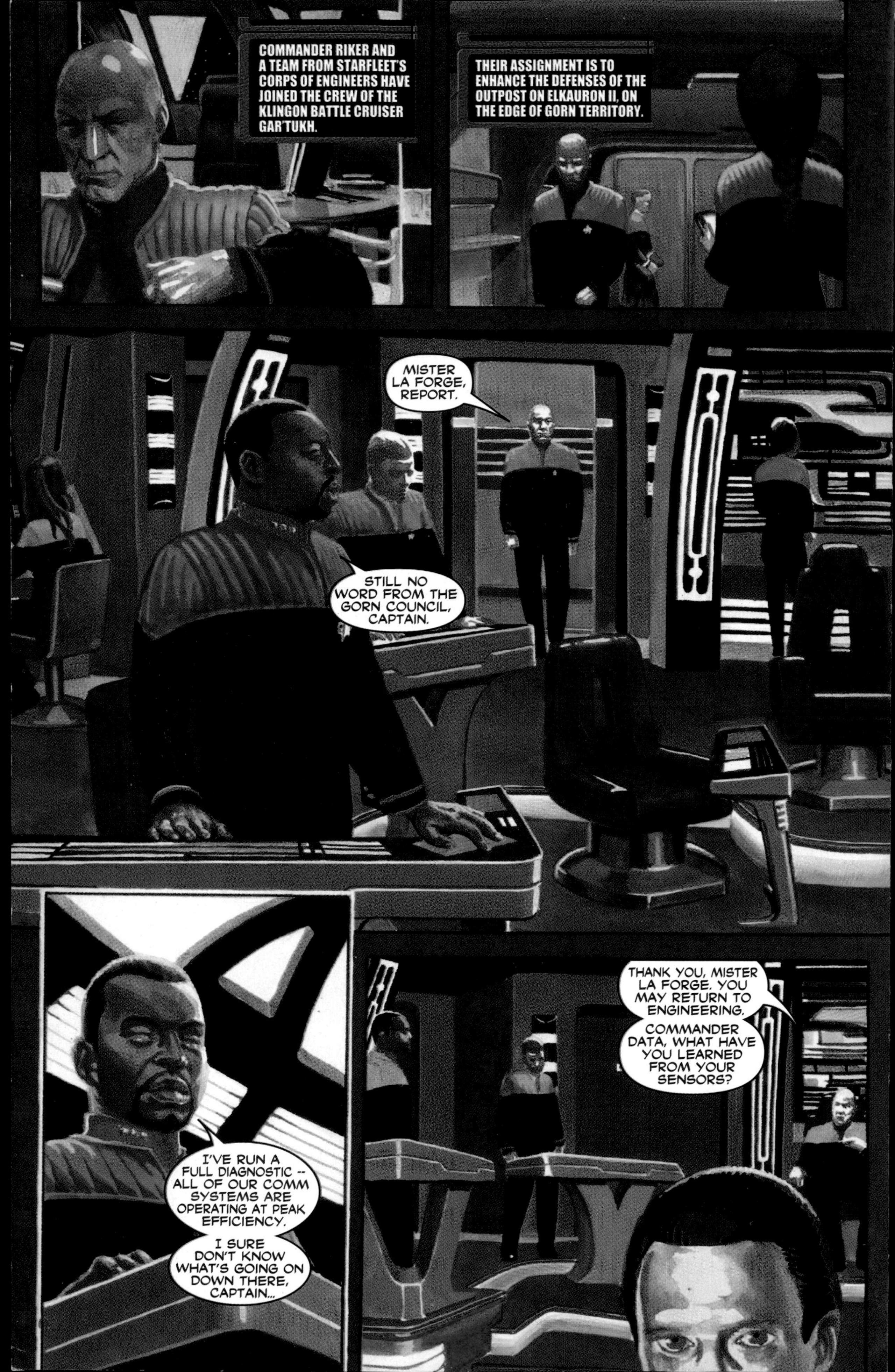
COMMANDER RIKER AND A TEAM FROM STARFLEET'S CORPS OF ENGINEERS HAVE JOINED THE CREW OF THE KLINGON BATTLE CRUISER GAR'TUKH.
THEIR ASSIGNMENT IS TO ENHANCE THE DEFENSES OF THE OUTPOST ON ELKAURON II, ON THE EDGE OF GORN TERRITORY.
MISTER LA FORGE, REPORT.
STILL NO WORD FROM THE GORN COUNCIL, CAPTAIN.
I'VE RUN A FULL DIAGNOSTIC -- ALL OF OUR COMM SYSTEMS ARE OPERATING AT PEAK EFFICIENCY.
I SURE DON'T KNOW WHAT'S GOING ON DOWN THERE, CAPTAIN...
THANK YOU, MISTER LA FORGE. YOU MAY RETURN TO ENGINEERING.
COMMANDER DATA, WHAT HAVE YOU LEARNED FROM YOUR SENSORS?

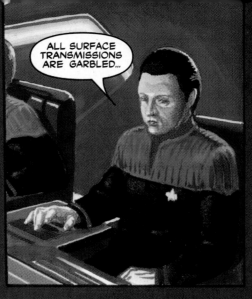

I HAVE BEEN ATTEMPTING TO TAP INTO GROUND-BASED BROADCASTS, CAPTAIN.

ALL SURFACE TRANSMISSIONS ARE GARBLED...

SENSORS DETECT NUMEROUS SMALL-SCALE EXPLOSIONS.

"COMING UP OVER CAPITAL CITY NOW, CAPTAIN.

"WILDFIRES ARE SPREADING IN URBAN AREAS."

ALL EVIDENCE POINTS TO CIVIL UNREST, SIR.

THAT SEEMS TO BE AN UNDERSTATEMENT, MR. DATA.

THEN PERHAPS WE'LL FINALLY GET SOME ANSWERS...

ON SCREEN, ENSIGN.

CAPTAIN, WE'RE RECEIVING A TRANSMISSION...
IT'S FROM THE GORN COUNCIL CHAMBER.

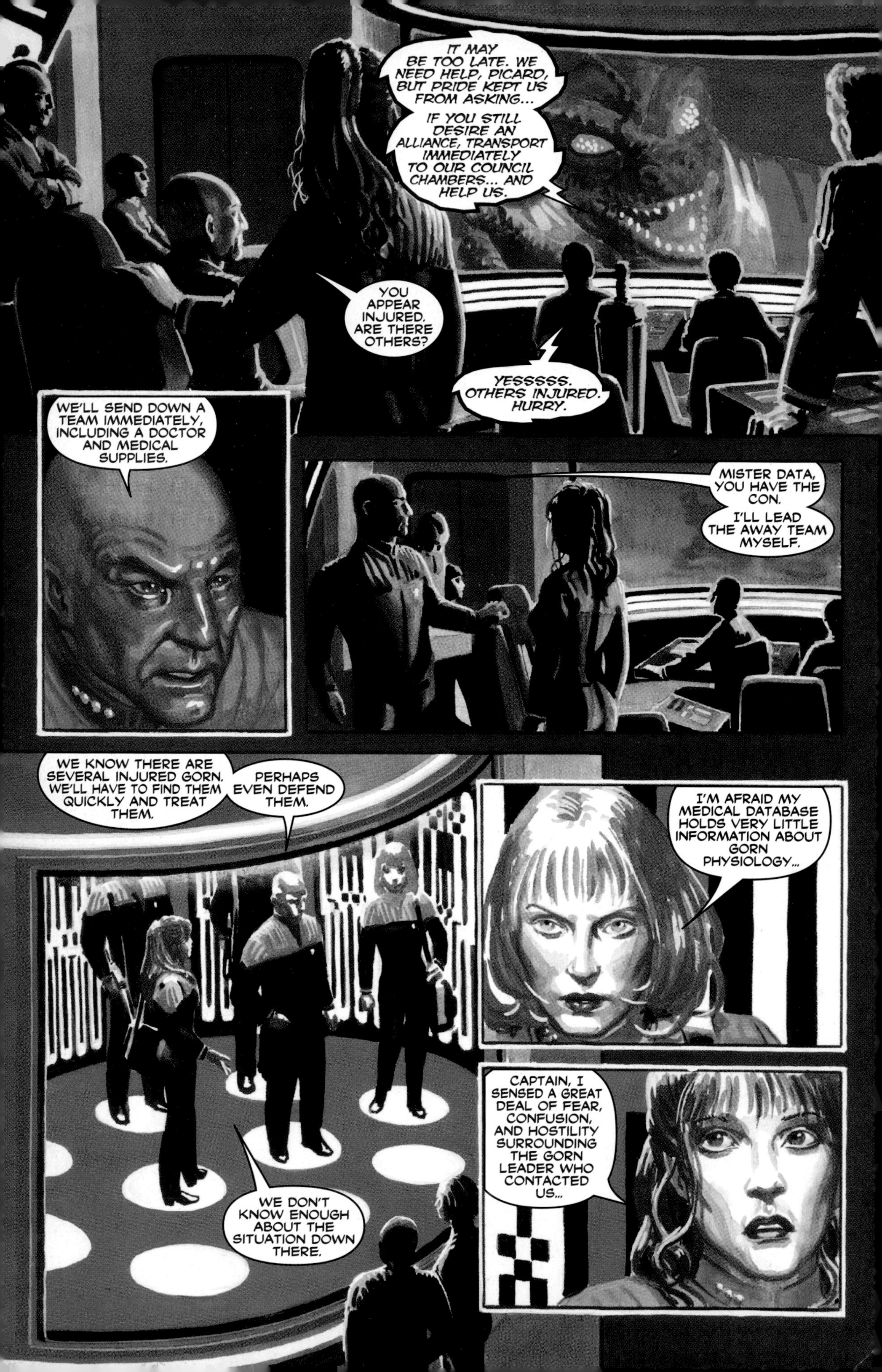
IT MAY BE TOO LATE. WE NEED HELP, PICARD, BUT PRIDE KEPT US FROM ASKING...
IF YOU STILL DESIRE AN ALLIANCE, TRANSPORT IMMEDIATELY TO OUR COUNCIL CHAMBERS... AND HELP US.
YOU APPEAR INJURED. ARE THERE OTHERS?
YESSSSS. OTHERS INJURED. HURRY.
WE'LL SEND DOWN A TEAM IMMEDIATELY, INCLUDING A DOCTOR AND MEDICAL SUPPLIES.
MISTER DATA, YOU HAVE THE CON.
I'LL LEAD THE AWAY TEAM MYSELF.
WE KNOW THERE ARE SEVERAL INJURED GORN. WE'LL HAVE TO FIND THEM QUICKLY AND TREAT THEM.
PERHAPS EVEN DEFEND THEM.
I'M AFRAID MY MEDICAL DATABASE HOLDS VERY LITTLE INFORMATION ABOUT GORN PHYSIOLOGY...
WE DON'T KNOW ENOUGH ABOUT THE SITUATION DOWN THERE.
CAPTAIN, I SENSED A GREAT DEAL OF FEAR, CONFUSION, AND HOSTILITY SURROUNDING THE GORN LEADER WHO CONTACTED US...

UNDERSTOOD. WE MUST EXERCISE ALL DUE CAUTION.
ENERGIZE.
IT APPEARS WE HAVE ARRIVED TOO LATE.

ELKAURON II, KLINGON CRUISER GAR'TUKH

KLINGON AND FEDERATION COOPERATIVE WORK CREW...

...ASSIGNED TO DELBLAD FORTRESS WITH ORDERS TO RESTORE THE OUTPOST TO BATTLE READINESS...

IN PREPARATION FOR AN ALLIANCE WITH THE GORN, AND AS AN OBSERVATION POINT FOR DOMINION ACTIVITY IN THIS SECTOR.

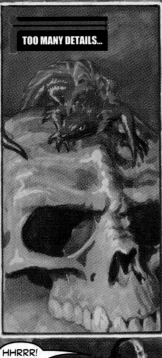

TOO MANY DETAILS...

BEEP!

TOO FAR FROM ACTION...

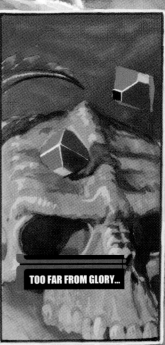

TOO FAR FROM GLORY...

HHRRR! MISSED AGAIN!

OUT OF THE WAY! MY THROW. YOU COULDN'T HIT THE EYE OF A KOLLA DRAGON.

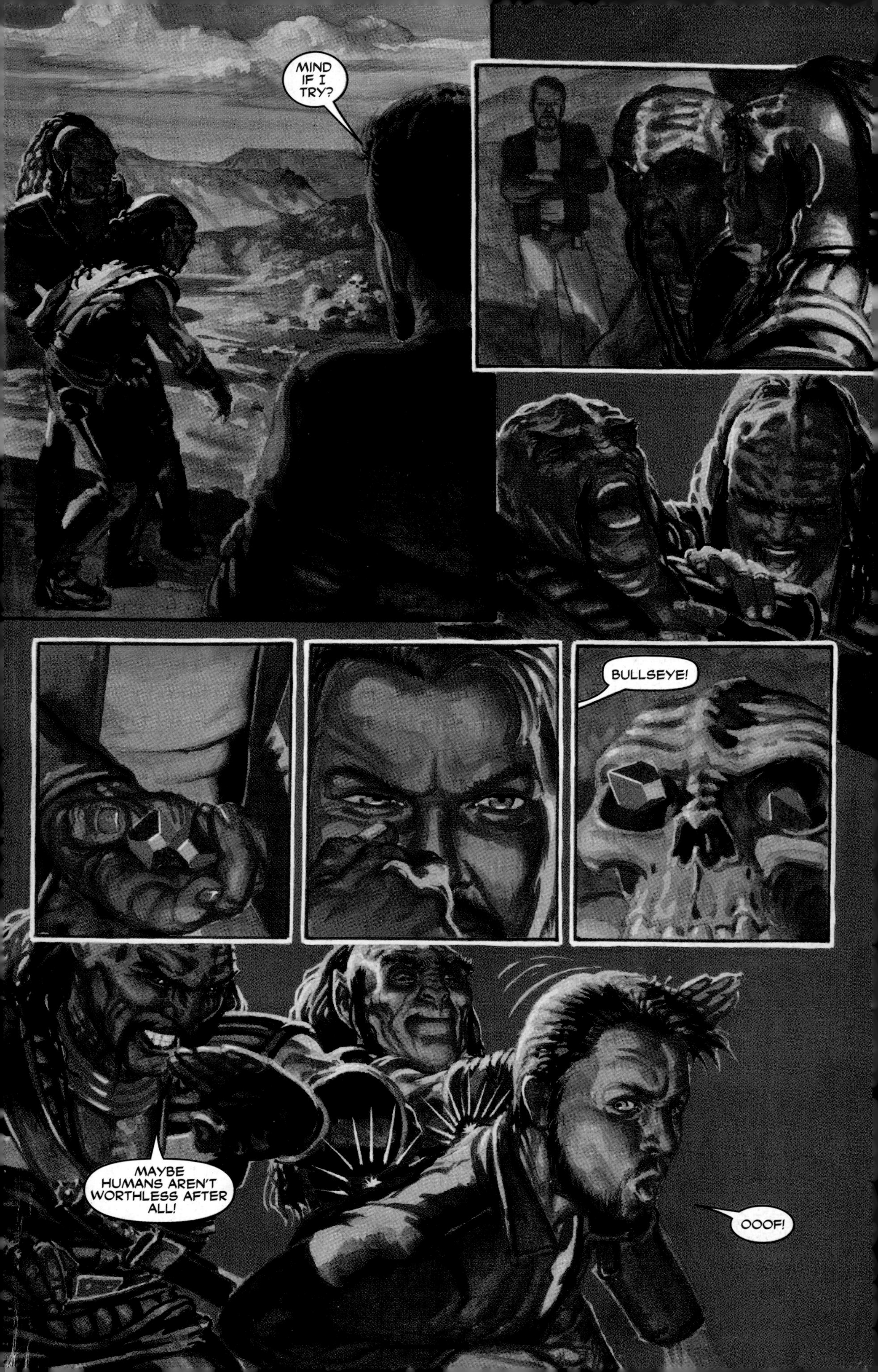
MIND IF I TRY?
BULLSEYE!
MAYBE HUMANS AREN'T WORTHLESS AFTER ALL!
OOOF!

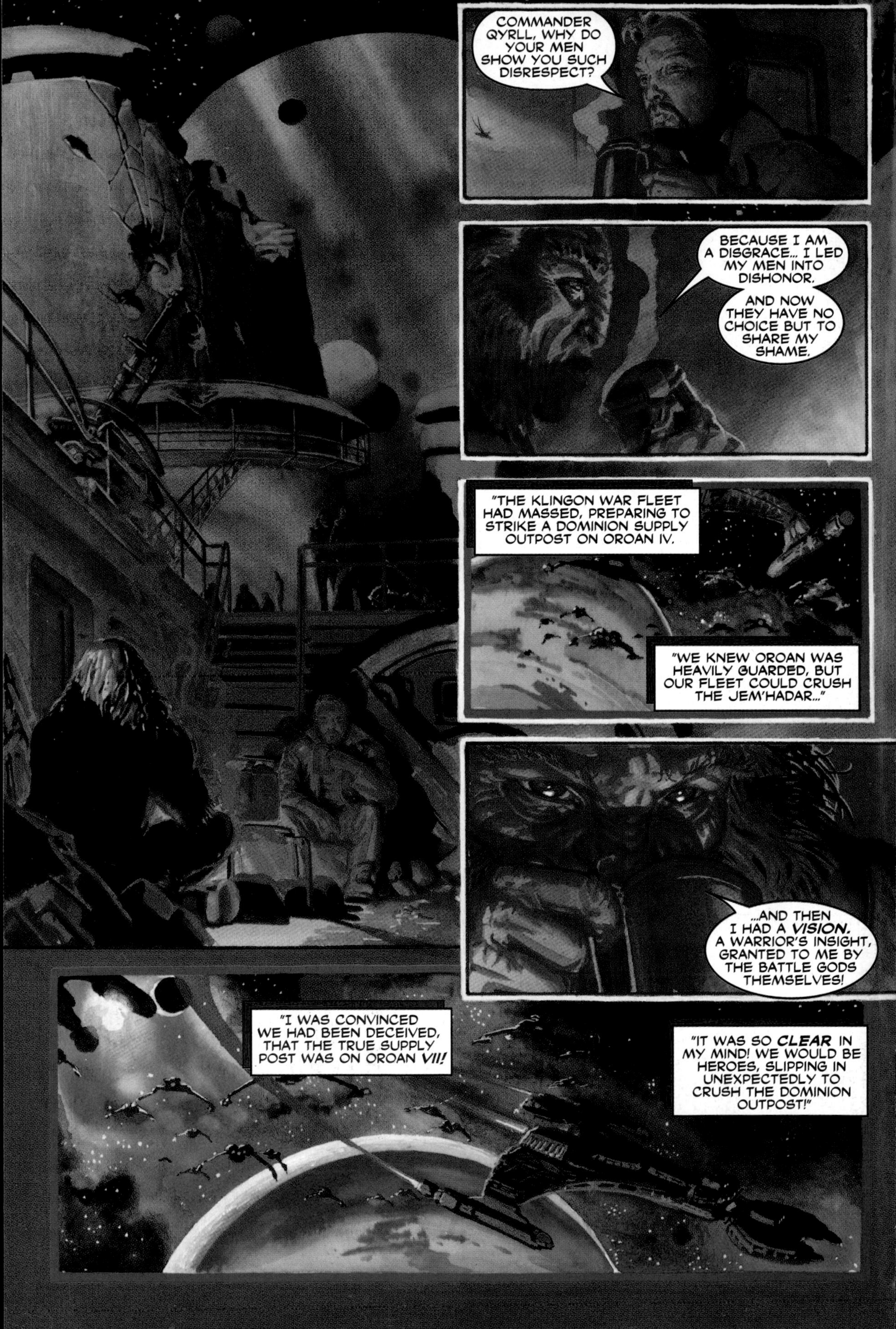
COMMANDER QYRLL, WHY DO YOUR MEN SHOW YOU SUCH DISRESPECT?
BECAUSE I AM A DISGRACE... I LED MY MEN INTO DISHONOR.
AND NOW THEY HAVE NO CHOICE BUT TO SHARE MY SHAME.
"THE KLINGON WAR FLEET HAD MASSED, PREPARING TO STRIKE A DOMINION SUPPLY OUTPOST ON OROAN IV.
"WE KNEW OROAN WAS HEAVILY GUARDED, BUT OUR FLEET COULD CRUSH THE JEM'HADAR..."
...AND THEN I HAD A *VISION.* A WARRIOR'S INSIGHT, GRANTED TO ME BY THE BATTLE GODS THEMSELVES!
"I WAS CONVINCED WE HAD BEEN DECEIVED, THAT THE TRUE SUPPLY POST WAS ON OROAN *VII!*
"IT WAS SO *CLEAR* IN MY MIND! WE WOULD BE HEROES, SLIPPING IN UNEXPECTEDLY TO CRUSH THE DOMINION OUTPOST!"

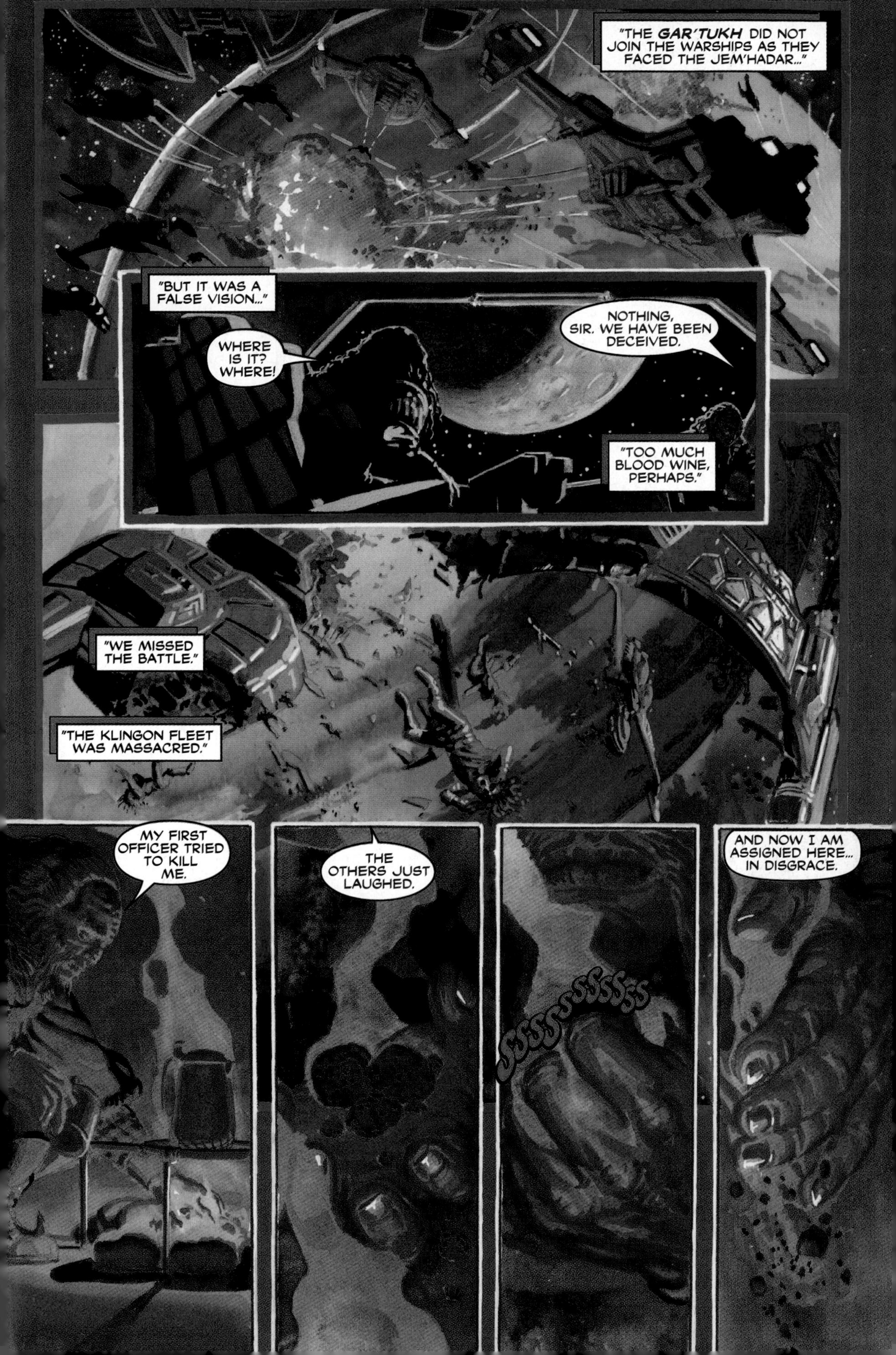
"THE GAR'TUKH DID NOT JOIN THE WARSHIPS AS THEY FACED THE JEM'HADAR..."
"BUT IT WAS A FALSE VISION..."
WHERE IS IT? WHERE!
NOTHING, SIR. WE HAVE BEEN DECEIVED.
"TOO MUCH BLOOD WINE, PERHAPS."
"WE MISSED THE BATTLE."
"THE KLINGON FLEET WAS MASSACRED."
MY FIRST OFFICER TRIED TO KILL ME.
THE OTHERS JUST LAUGHED.
SSSSS-SSSSSS
AND NOW I AM ASSIGNED HERE... IN DISGRACE.

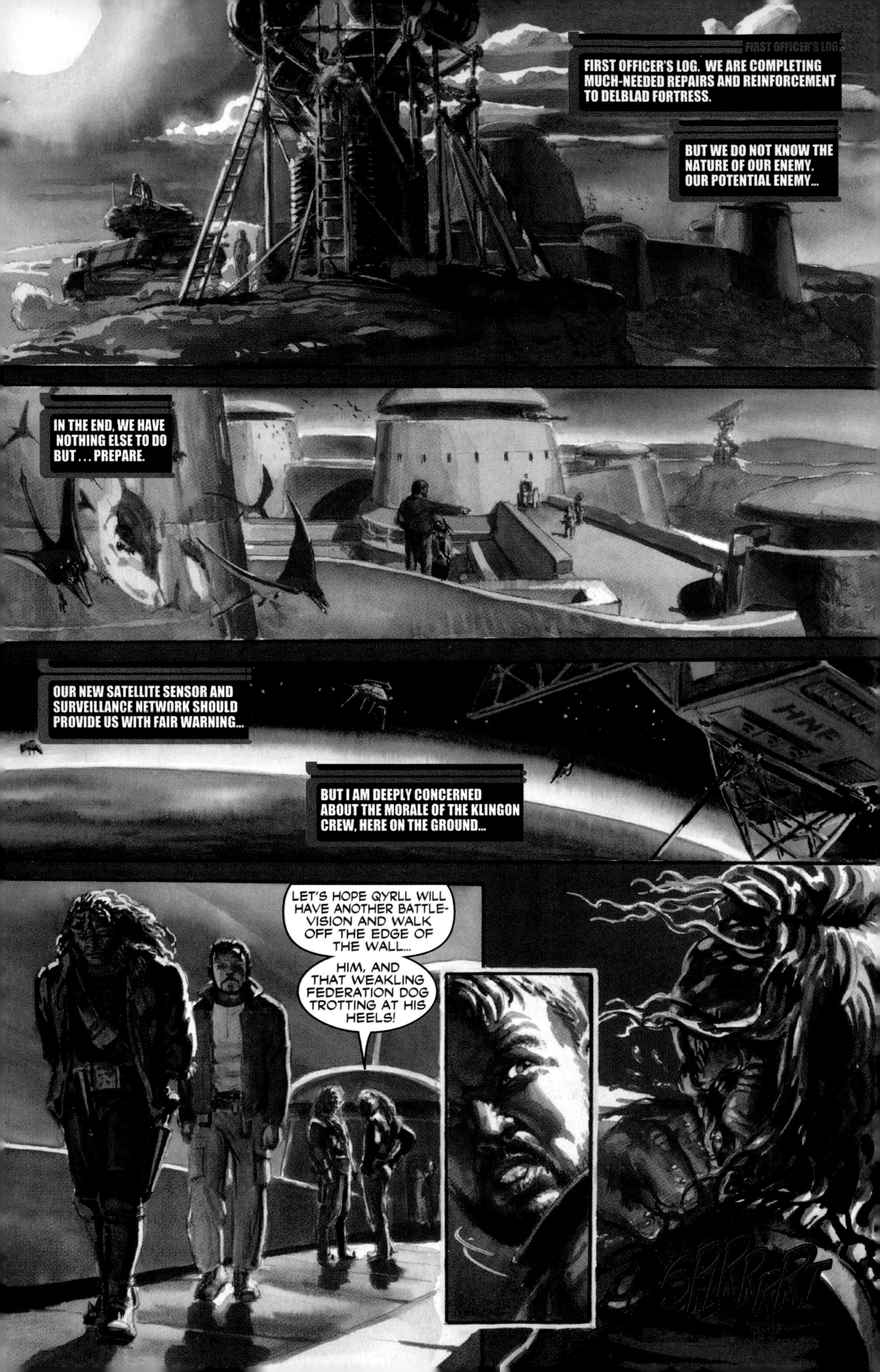
FIRST OFFICER'S LOG
FIRST OFFICER'S LOG. WE ARE COMPLETING MUCH-NEEDED REPAIRS AND REINFORCEMENT TO DELBLAD FORTRESS.
BUT WE DO NOT KNOW THE NATURE OF OUR ENEMY. OUR POTENTIAL ENEMY...
IN THE END, WE HAVE NOTHING ELSE TO DO BUT . . . PREPARE.
OUR NEW SATELLITE SENSOR AND SURVEILLANCE NETWORK SHOULD PROVIDE US WITH FAIR WARNING...
BUT I AM DEEPLY CONCERNED ABOUT THE MORALE OF THE KLINGON CREW, HERE ON THE GROUND...
LET'S HOPE QYRLL WILL HAVE ANOTHER BATTLE-VISION AND WALK OFF THE EDGE OF THE WALL...
HIM, AND THAT WEAKLING FEDERATION DOG TROTTING AT HIS HEELS!

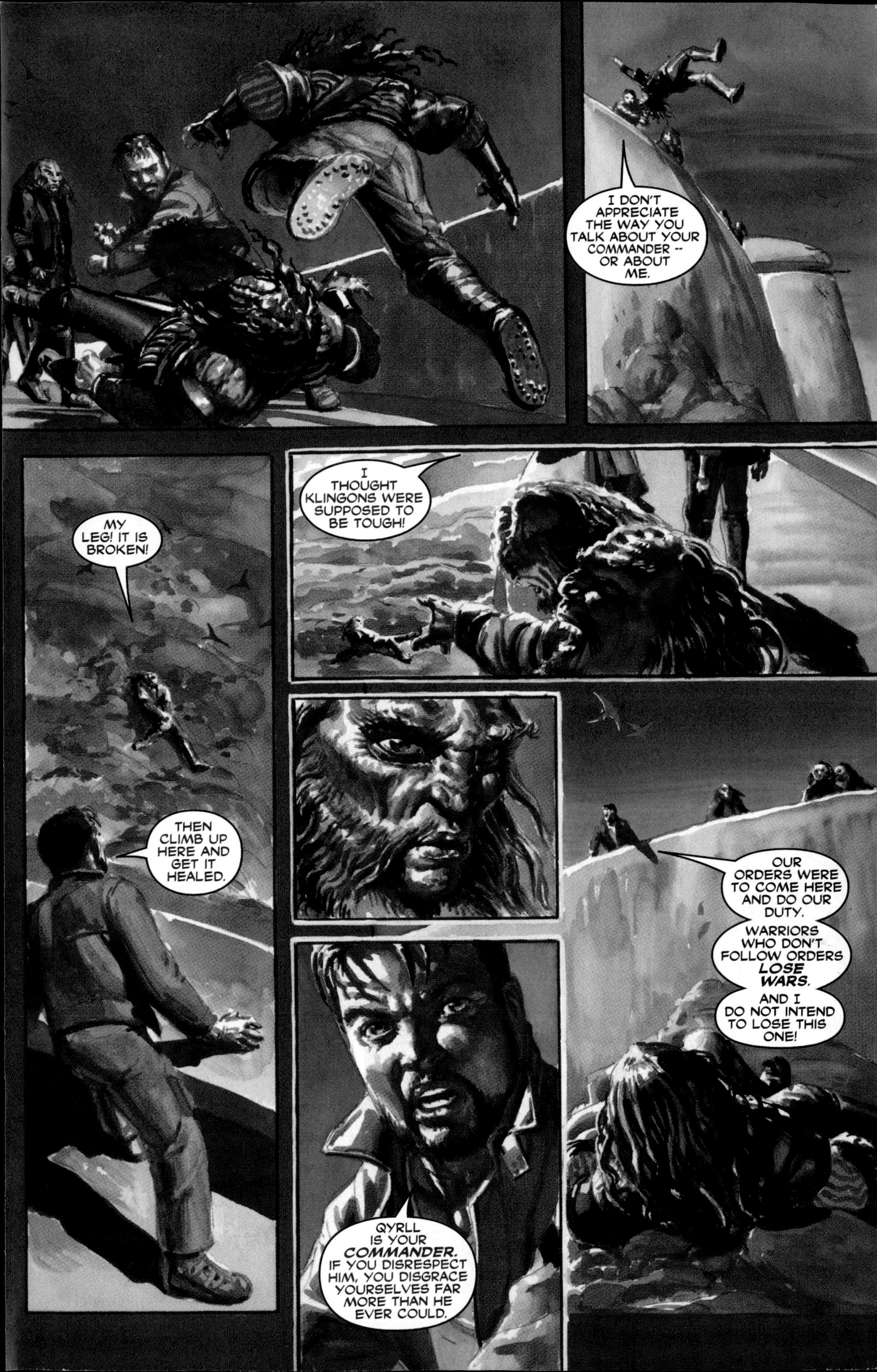
I DON'T APPRECIATE THE WAY YOU TALK ABOUT YOUR COMMANDER -- OR ABOUT ME.
MY LEG! IT IS BROKEN!
I THOUGHT KLINGONS WERE SUPPOSED TO BE TOUGH!
THEN CLIMB UP HERE AND GET IT HEALED.
OUR ORDERS WERE TO COME HERE AND DO OUR DUTY.
WARRIORS WHO DON'T FOLLOW ORDERS LOSE WARS.
AND I DO NOT INTEND TO LOSE THIS ONE!
QYRLL IS YOUR COMMANDER. IF YOU DISRESPECT HIM, YOU DISGRACE YOURSELVES FAR MORE THAN HE EVER COULD.

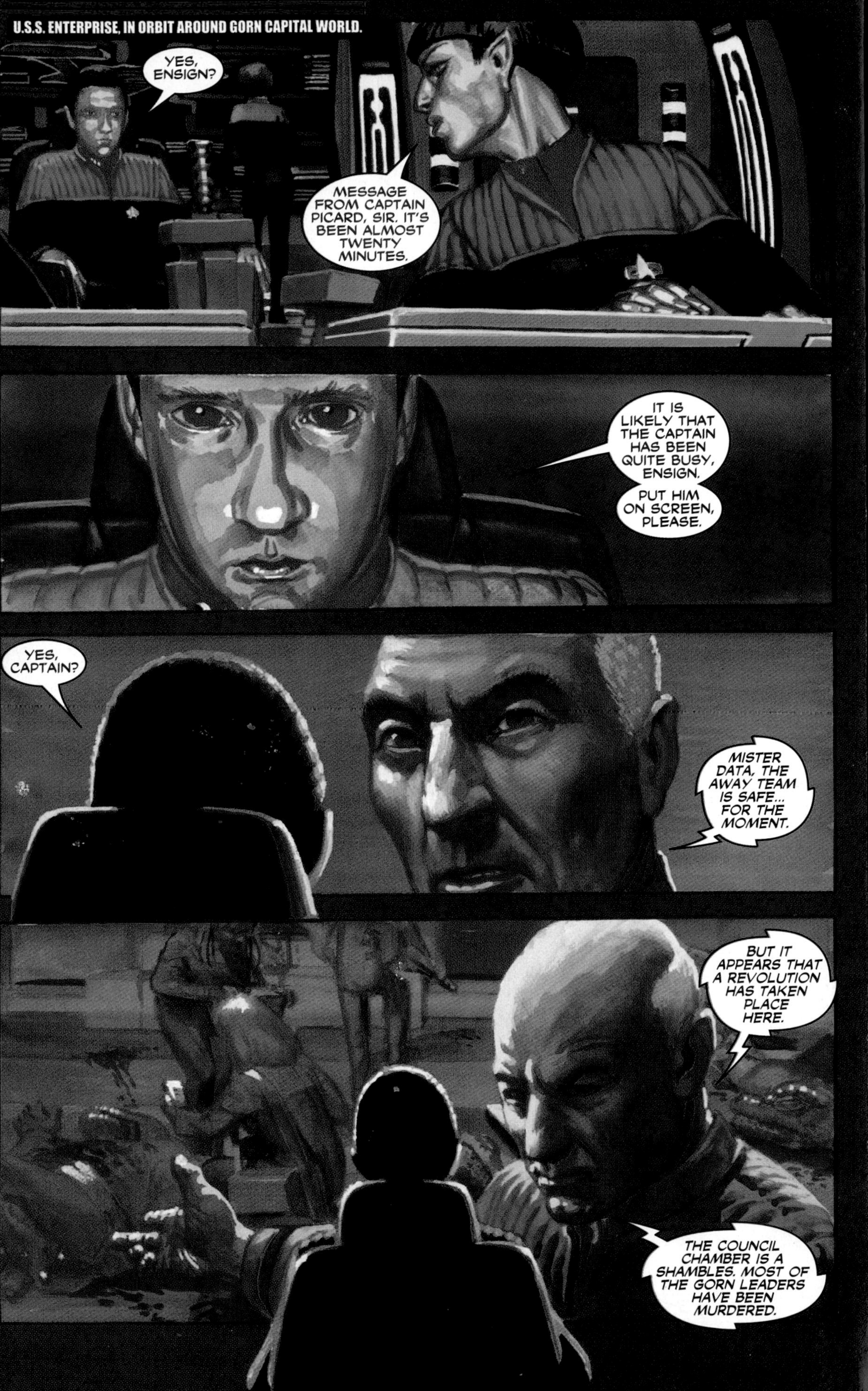
U.S.S. ENTERPRISE, IN ORBIT AROUND GORN CAPITAL WORLD.
YES, ENSIGN?
MESSAGE FROM CAPTAIN PICARD, SIR. IT'S BEEN ALMOST TWENTY MINUTES.
IT IS LIKELY THAT THE CAPTAIN HAS BEEN QUITE BUSY, ENSIGN.
PUT HIM ON SCREEN, PLEASE.
YES, CAPTAIN?
MISTER DATA, THE AWAY TEAM IS SAFE... FOR THE MOMENT.
BUT IT APPEARS THAT A REVOLUTION HAS TAKEN PLACE HERE.
THE COUNCIL CHAMBER IS A SHAMBLES. MOST OF THE GORN LEADERS HAVE BEEN MURDERED.

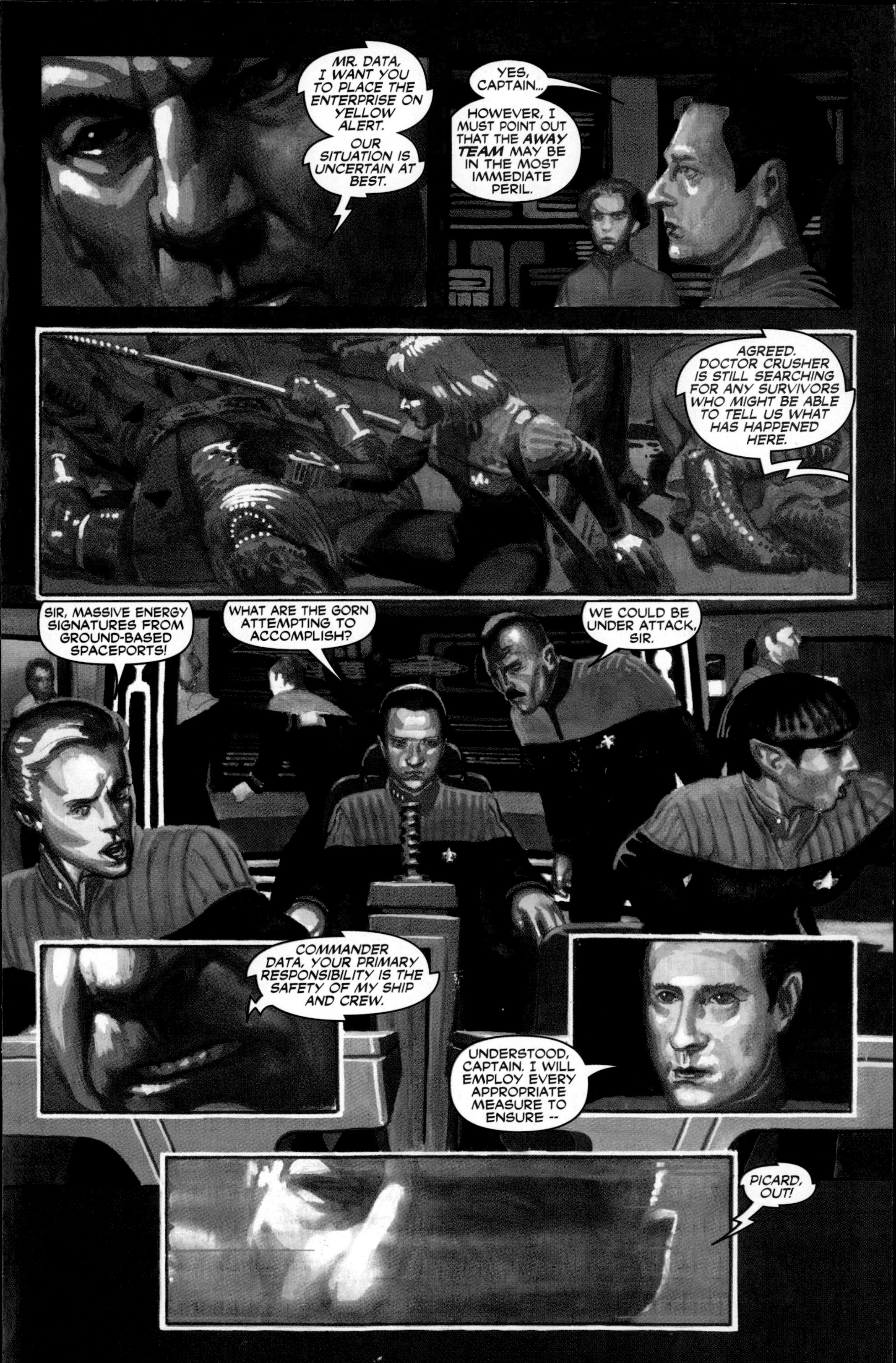
MR. DATA, I WANT YOU TO PLACE THE ENTERPRISE ON YELLOW ALERT.
OUR SITUATION IS UNCERTAIN AT BEST.
YES, CAPTAIN...
HOWEVER, I MUST POINT OUT THAT THE AWAY TEAM MAY BE IN THE MOST IMMEDIATE PERIL.
AGREED. DOCTOR CRUSHER IS STILL SEARCHING FOR ANY SURVIVORS WHO MIGHT BE ABLE TO TELL US WHAT HAS HAPPENED HERE.
SIR, MASSIVE ENERGY SIGNATURES FROM GROUND-BASED SPACEPORTS!
WHAT ARE THE GORN ATTEMPTING TO ACCOMPLISH?
WE COULD BE UNDER ATTACK, SIR.
COMMANDER DATA, YOUR PRIMARY RESPONSIBILITY IS THE SAFETY OF MY SHIP AND CREW.
UNDERSTOOD, CAPTAIN. I WILL EMPLOY EVERY APPROPRIATE MEASURE TO ENSURE --
PICARD, OUT!

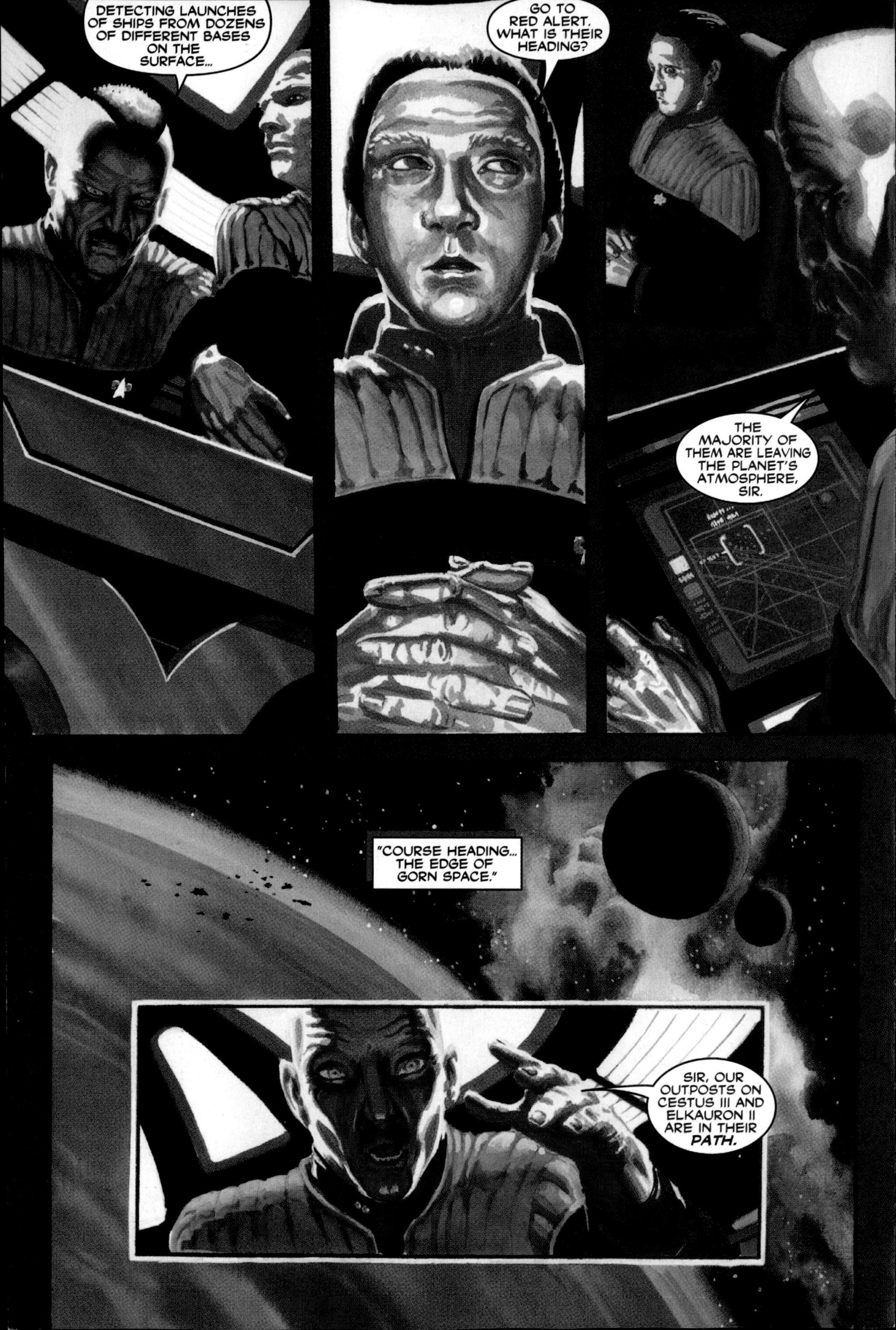
DETECTING LAUNCHES OF SHIPS FROM DOZENS OF DIFFERENT BASES ON THE SURFACE...
GO TO RED ALERT. WHAT IS THEIR HEADING?
THE MAJORITY OF THEM ARE LEAVING THE PLANET'S ATMOSPHERE, SIR.
"COURSE HEADING... THE EDGE OF GORN SPACE."
SIR, OUR OUTPOSTS ON CESTUS III AND ELKAURON II ARE IN THEIR *PATH*.

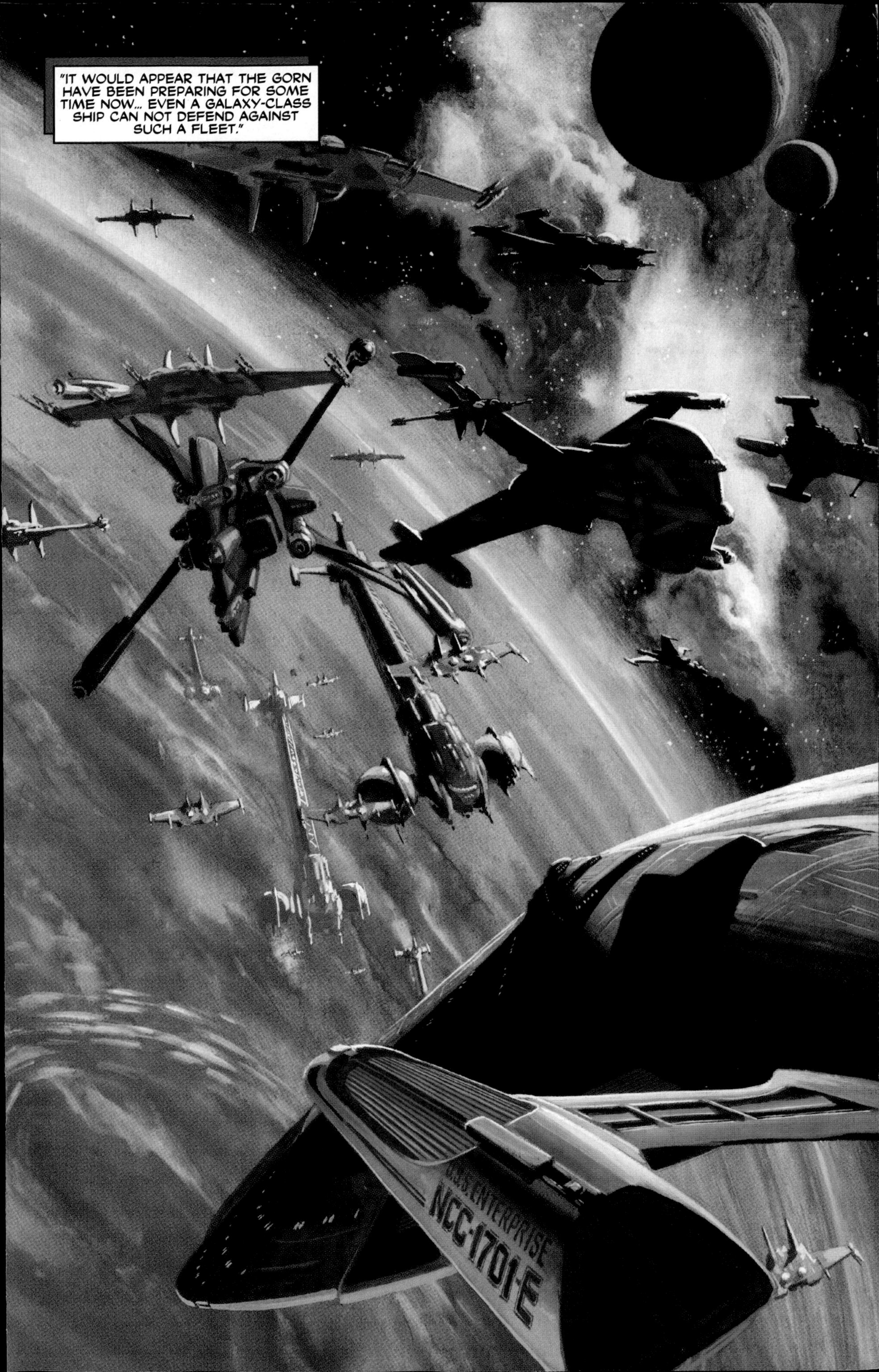
"IT WOULD APPEAR THAT THE GORN HAVE BEEN PREPARING FOR SOME TIME NOW... EVEN A GALAXY-CLASS SHIP CAN NOT DEFEND AGAINST SUCH A FLEET."
U.S.S. ENTERPRISE
NCC-1701-E

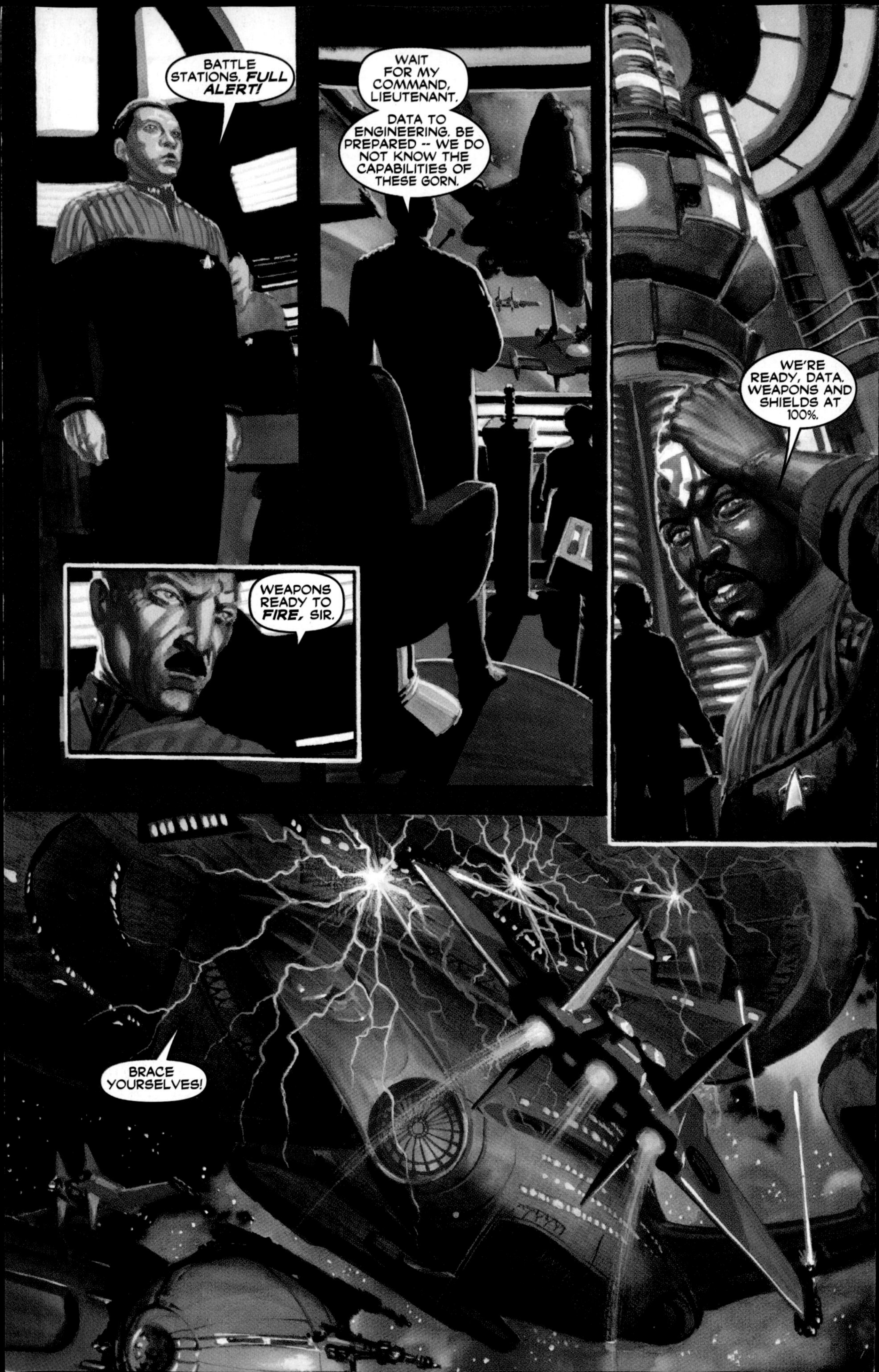
BATTLE STATIONS, FULL ALERT!
WAIT FOR MY COMMAND, LIEUTENANT.
DATA TO ENGINEERING. BE PREPARED -- WE DO NOT KNOW THE CAPABILITIES OF THESE GORN.
WE'RE READY, DATA. WEAPONS AND SHIELDS AT 100%.
WEAPONS READY TO FIRE, SIR.
BRACE YOURSELVES!

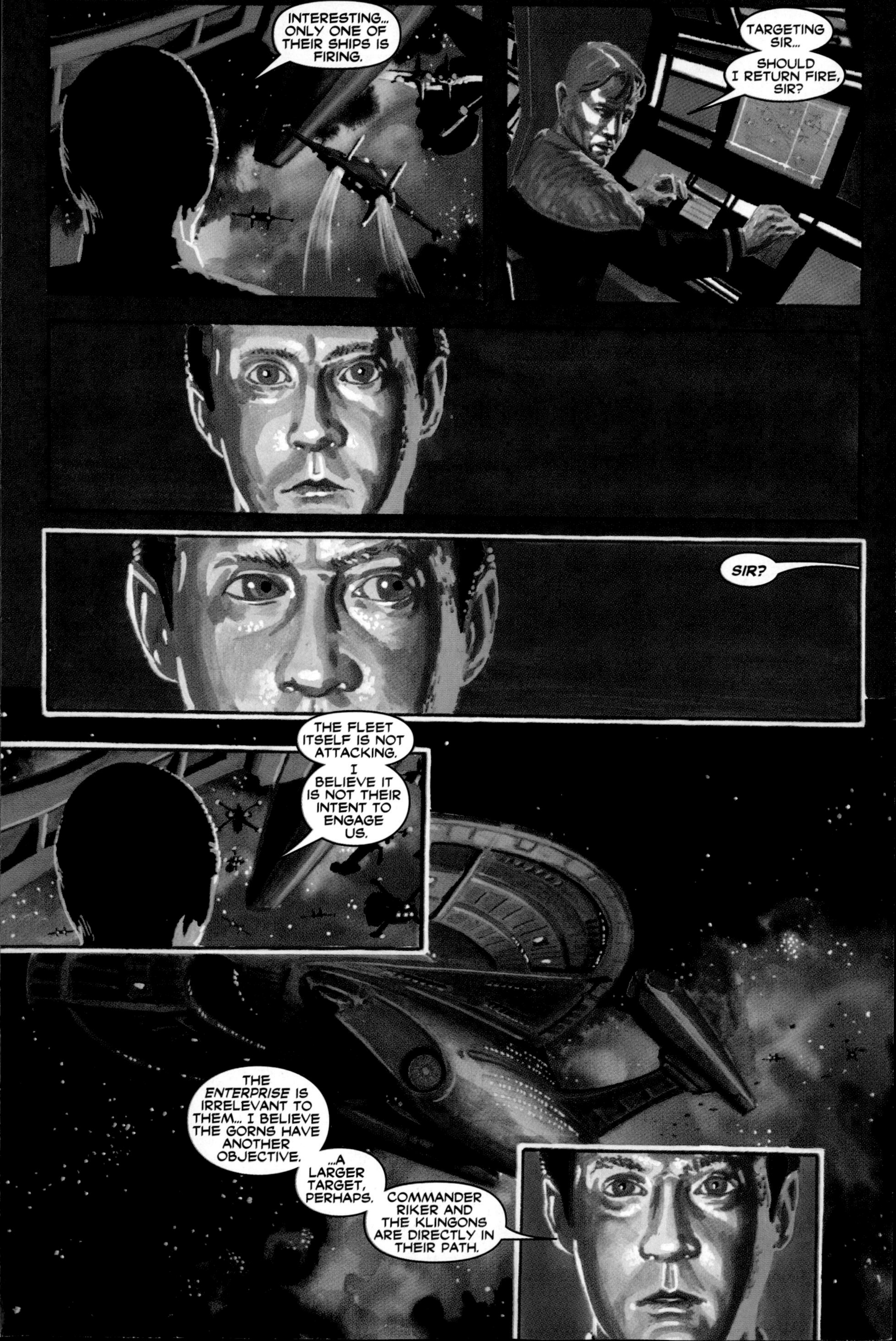
INTERESTING... ONLY ONE OF THEIR SHIPS IS FIRING.
TARGETING SIR...
SHOULD I RETURN FIRE, SIR?
SIR?
THE FLEET ITSELF IS NOT ATTACKING.
I BELIEVE IT IS NOT THEIR INTENT TO ENGAGE US.
THE *ENTERPRISE* IS IRRELEVANT TO THEM... I BELIEVE THE GORNS HAVE ANOTHER OBJECTIVE.
...A LARGER TARGET, PERHAPS.
COMMANDER RIKER AND THE KLINGONS ARE DIRECTLY IN THEIR PATH.

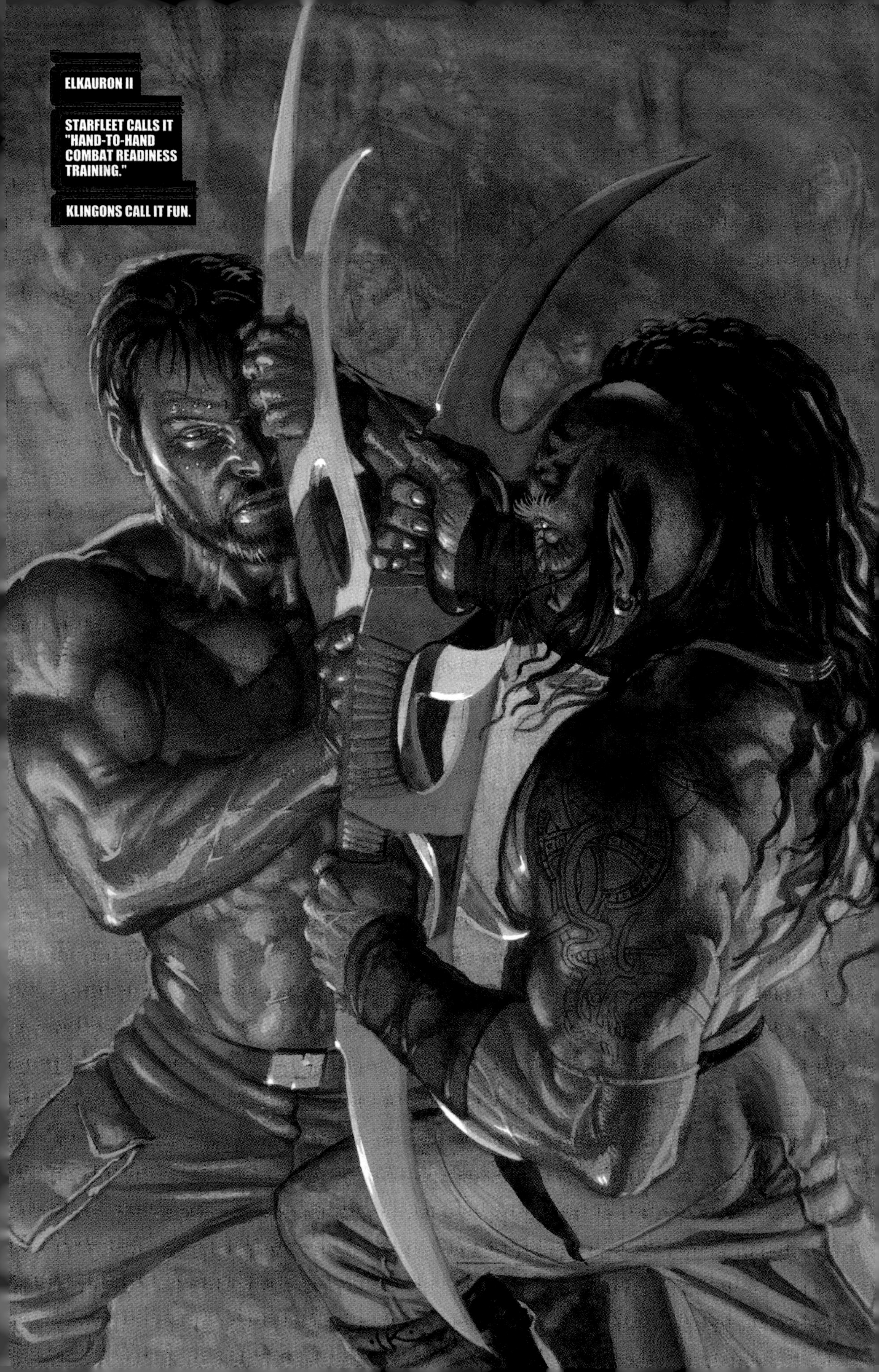
ELKAURON II
STARFLEET CALLS IT "HAND-TO-HAND COMBAT READINESS TRAINING."
KLINGONS CALL IT FUN.

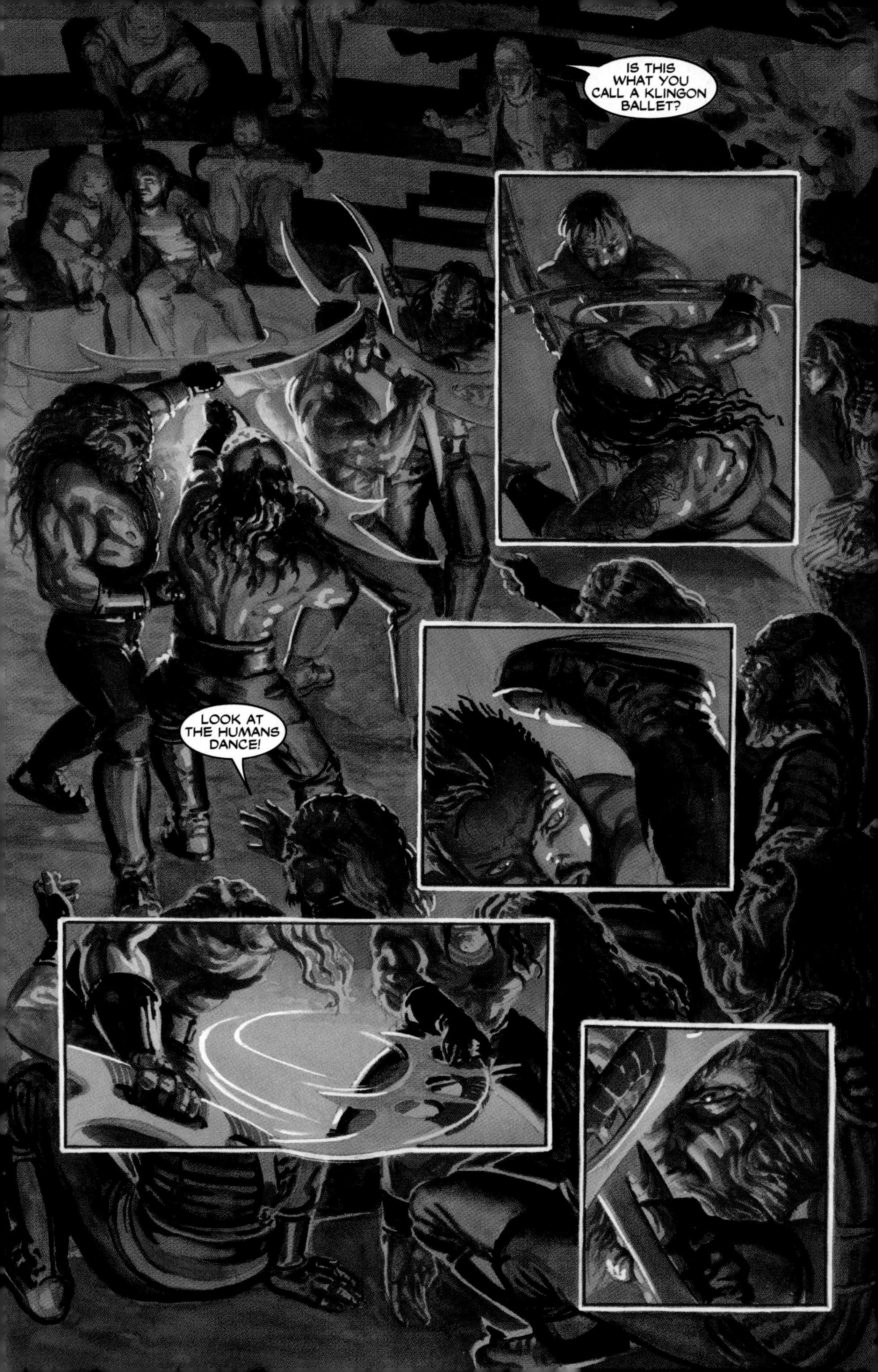
IS THIS WHAT YOU CALL A KLINGON BALLET?
LOOK AT THE HUMANS DANCE!

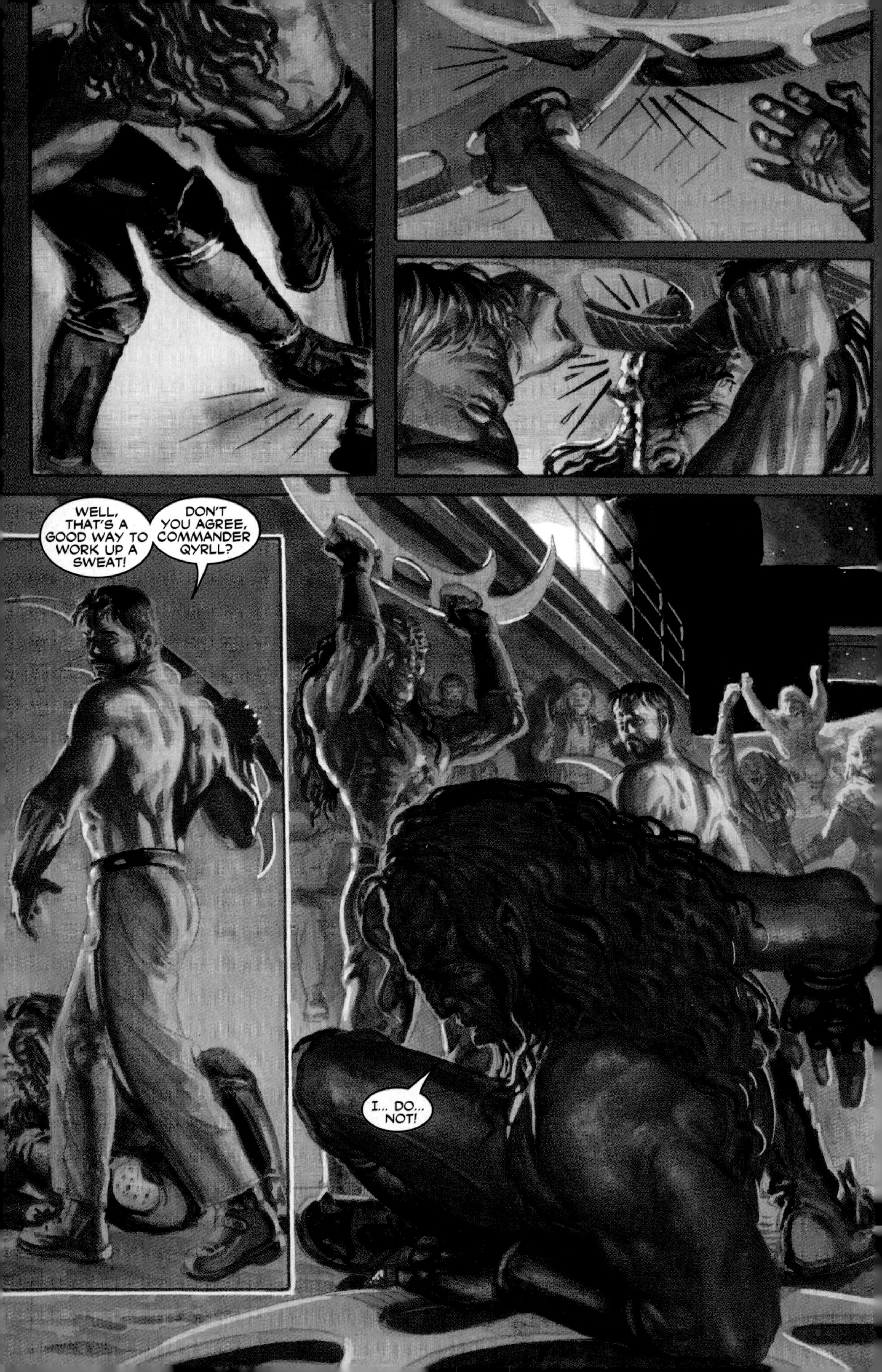
WELL, THAT'S A GOOD WAY TO WORK UP A SWEAT!
DON'T YOU AGREE, COMMANDER QYRLL?
I... DO... NOT!

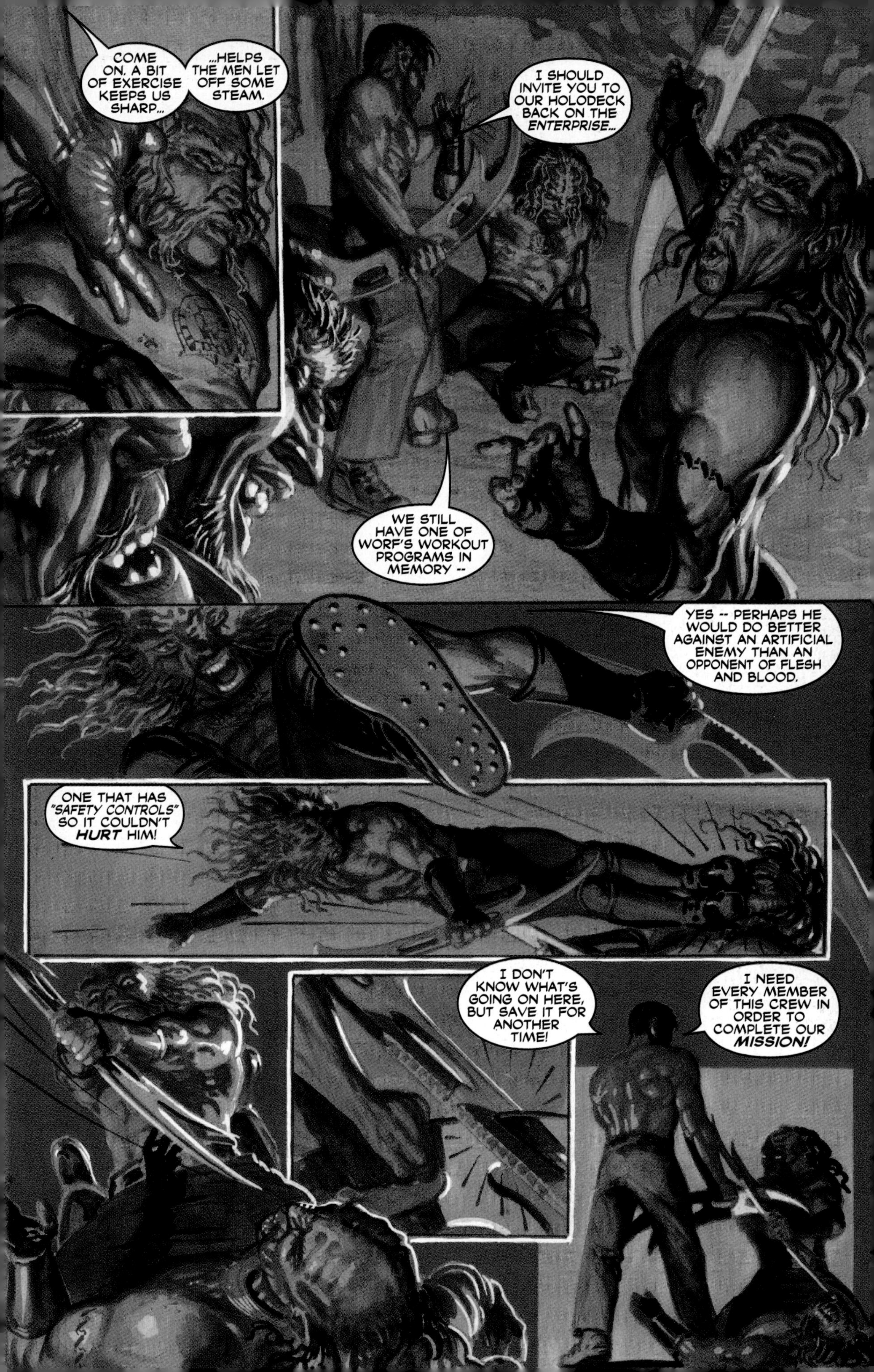
COME ON. A BIT OF EXERCISE KEEPS US SHARP...
...HELPS THE MEN LET OFF SOME STEAM.
I SHOULD INVITE YOU TO OUR HOLODECK BACK ON THE *ENTERPRISE*...
WE STILL HAVE ONE OF WORF'S WORKOUT PROGRAMS IN MEMORY --
YES -- PERHAPS HE WOULD DO BETTER AGAINST AN ARTIFICIAL ENEMY THAN AN OPPONENT OF FLESH AND BLOOD.
ONE THAT HAS *"SAFETY CONTROLS"* SO IT COULDN'T ***HURT*** HIM!
I DON'T KNOW WHAT'S GOING ON HERE, BUT SAVE IT FOR ANOTHER TIME!
I NEED EVERY MEMBER OF THIS CREW IN ORDER TO COMPLETE OUR ***MISSION!***

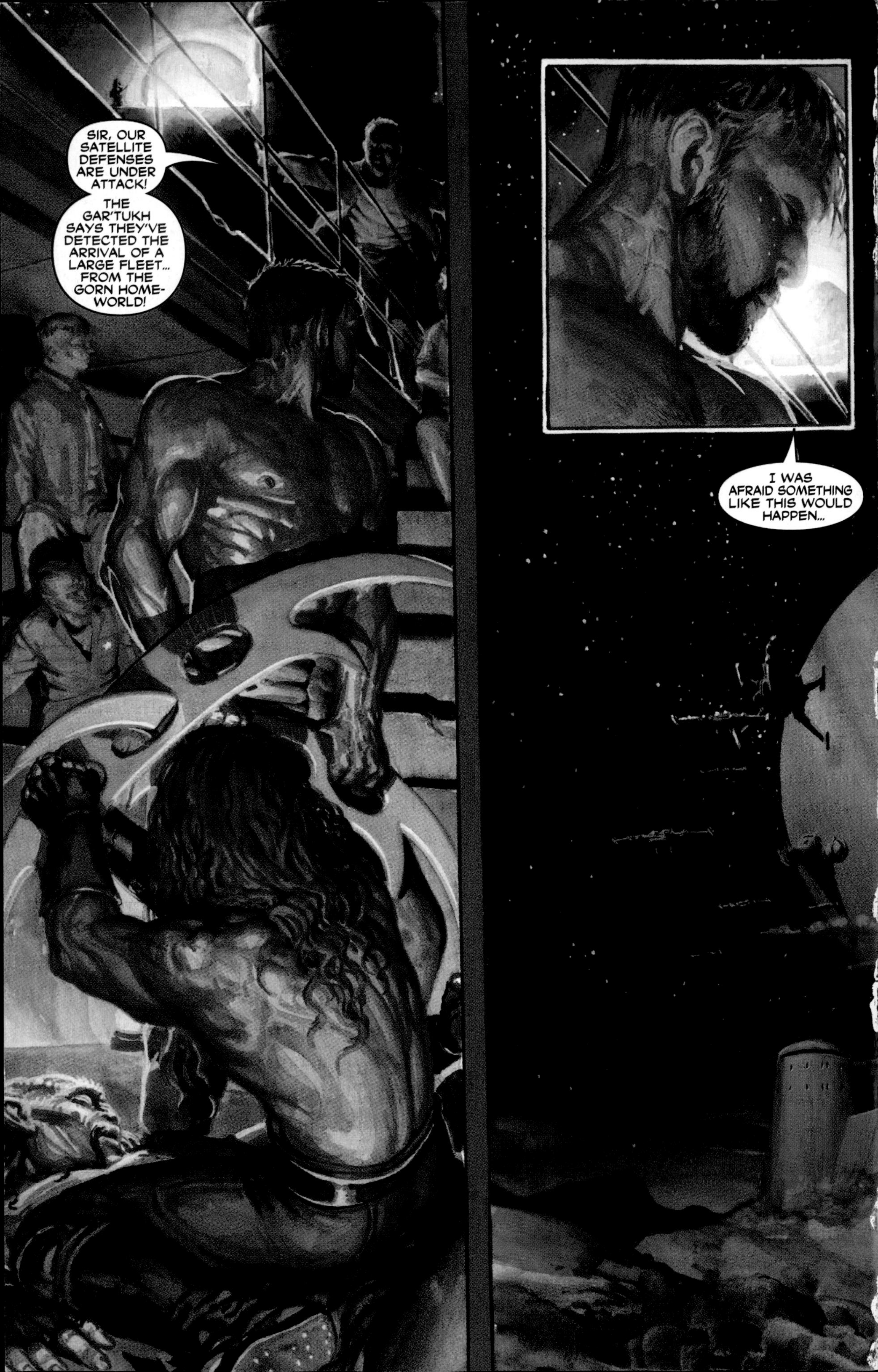
SIR, OUR SATELLITE DEFENSES ARE UNDER ATTACK!
THE GAR'TUKH SAYS THEY'VE DETECTED THE ARRIVAL OF A LARGE FLEET... FROM THE GORN HOME-WORLD!
I WAS AFRAID SOMETHING LIKE THIS WOULD HAPPEN...

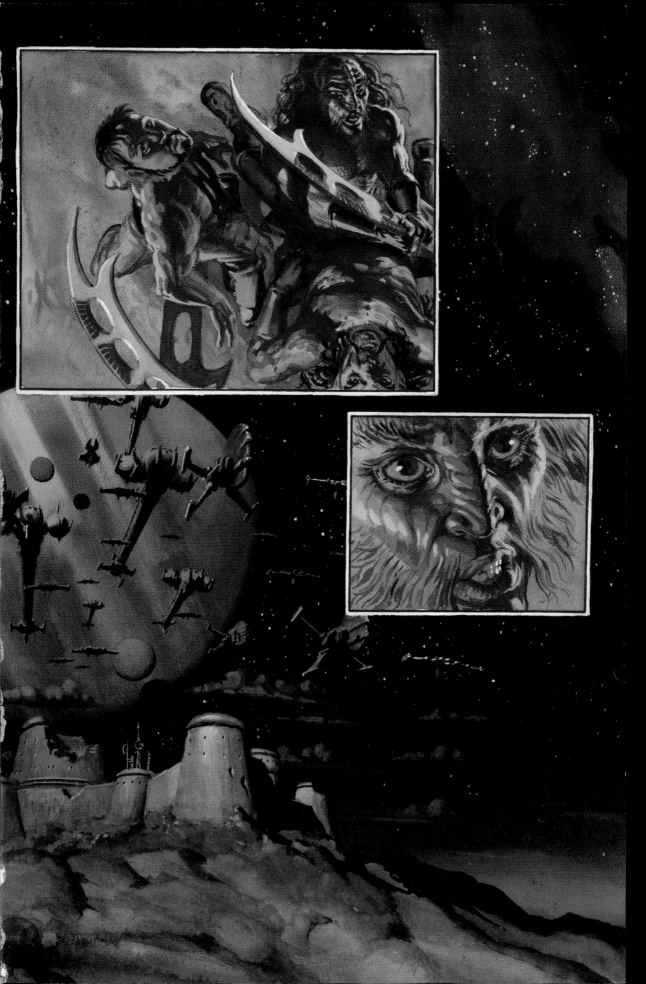

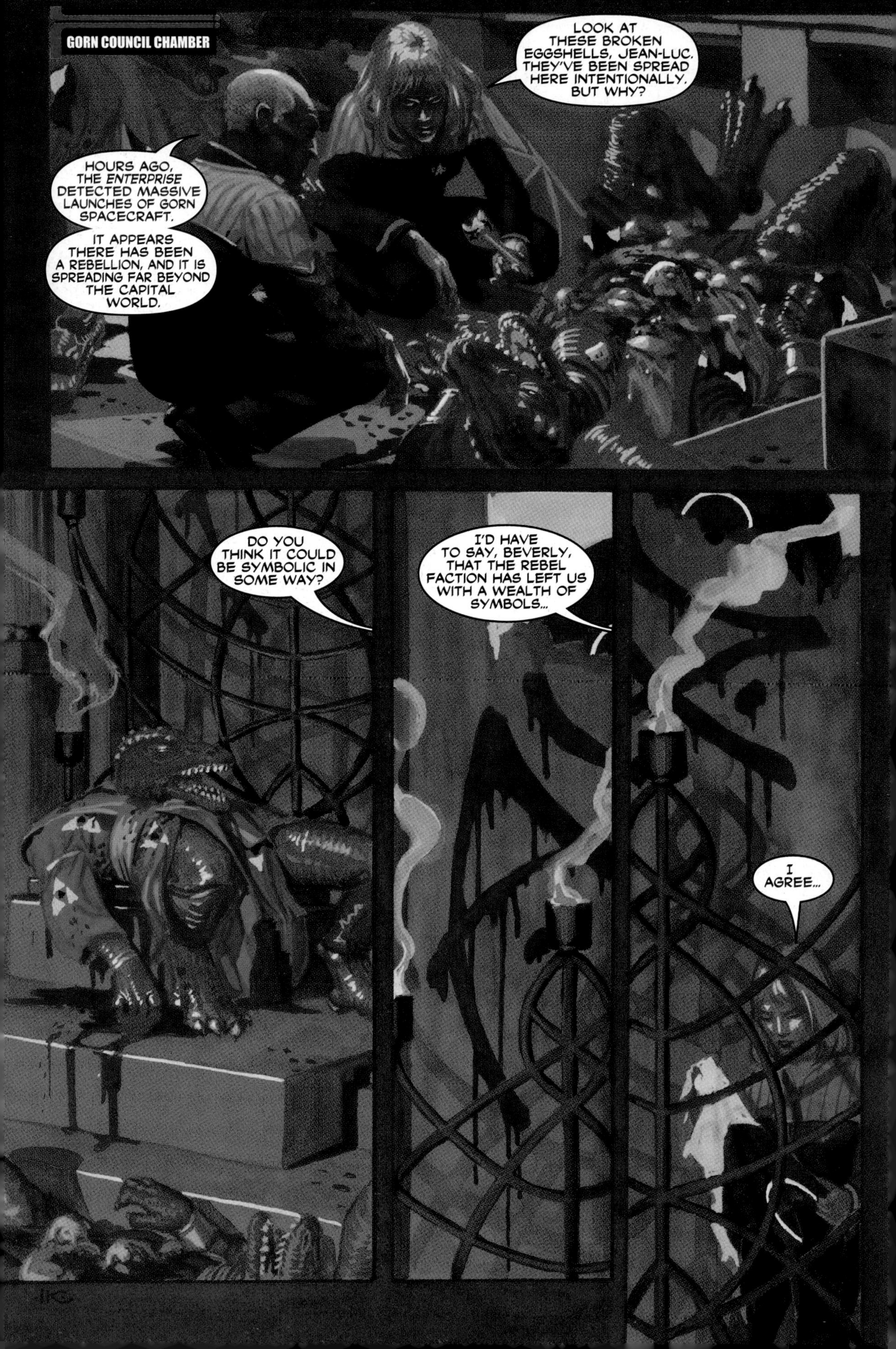
GORN COUNCIL CHAMBER
LOOK AT THESE BROKEN EGGSHELLS, JEAN-LUC. THEY'VE BEEN SPREAD HERE INTENTIONALLY. BUT WHY?
HOURS AGO, THE *ENTERPRISE* DETECTED MASSIVE LAUNCHES OF GORN SPACECRAFT.
IT APPEARS THERE HAS BEEN A REBELLION, AND IT IS SPREADING FAR BEYOND THE CAPITAL WORLD.
DO YOU THINK IT COULD BE SYMBOLIC IN SOME WAY?
I'D HAVE TO SAY, BEVERLY, THAT THE REBEL FACTION HAS LEFT US WITH A WEALTH OF SYMBOLS...
I AGREE...

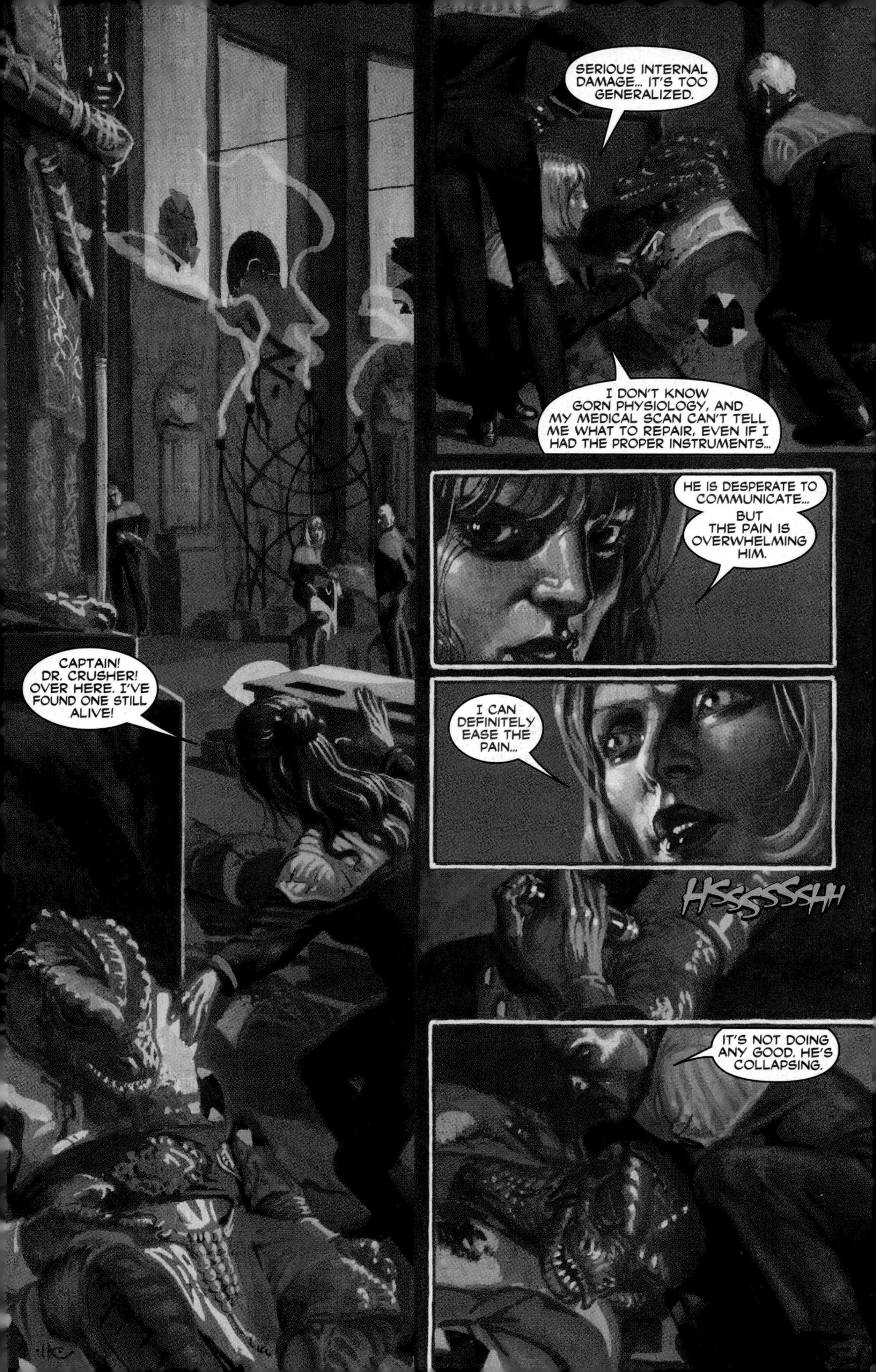
CAPTAIN! DR. CRUSHER! OVER HERE. I'VE FOUND ONE STILL ALIVE!
SERIOUS INTERNAL DAMAGE... IT'S TOO GENERALIZED.
I DON'T KNOW GORN PHYSIOLOGY, AND MY MEDICAL SCAN CAN'T TELL ME WHAT TO REPAIR, EVEN IF I HAD THE PROPER INSTRUMENTS...
HE IS DESPERATE TO COMMUNICATE... BUT THE PAIN IS OVERWHELMING HIM.
I CAN DEFINITELY EASE THE PAIN...
HSSSSSSHH
IT'S NOT DOING ANY GOOD. HE'S COLLAPSING.

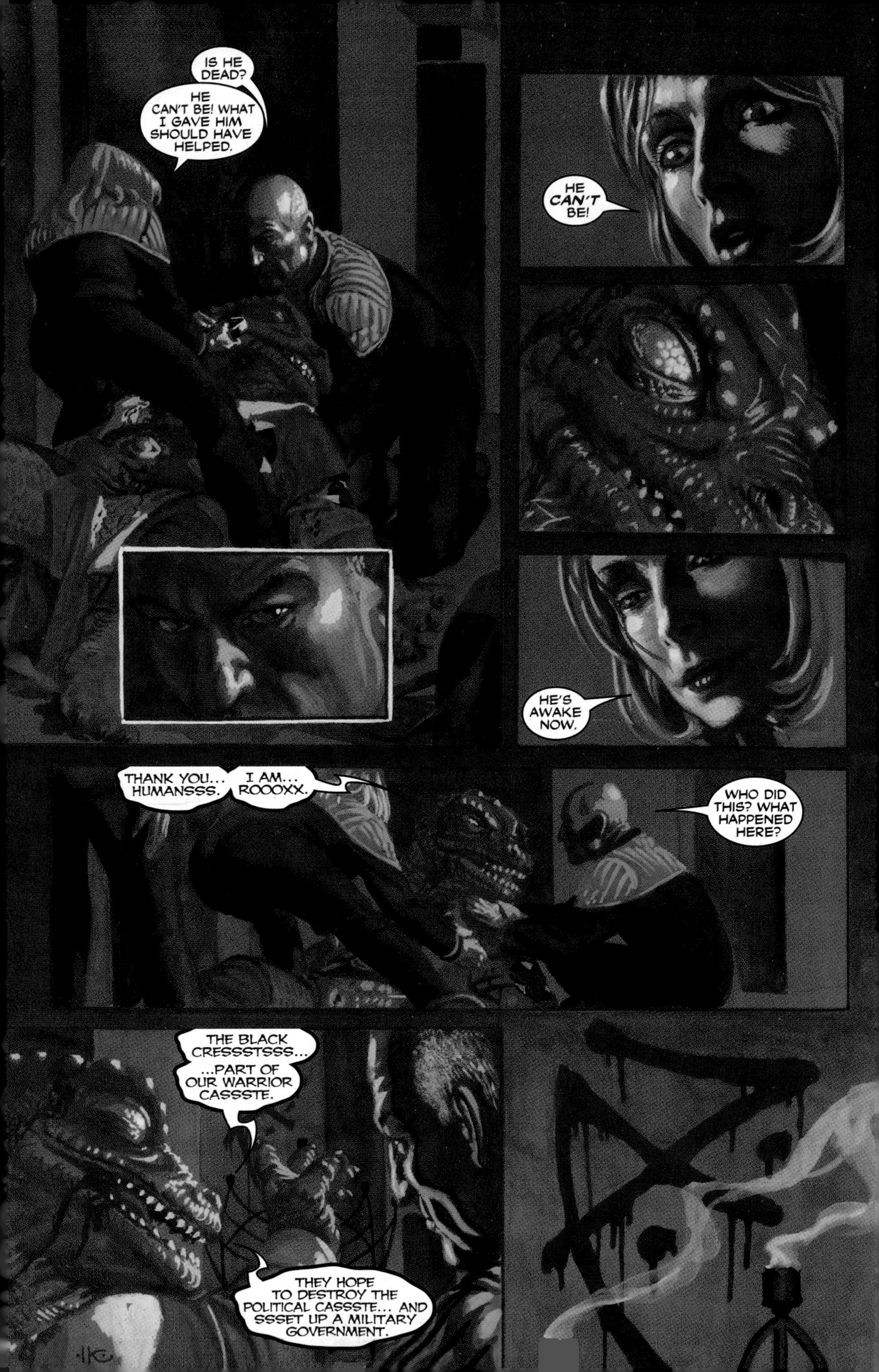
IS HE DEAD?
HE CAN'T BE! WHAT I GAVE HIM SHOULD HAVE HELPED.
HE CAN'T BE!
HE'S AWAKE NOW.
THANK YOU... HUMANSSS.
I AM... ROOOXX.
WHO DID THIS? WHAT HAPPENED HERE?
THE BLACK CRESSSTSSS... ...PART OF OUR WARRIOR CASSSTE.
THEY HOPE TO DESTROY THE POLITICAL CASSSTE... AND SSSET UP A MILITARY GOVERNMENT.

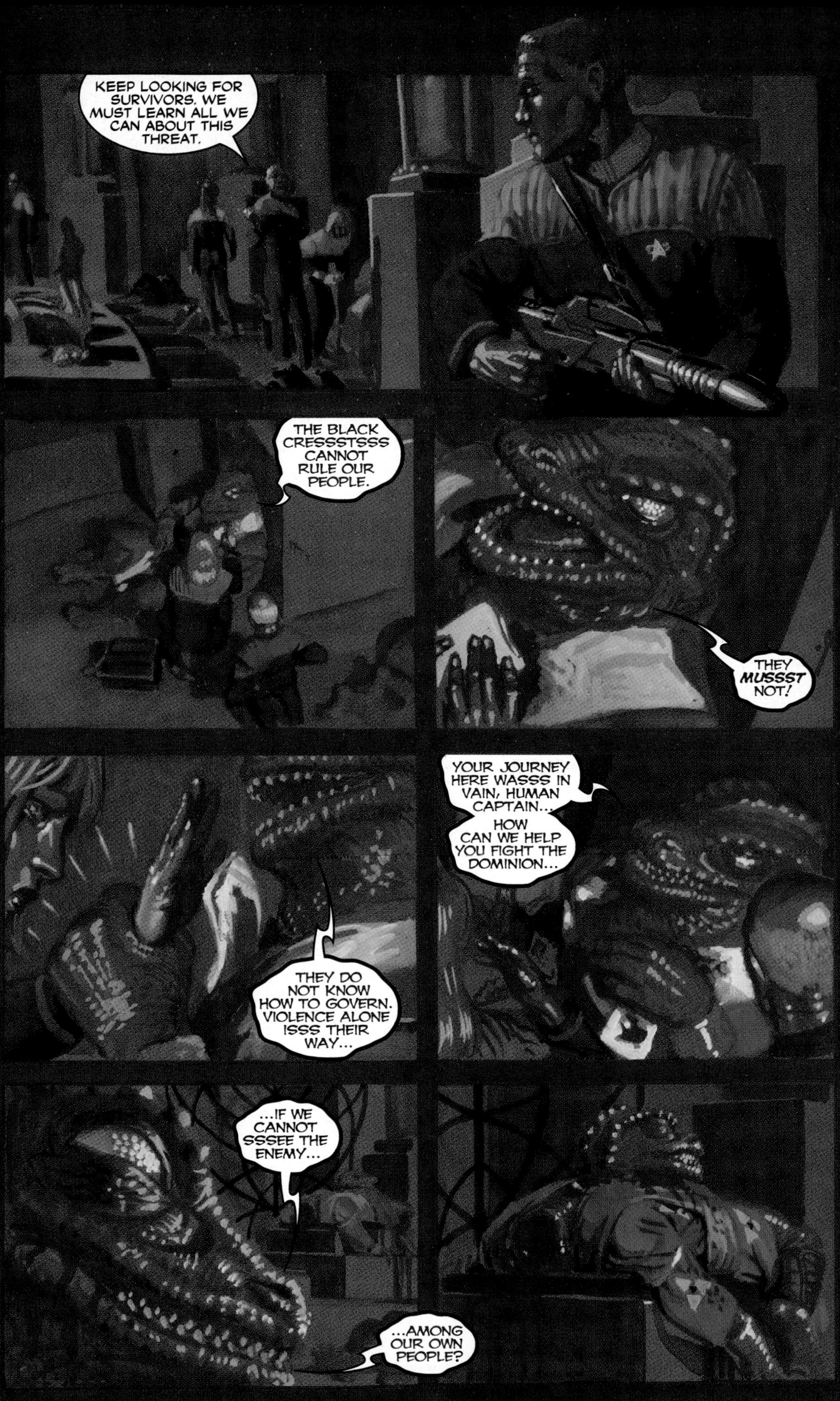
KEEP LOOKING FOR SURVIVORS. WE MUST LEARN ALL WE CAN ABOUT THIS THREAT.
THE BLACK CRESSSTSSS CANNOT RULE OUR PEOPLE.
THEY **MUSSST** NOT!
THEY DO NOT KNOW HOW TO GOVERN. VIOLENCE ALONE ISSS THEIR WAY...
YOUR JOURNEY HERE WASSS IN VAIN, HUMAN CAPTAIN...
HOW CAN WE HELP YOU FIGHT THE DOMINION...
...IF WE CANNOT SSSEE THE ENEMY...
...AMONG OUR OWN PEOPLE?

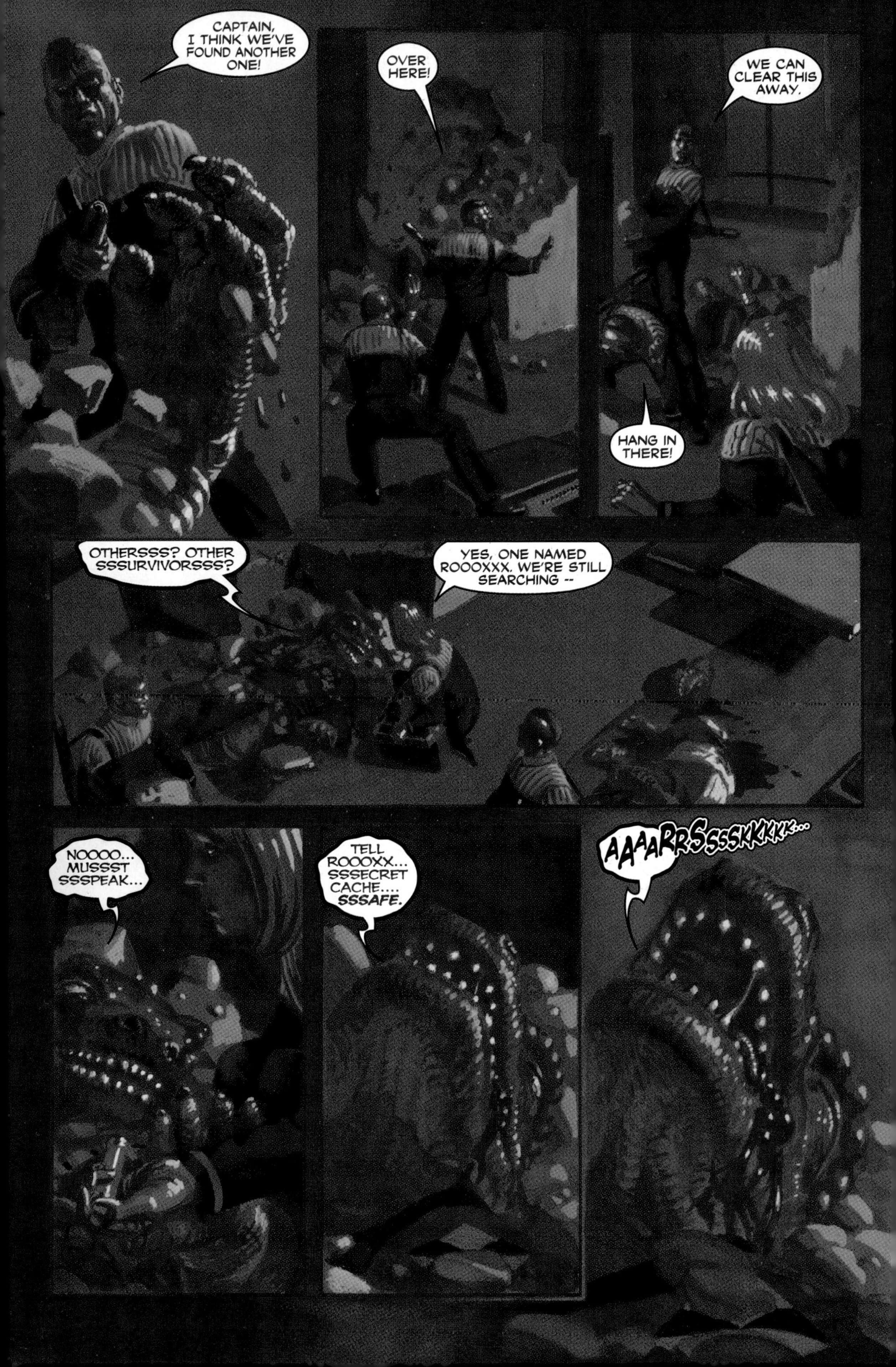
CAPTAIN, I THINK WE'VE FOUND ANOTHER ONE!
OVER HERE!
WE CAN CLEAR THIS AWAY.
HANG IN THERE!
OTHERSSS? OTHER SSSURVIVORSSS?
YES, ONE NAMED ROOOXXX. WE'RE STILL SEARCHING --
NOOOO... MUSSST SSSPEAK...
TELL ROOOXX... SSSECRET CACHE.... SSSAFE.
AAAARRSSSSKKKKK...

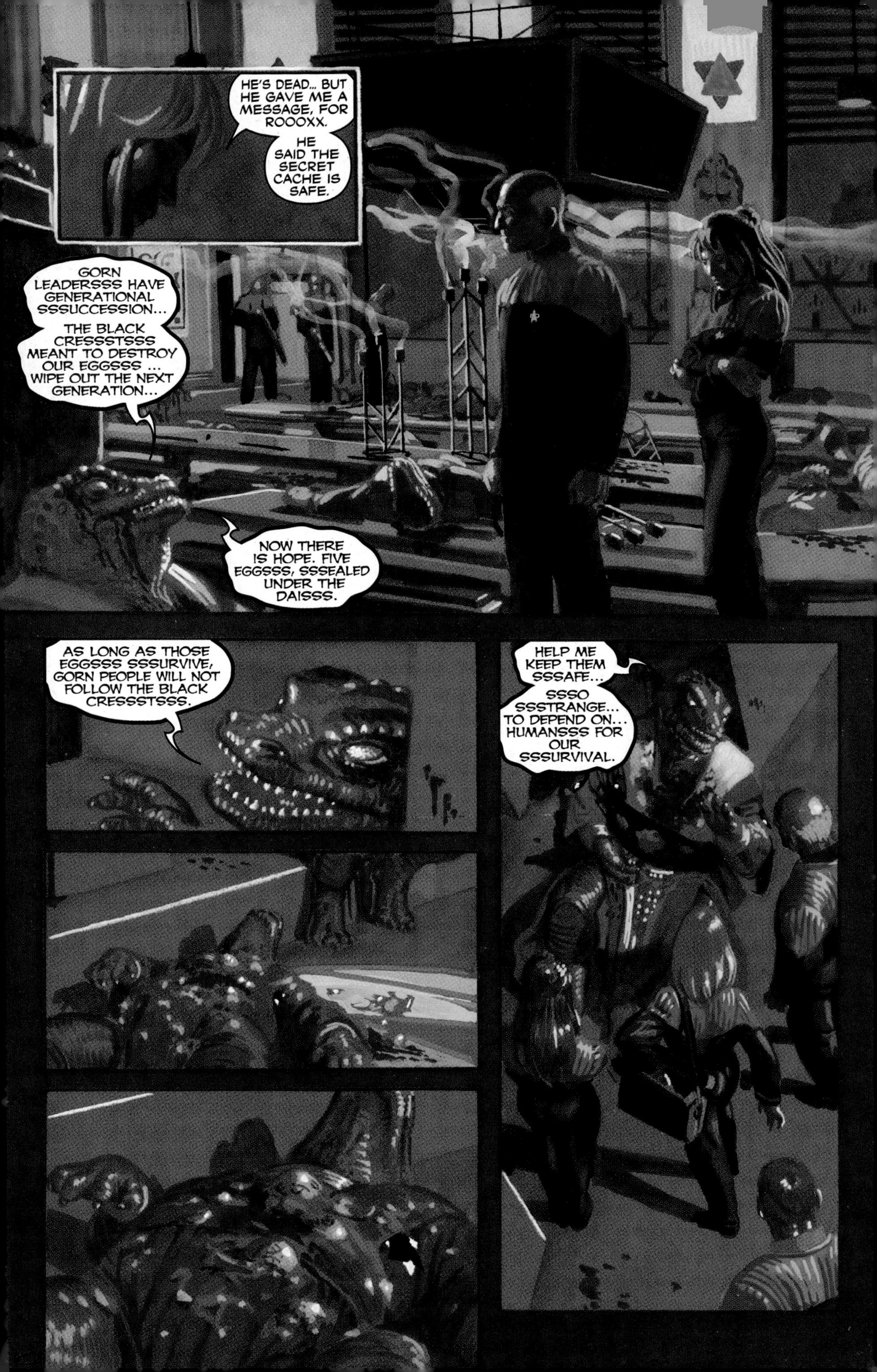
HE'S DEAD... BUT HE GAVE ME A MESSAGE, FOR ROOOXX.
HE SAID THE SECRET CACHE IS SAFE.
GORN LEADERSSS HAVE GENERATIONAL SSSUCCESSION...
THE BLACK CRESSSTSSS MEANT TO DESTROY OUR EGGSSS ... WIPE OUT THE NEXT GENERATION...
NOW THERE IS HOPE. FIVE EGGSSS, SSSEALED UNDER THE DAISSS.
AS LONG AS THOSE EGGSSS SSSURVIVE, GORN PEOPLE WILL NOT FOLLOW THE BLACK CRESSSTSSS.
HELP ME KEEP THEM SSSAFE...
SSSO SSSTRANGE... TO DEPEND ON... HUMANSSS FOR OUR SSSURVIVAL.

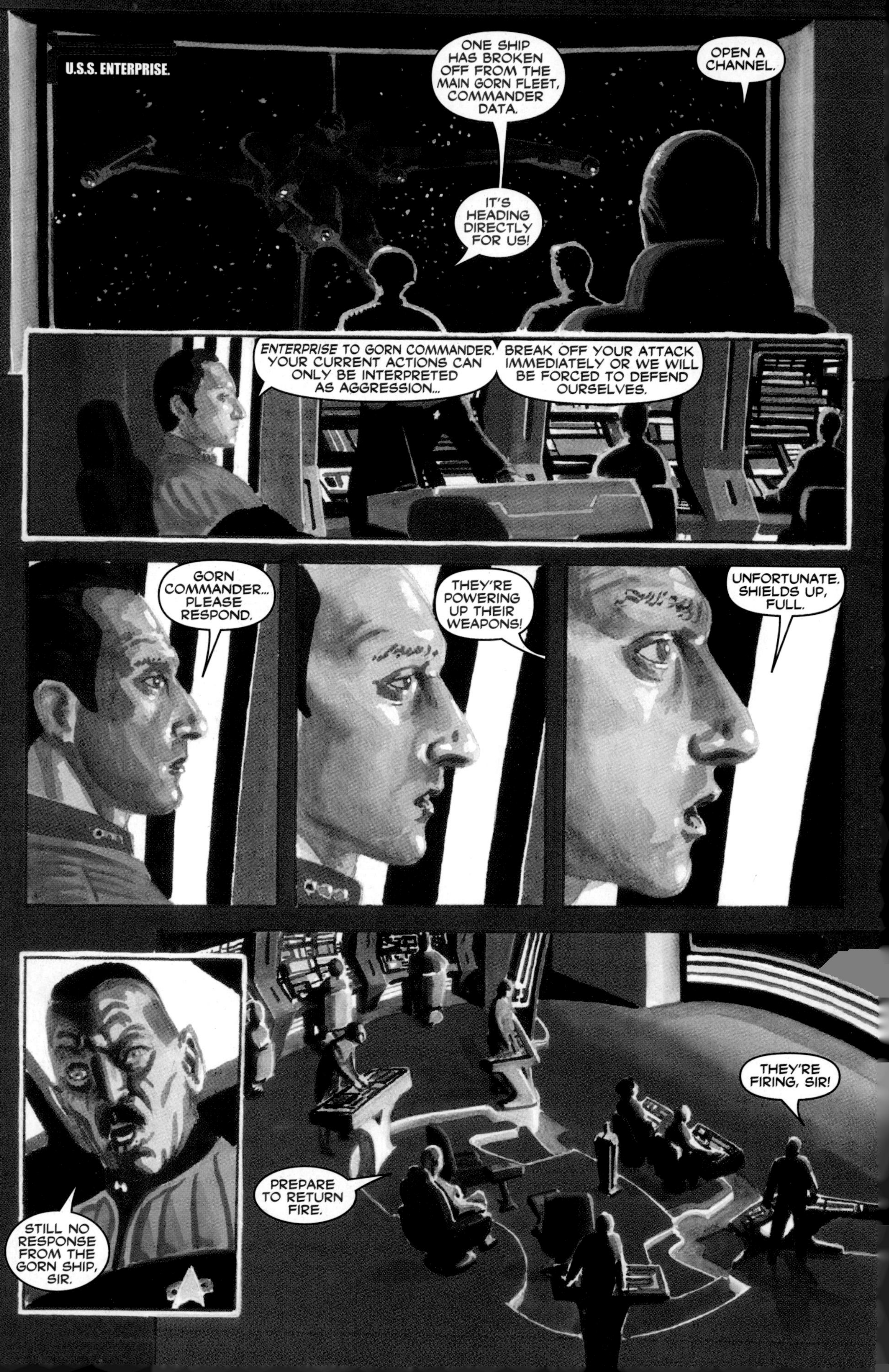
U.S.S. ENTERPRISE.
ONE SHIP HAS BROKEN OFF FROM THE MAIN GORN FLEET, COMMANDER DATA.
IT'S HEADING DIRECTLY FOR US!
OPEN A CHANNEL.
ENTERPRISE TO GORN COMMANDER. YOUR CURRENT ACTIONS CAN ONLY BE INTERPRETED AS AGGRESSION...
BREAK OFF YOUR ATTACK IMMEDIATELY OR WE WILL BE FORCED TO DEFEND OURSELVES.
GORN COMMANDER... PLEASE RESPOND.
THEY'RE POWERING UP THEIR WEAPONS!
UNFORTUNATE. SHIELDS UP, FULL.
STILL NO RESPONSE FROM THE GORN SHIP, SIR.
PREPARE TO RETURN FIRE.
THEY'RE FIRING, SIR!

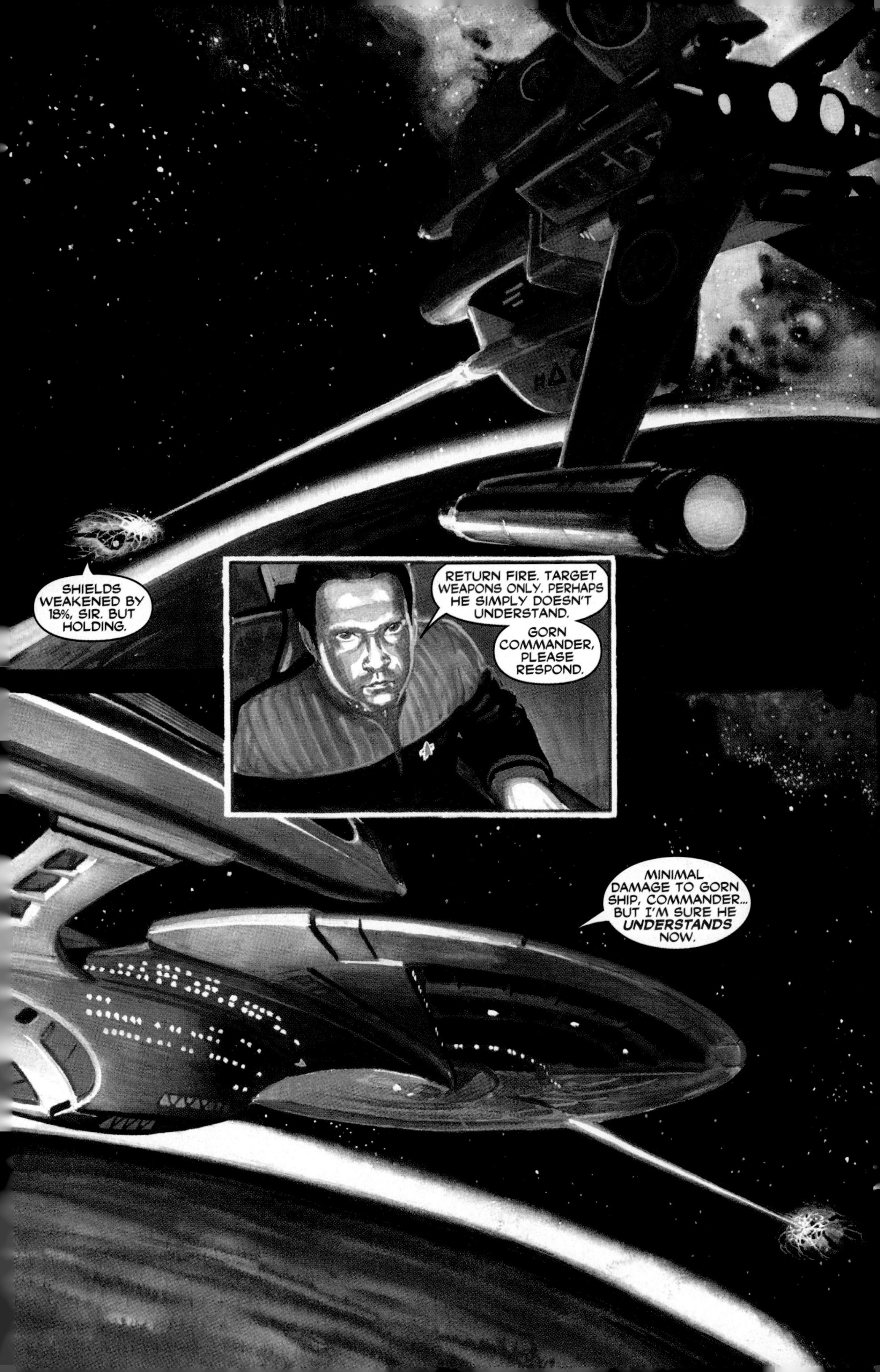
SHIELDS WEAKENED BY 18%, SIR. BUT HOLDING.
RETURN FIRE. TARGET WEAPONS ONLY. PERHAPS HE SIMPLY DOESN'T UNDERSTAND.
GORN COMMANDER, PLEASE RESPOND.
MINIMAL DAMAGE TO GORN SHIP, COMMANDER... BUT I'M SURE HE *UNDERSTANDS* NOW.

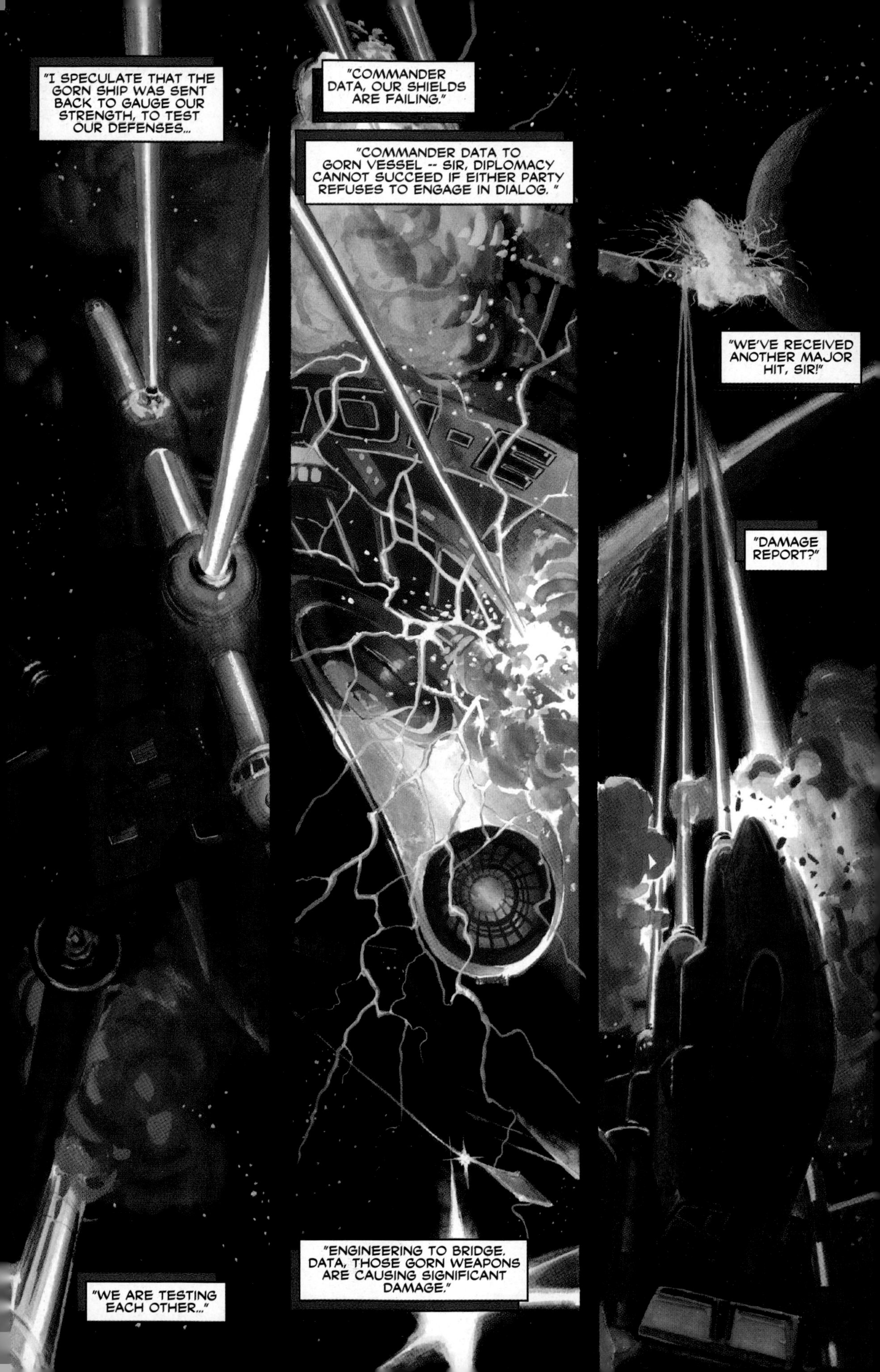
"I SPECULATE THAT THE GORN SHIP WAS SENT BACK TO GAUGE OUR STRENGTH, TO TEST OUR DEFENSES...
"WE ARE TESTING EACH OTHER..."
"COMMANDER DATA, OUR SHIELDS ARE FAILING."
"COMMANDER DATA TO GORN VESSEL -- SIR, DIPLOMACY CANNOT SUCCEED IF EITHER PARTY REFUSES TO ENGAGE IN DIALOG."
"ENGINEERING TO BRIDGE. DATA, THOSE GORN WEAPONS ARE CAUSING SIGNIFICANT DAMAGE."
"WE'VE RECEIVED ANOTHER MAJOR HIT, SIR!"
"DAMAGE REPORT?"

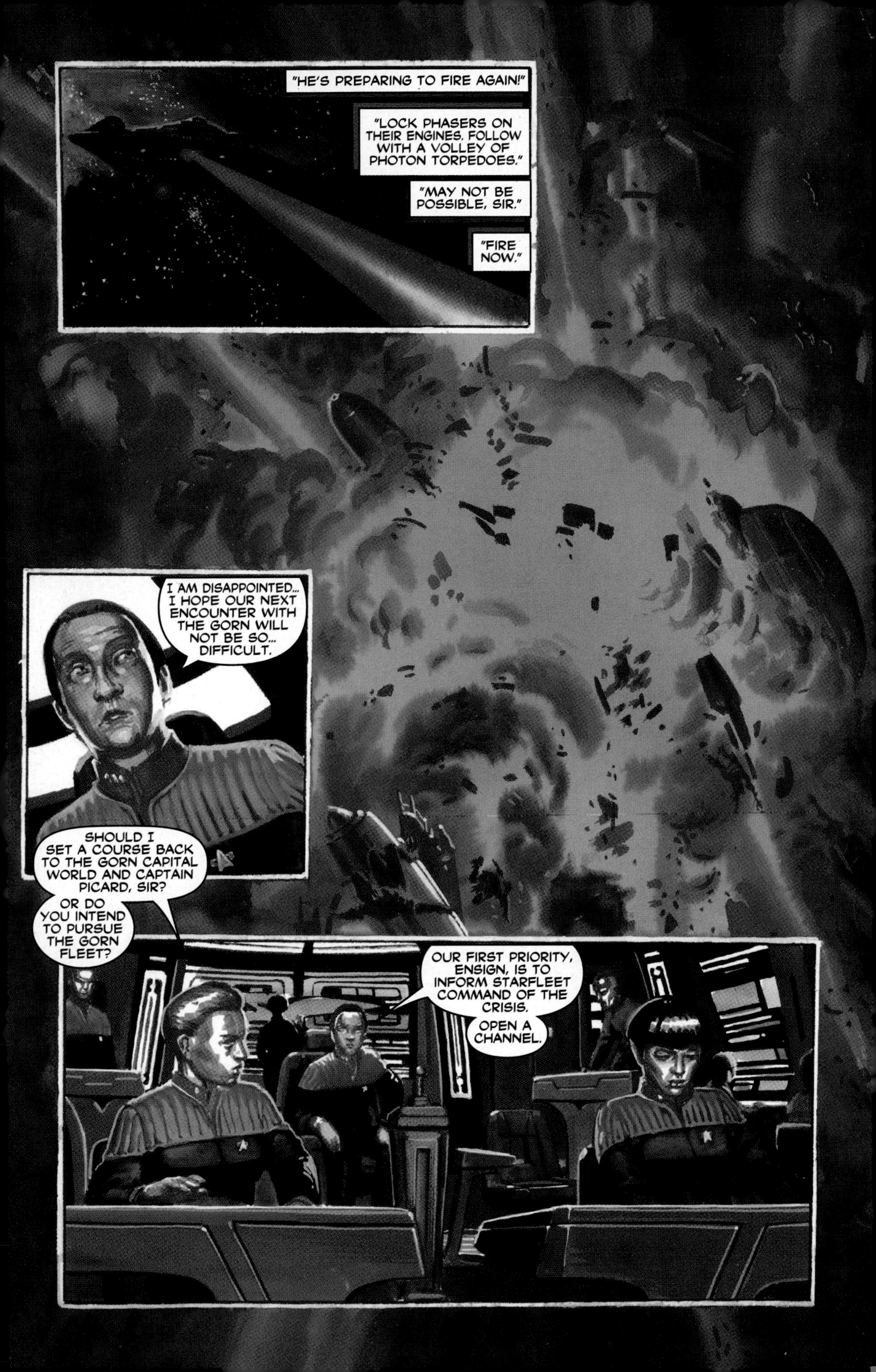
"HE'S PREPARING TO FIRE AGAIN!"
"LOCK PHASERS ON THEIR ENGINES. FOLLOW WITH A VOLLEY OF PHOTON TORPEDOES."
"MAY NOT BE POSSIBLE, SIR."
"FIRE NOW."
I AM DISAPPOINTED... I HOPE OUR NEXT ENCOUNTER WITH THE GORN WILL NOT BE SO... DIFFICULT.
SHOULD I SET A COURSE BACK TO THE GORN CAPITAL WORLD AND CAPTAIN PICARD, SIR?
OR DO YOU INTEND TO PURSUE THE GORN FLEET?
OUR FIRST PRIORITY, ENSIGN, IS TO INFORM STARFLEET COMMAND OF THE CRISIS.
OPEN A CHANNEL.

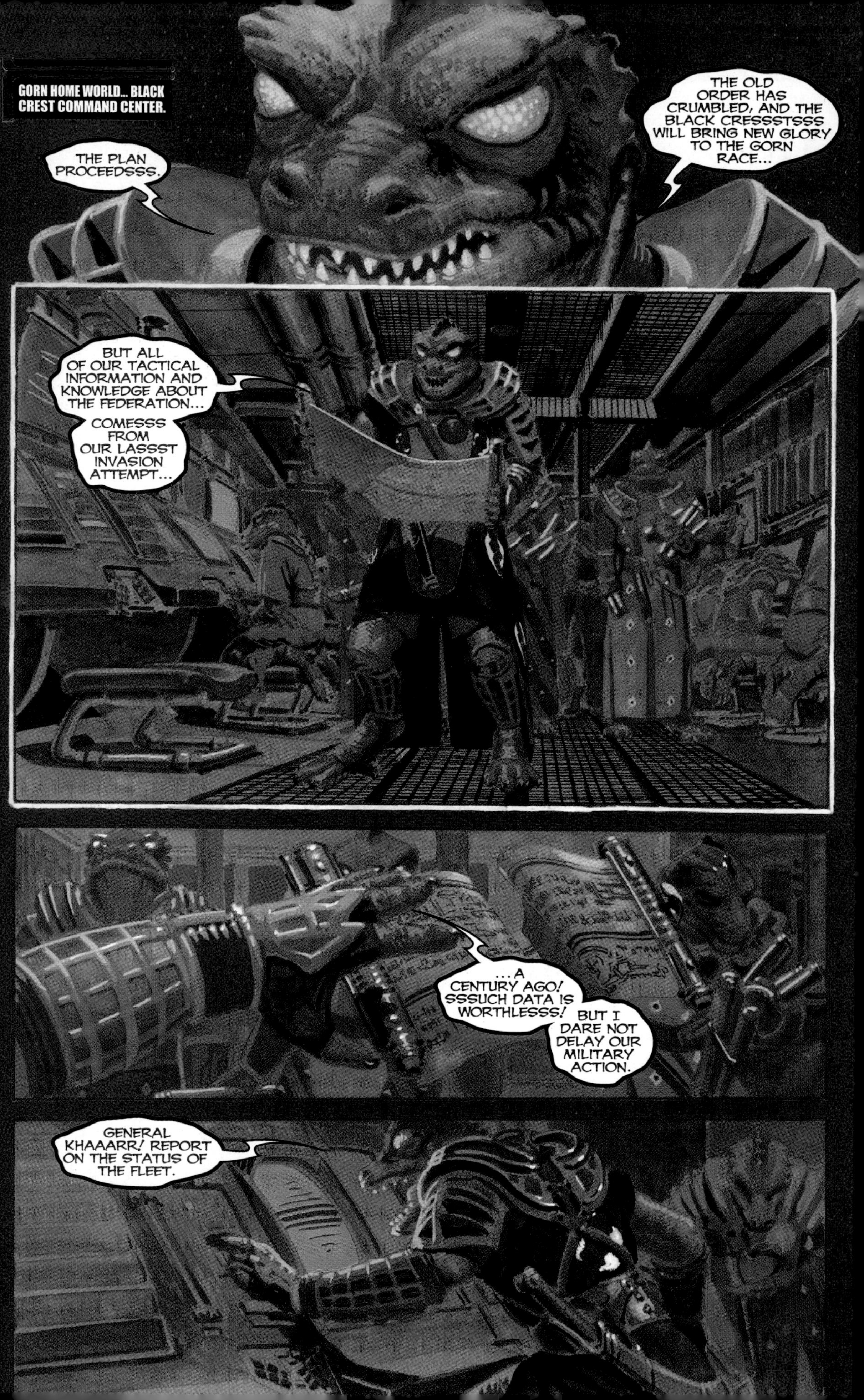
GORN HOME WORLD... BLACK CREST COMMAND CENTER.
THE PLAN PROCEEDSSS.
THE OLD ORDER HAS CRUMBLED, AND THE BLACK CRESSSTSSS WILL BRING NEW GLORY TO THE GORN RACE...
BUT ALL OF OUR TACTICAL INFORMATION AND KNOWLEDGE ABOUT THE FEDERATION...
COMESSS FROM OUR LASSST INVASION ATTEMPT...
...A CENTURY AGO! SSSUCH DATA IS WORTHLESSS!
BUT I DARE NOT DELAY OUR MILITARY ACTION.
GENERAL KHAAARR! REPORT ON THE STATUS OF THE FLEET.

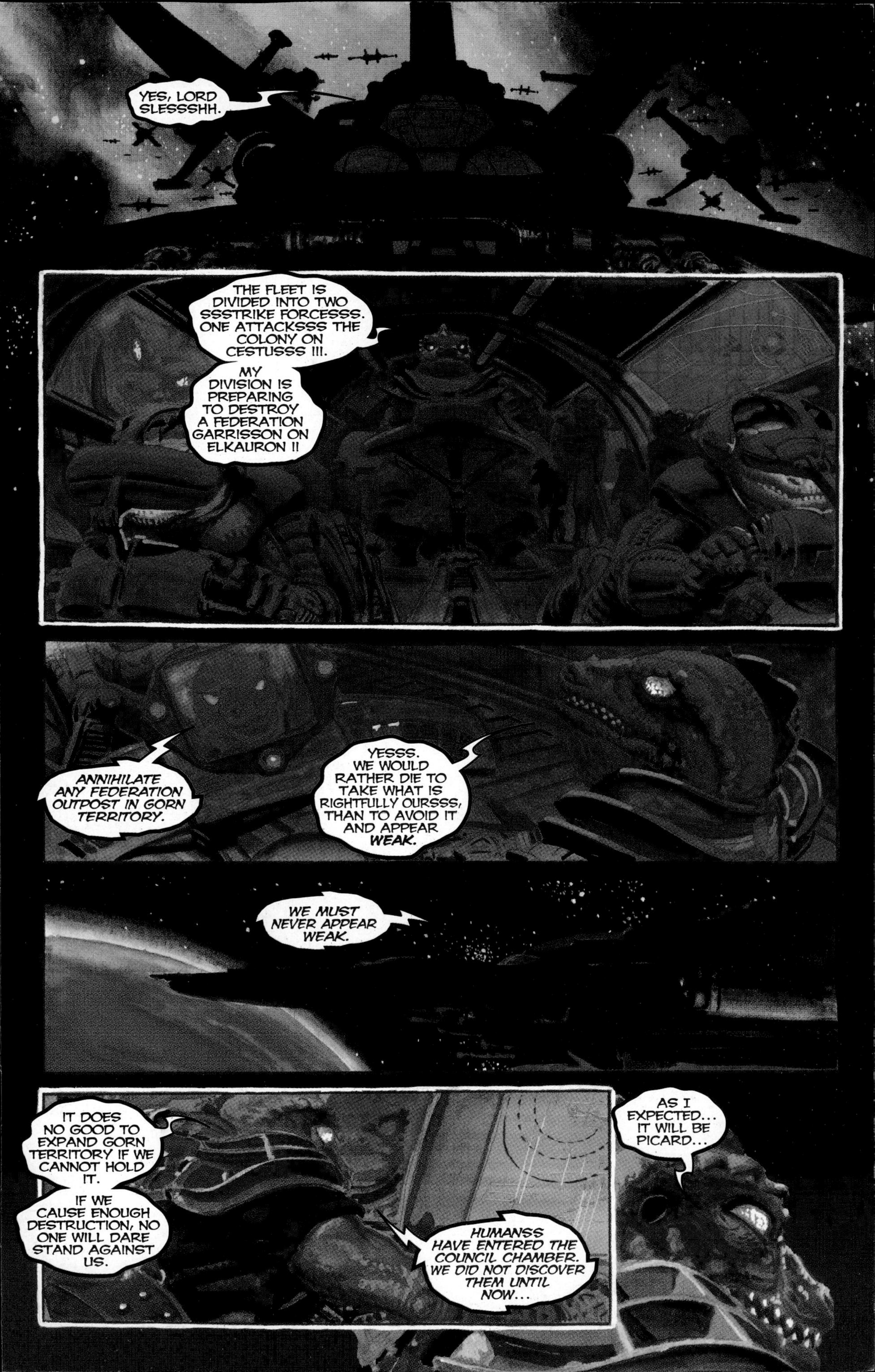
YES, LORD SLESSSHH.
THE FLEET IS DIVIDED INTO TWO SSSTRIKE FORCESSS. ONE ATTACKSSS THE COLONY ON CESTUSSS III.
MY DIVISION IS PREPARING TO DESTROY A FEDERATION GARRISSON ON ELKAURON II!
ANNIHILATE ANY FEDERATION OUTPOST IN GORN TERRITORY.
YESSS. WE WOULD RATHER DIE TO TAKE WHAT IS RIGHTFULLY OURSSS, THAN TO AVOID IT AND APPEAR WEAK.
WE MUST NEVER APPEAR WEAK.
IT DOES NO GOOD TO EXPAND GORN TERRITORY IF WE CANNOT HOLD IT.
IF WE CAUSE ENOUGH DESTRUCTION, NO ONE WILL DARE STAND AGAINST US.
HUMANSS HAVE ENTERED THE COUNCIL CHAMBER. WE DID NOT DISCOVER THEM UNTIL NOW...
AS I EXPECTED... IT WILL BE PICARD...

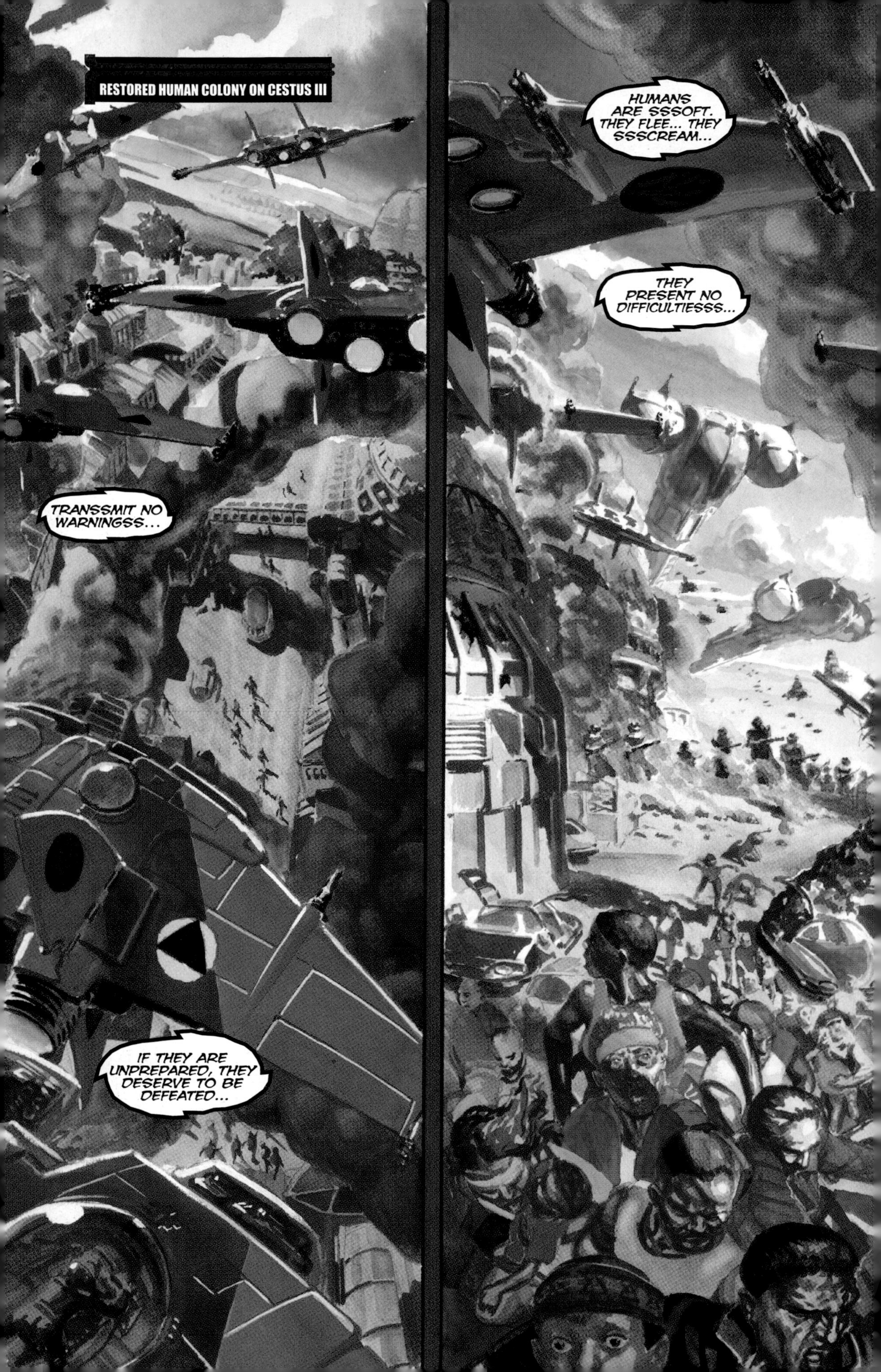
RESTORED HUMAN COLONY ON CESTUS III
TRANSMIT NO WARNINGSS...
IF THEY ARE UNPREPARED, THEY DESERVE TO BE DEFEATED...
HUMANS ARE SSSOFT. THEY FLEE... THEY SSSCREAM...
THEY PRESENT NO DIFFICULTIESSS...

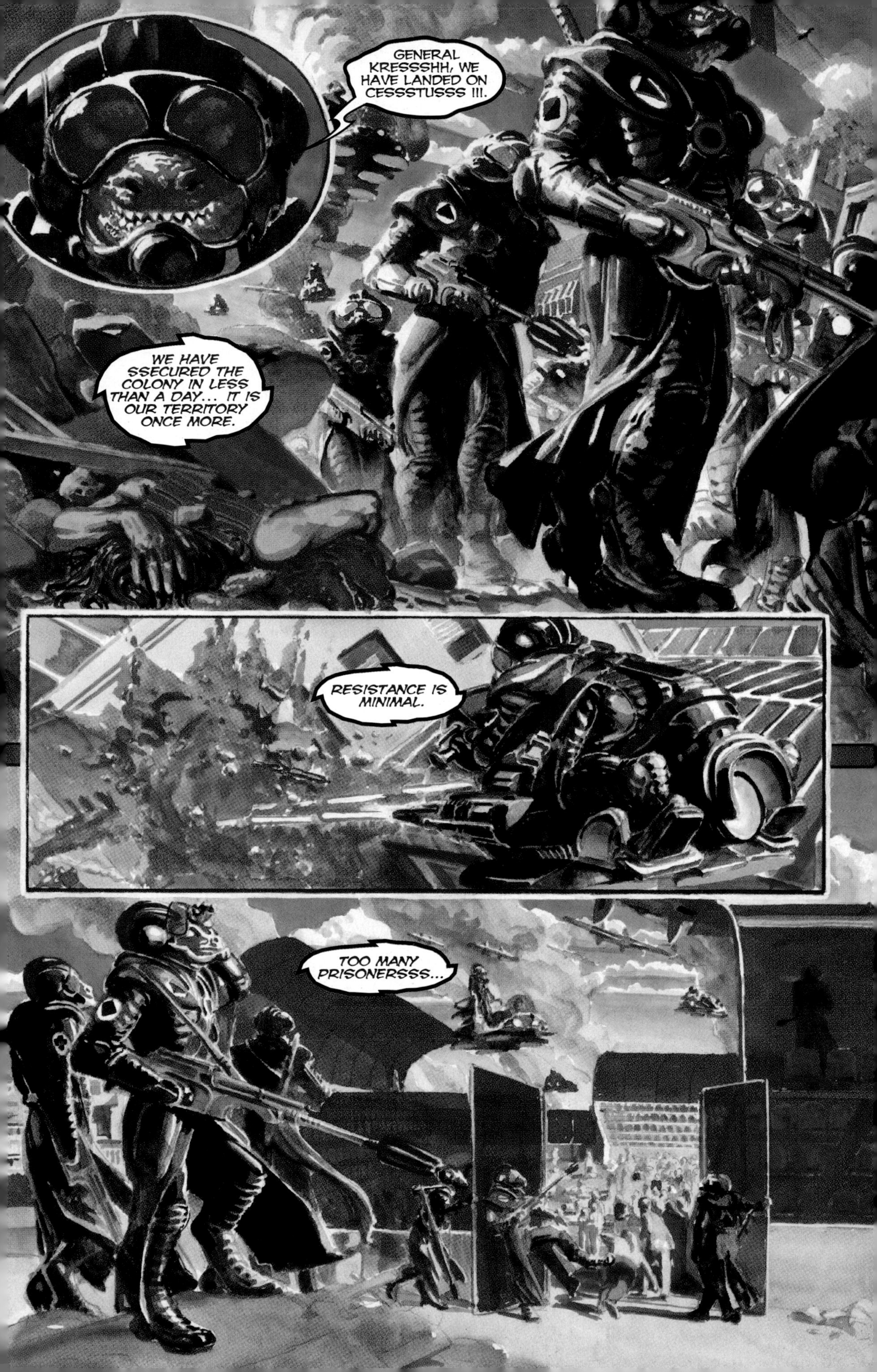
GENERAL KRESSSHH, WE HAVE LANDED ON CESSSTUSSS !!!.
WE HAVE SSECURED THE COLONY IN LESS THAN A DAY... IT IS OUR TERRITORY ONCE MORE.
RESISTANCE IS MINIMAL.
TOO MANY PRISONERSSS...

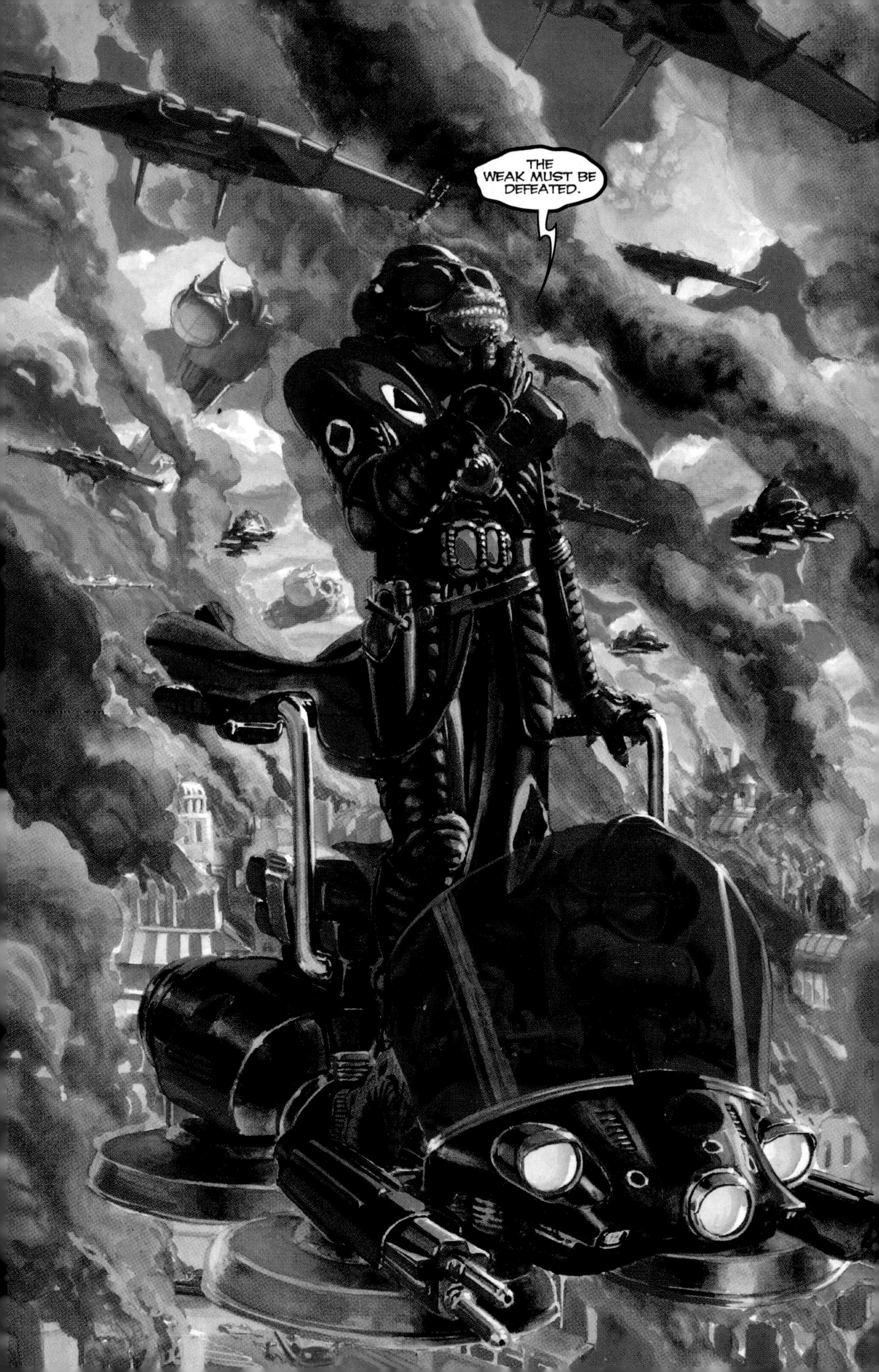
THE WEAK MUST BE DEFEATED.

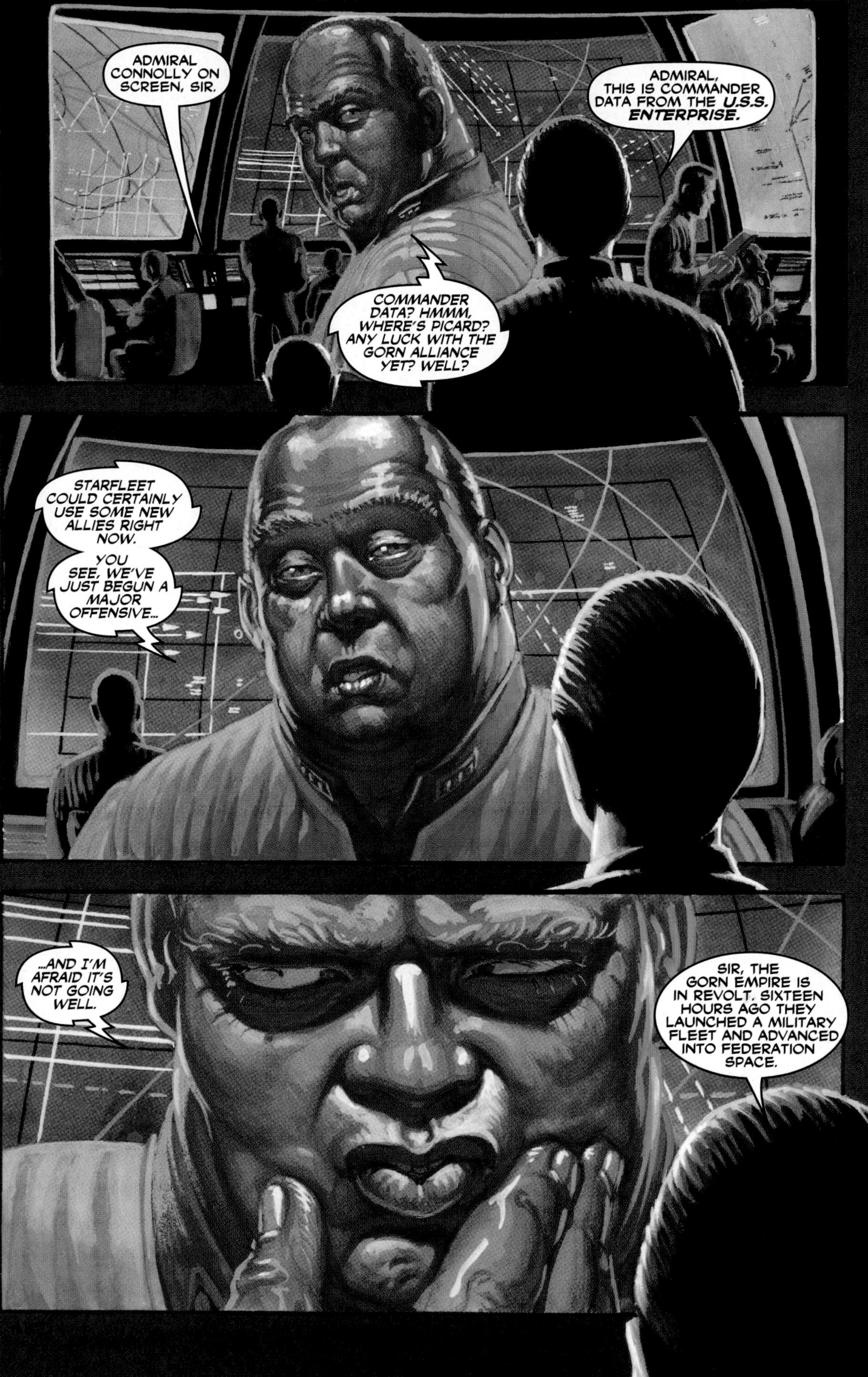
ADMIRAL CONNOLLY ON SCREEN, SIR.
ADMIRAL, THIS IS COMMANDER DATA FROM THE U.S.S. ENTERPRISE.
COMMANDER DATA? HMMM, WHERE'S PICARD? ANY LUCK WITH THE GORN ALLIANCE YET? WELL?
STARFLEET COULD CERTAINLY USE SOME NEW ALLIES RIGHT NOW.
YOU SEE, WE'VE JUST BEGUN A MAJOR OFFENSIVE...
...AND I'M AFRAID IT'S NOT GOING WELL.
SIR, THE GORN EMPIRE IS IN REVOLT. SIXTEEN HOURS AGO THEY LAUNCHED A MILITARY FLEET AND ADVANCED INTO FEDERATION SPACE.

I WAS HOPING TO REQUEST STARFLEET ASSISTANCE, SIR.

THE GORN HAVE BEGUN ATTACKING OUR OUTPOSTS...

ONE OF THEIR WARSHIPS FIRED ON THE *ENTERPRISE*, SIR. IN THE SUBSEQUENT ENGAGEMENT, THE GORN VESSEL WAS DESTROYED.

THAT'S BAD NEWS. BUT THERE'S NO WAY STARFLEET CAN MOUNT A RESPONSE, I'M AFRAID.

NOT NOW.

ADMIRAL, WE'VE HAD ANOTHER SETBACK. TACTICAL HAS REQUESTED --

COMMANDER, I CAN'T CONTINUE THIS CONVERSATION.

HMMM, I SUGGEST YOU USE DIPLOMACY, OR PHASERS -- WHATEVER WORKS!

I'M AFRAID YOU'RE ON YOUR OWN, COMMANDER DATA.

CONNOLLY, OUT.

DATA TO ENGINEERING, PLEASE PROVIDE A FULL DAMAGE REPORT. PRIORITY REPAIRS TO SHIELDS AND WEAPONS.

THE *ENTERPRISE* HAS A LOT OF WORK TO DO.

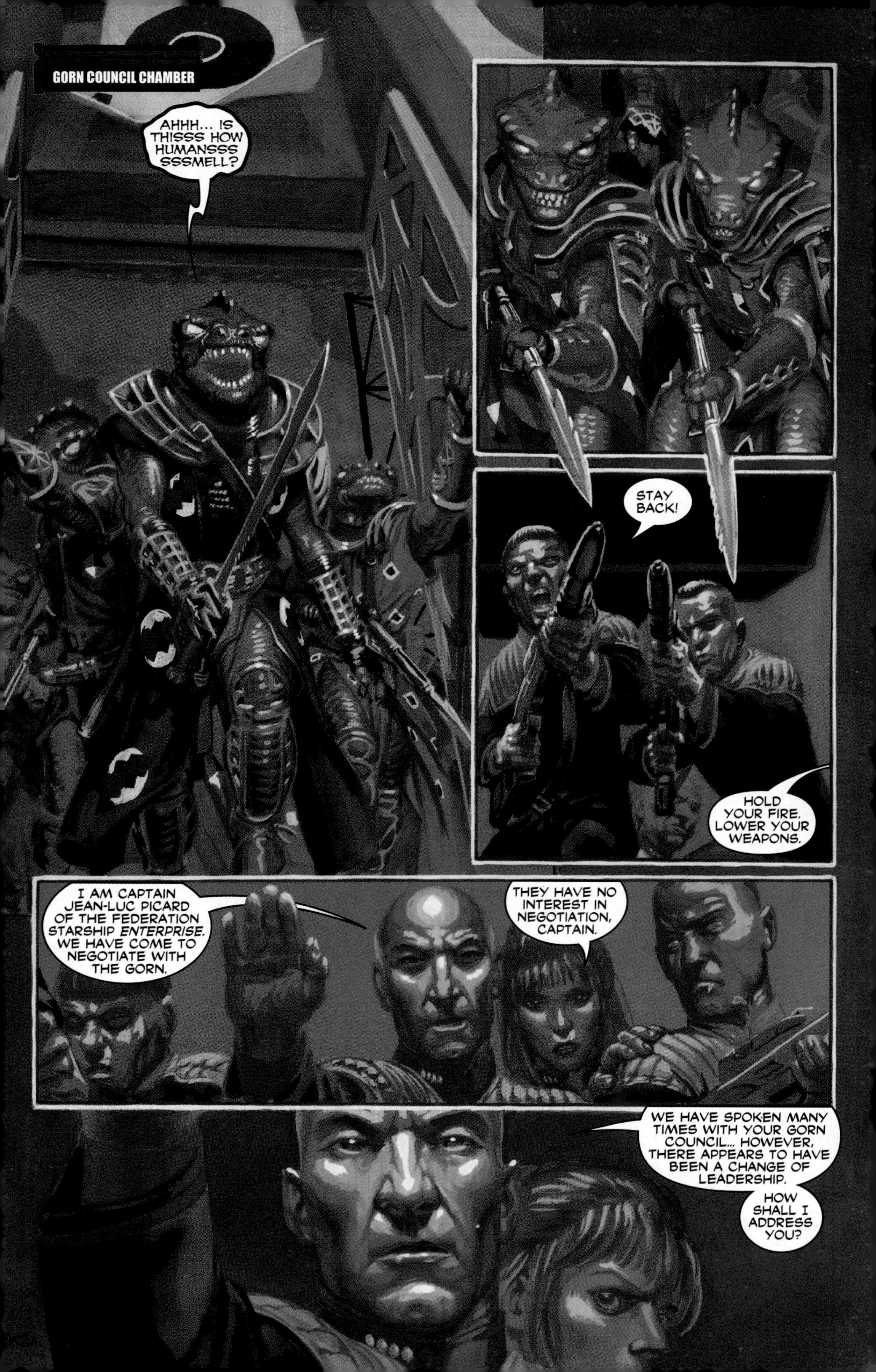
GORN COUNCIL CHAMBER
AHHH... IS THISSS HOW HUMANSSS SSSMELL?
STAY BACK!
HOLD YOUR FIRE. LOWER YOUR WEAPONS.
I AM CAPTAIN JEAN-LUC PICARD OF THE FEDERATION STARSHIP *ENTERPRISE*. WE HAVE COME TO NEGOTIATE WITH THE GORN.
THEY HAVE NO INTEREST IN NEGOTIATION, CAPTAIN.
WE HAVE SPOKEN MANY TIMES WITH YOUR GORN COUNCIL... HOWEVER, THERE APPEARS TO HAVE BEEN A CHANGE OF LEADERSHIP.
HOW SHALL I ADDRESS YOU?

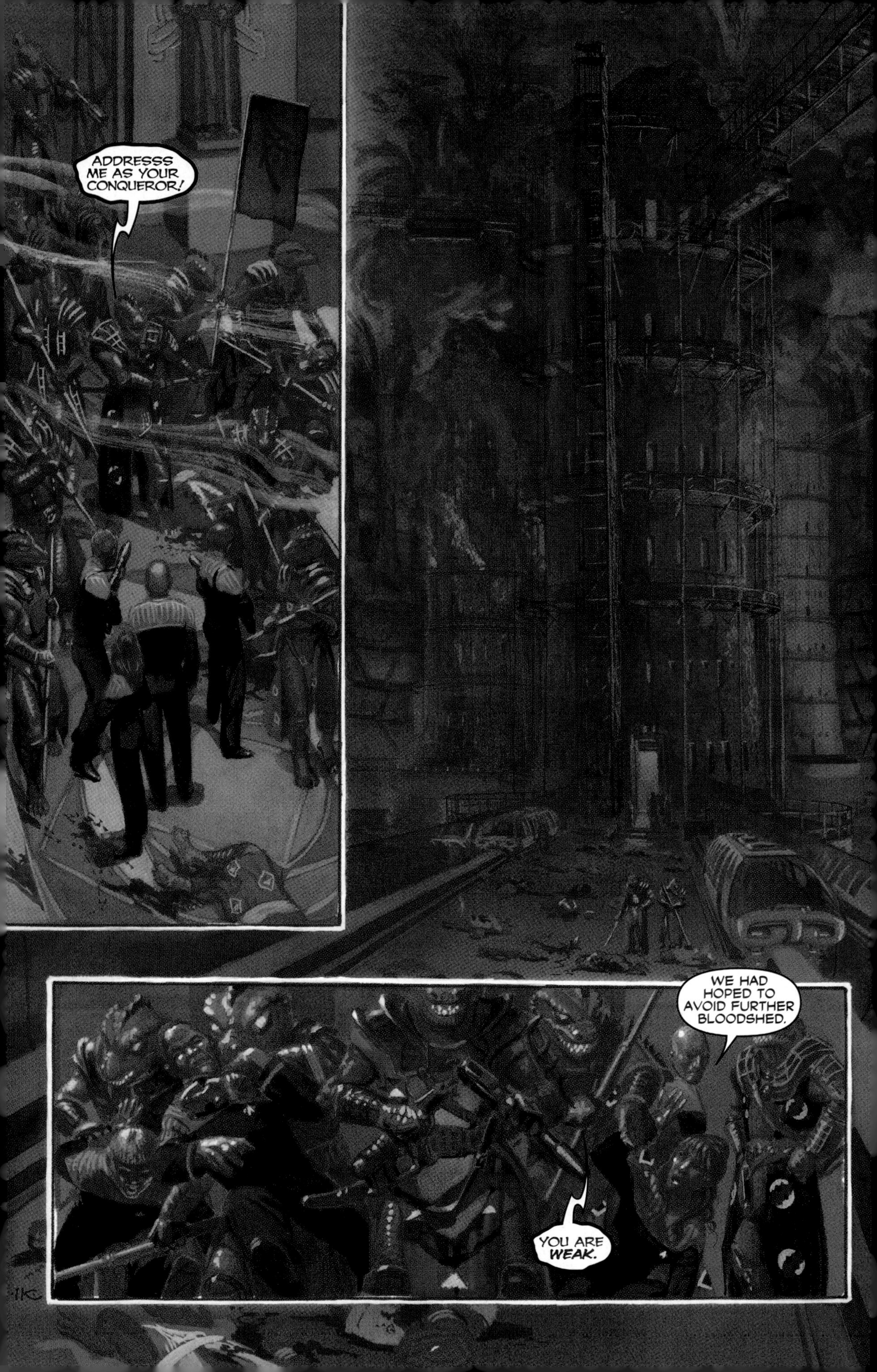
ADDRESSS ME AS YOUR CONQUEROR!
WE HAD HOPED TO AVOID FURTHER BLOODSHED.
YOU ARE WEAK.

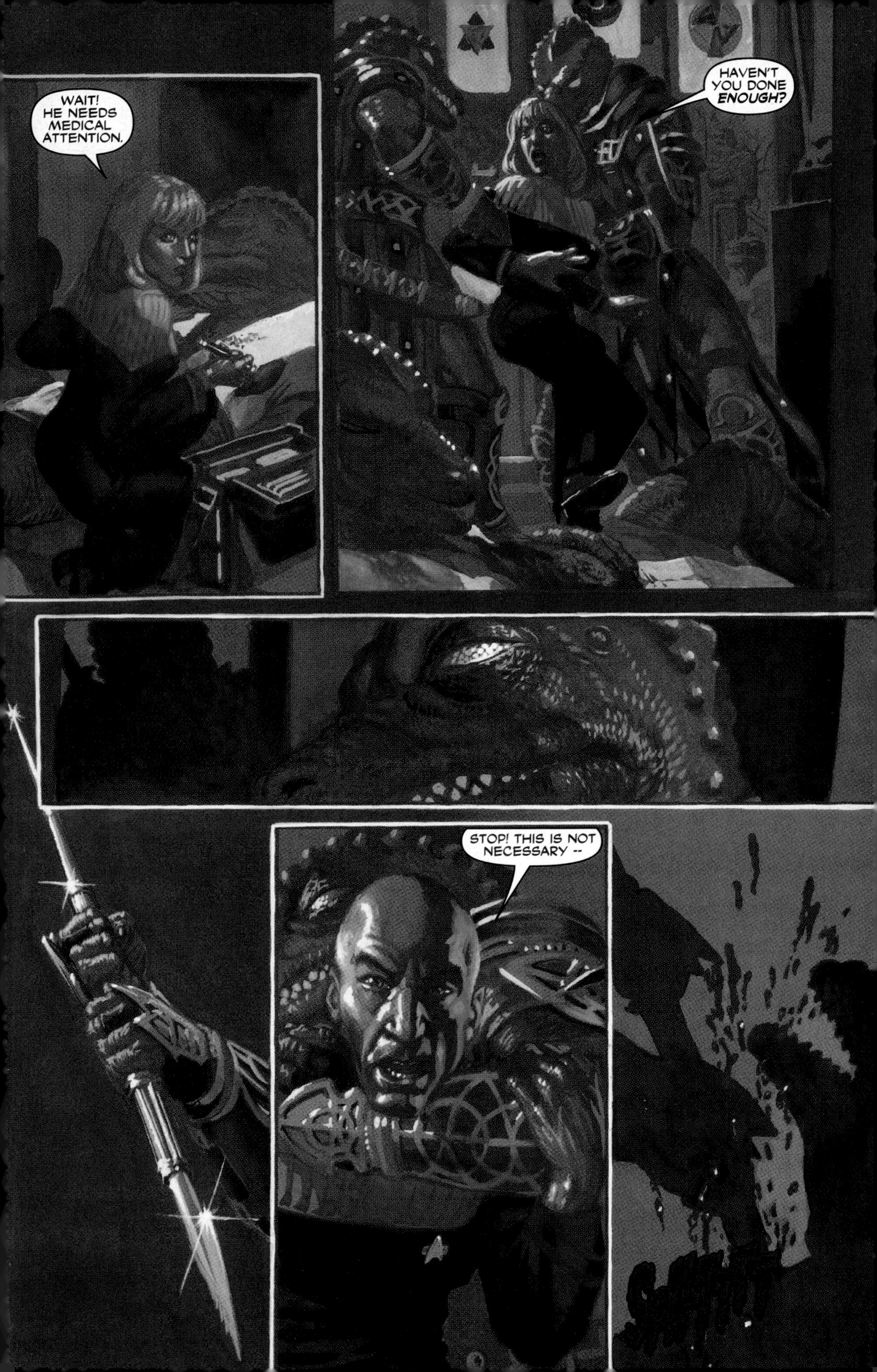
WAIT! HE NEEDS MEDICAL ATTENTION.
HAVEN'T YOU DONE ENOUGH?
STOP! THIS IS NOT NECESSARY --

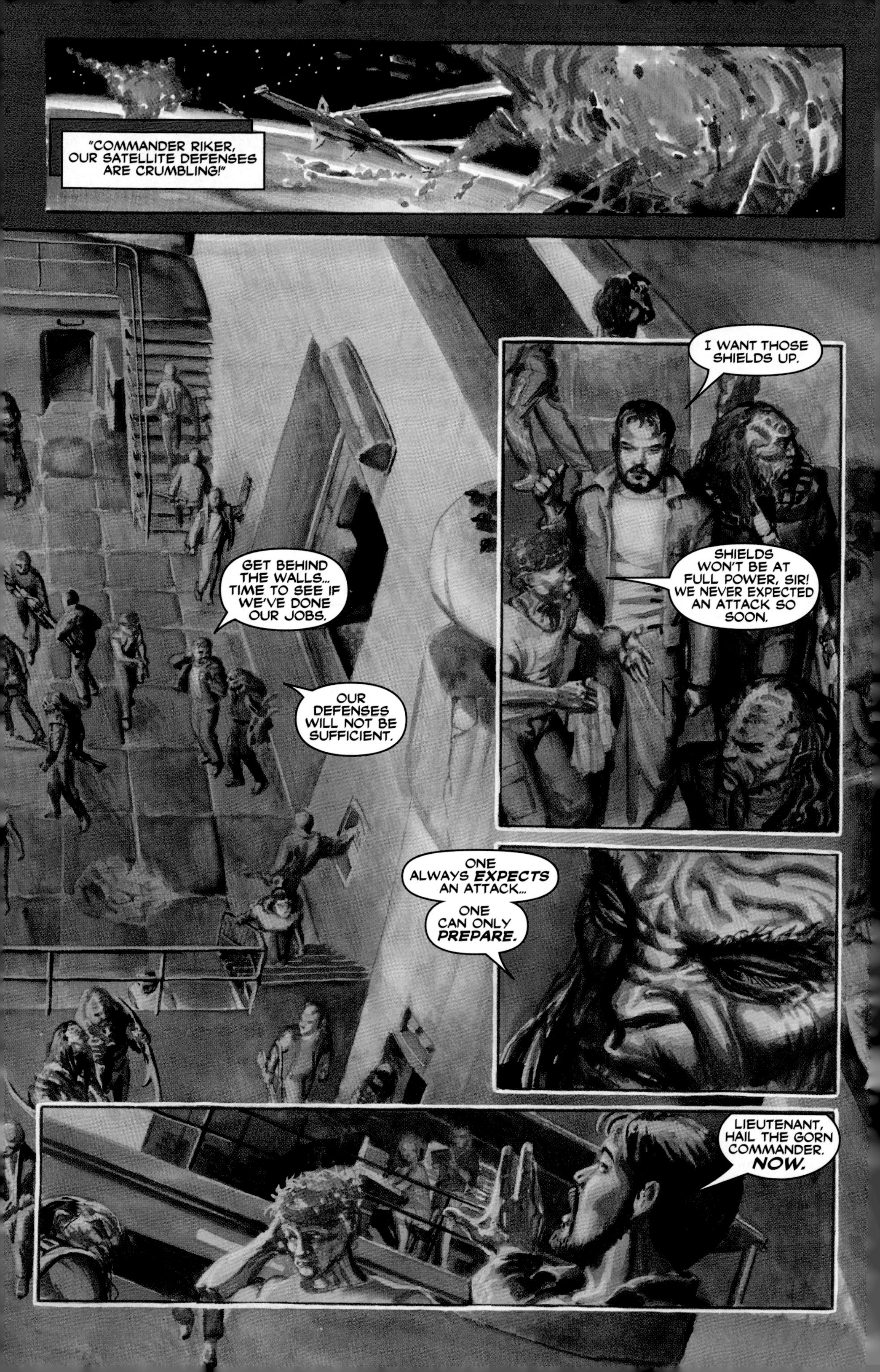
"COMMANDER RIKER, OUR SATELLITE DEFENSES ARE CRUMBLING!"
GET BEHIND THE WALLS... TIME TO SEE IF WE'VE DONE OUR JOBS.
OUR DEFENSES WILL NOT BE SUFFICIENT.
I WANT THOSE SHIELDS UP.
SHIELDS WON'T BE AT FULL POWER, SIR! WE NEVER EXPECTED AN ATTACK SO SOON.
ONE ALWAYS EXPECTS AN ATTACK...
ONE CAN ONLY PREPARE.
LIEUTENANT, HAIL THE GORN COMMANDER. NOW.

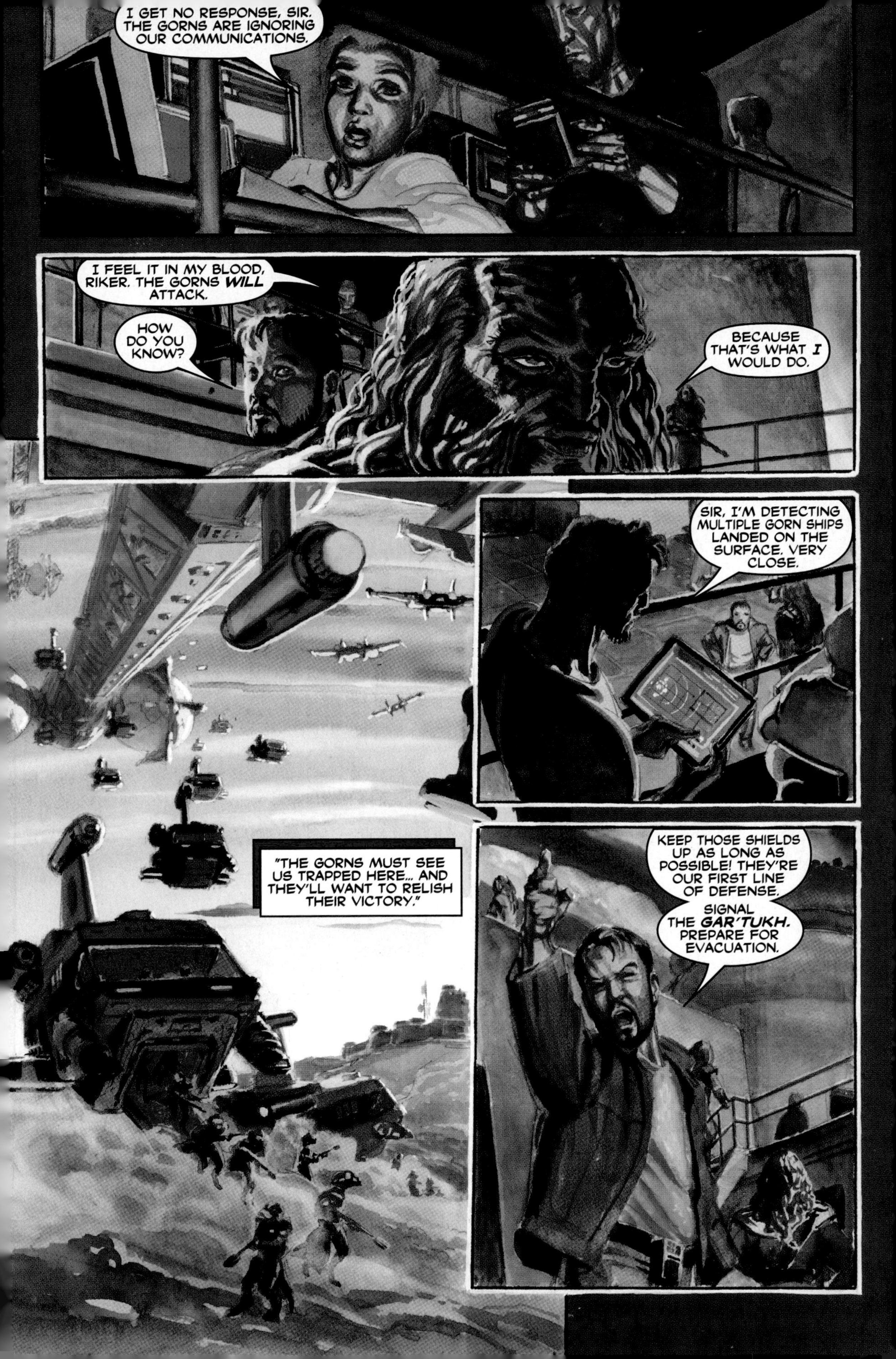
I GET NO RESPONSE, SIR. THE GORNS ARE IGNORING OUR COMMUNICATIONS.
I FEEL IT IN MY BLOOD, RIKER. THE GORNS *WILL* ATTACK.
HOW DO YOU KNOW?
BECAUSE THAT'S WHAT *I* WOULD DO.
SIR, I'M DETECTING MULTIPLE GORN SHIPS LANDED ON THE SURFACE. VERY CLOSE.
"THE GORNS MUST SEE US TRAPPED HERE... AND THEY'LL WANT TO RELISH THEIR VICTORY."
KEEP THOSE SHIELDS UP AS LONG AS POSSIBLE! THEY'RE OUR FIRST LINE OF DEFENSE.
SIGNAL THE *GAR'TUKH.* PREPARE FOR EVACUATION.

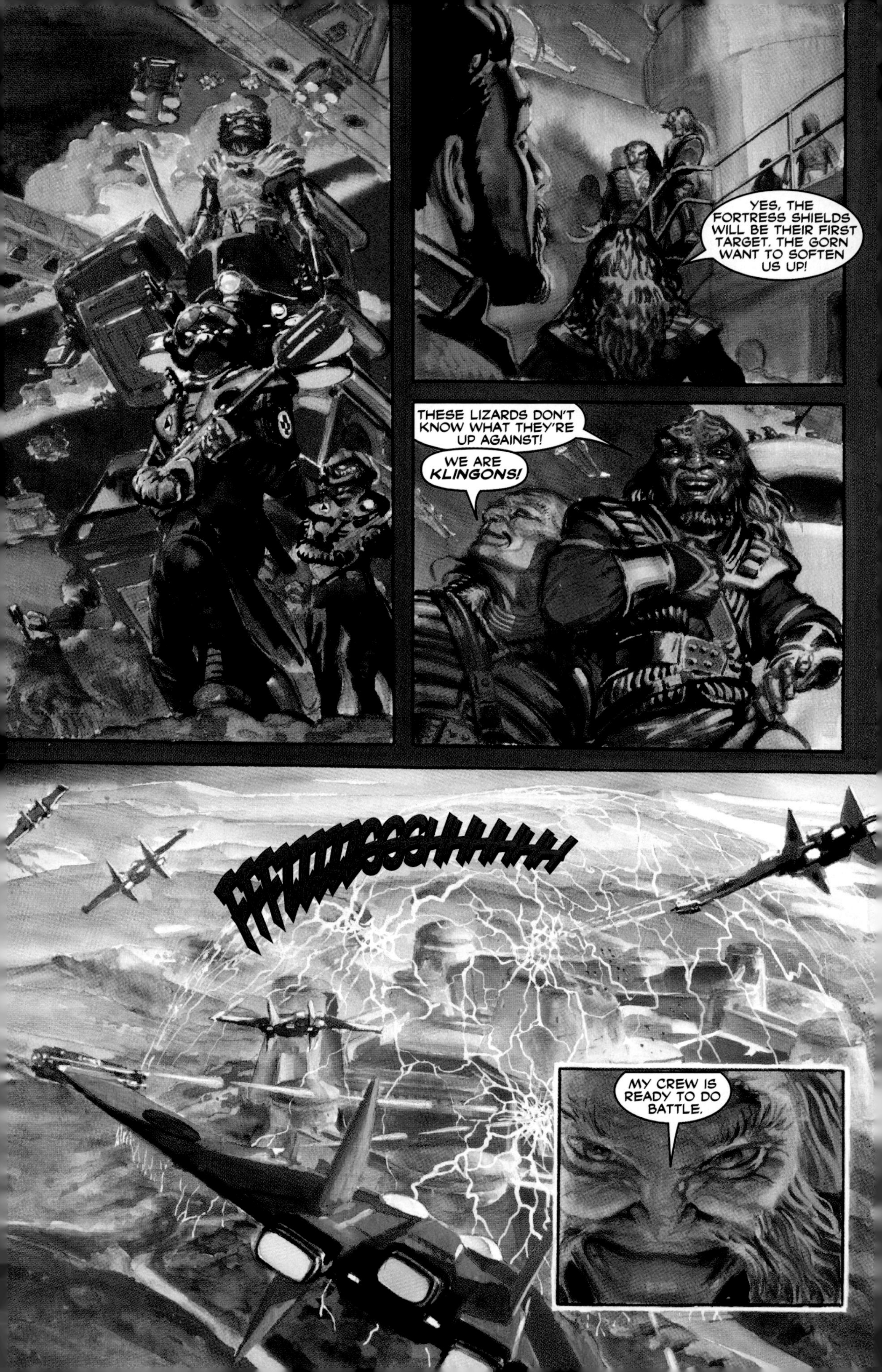
YES, THE FORTRESS SHIELDS WILL BE THEIR FIRST TARGET. THE GORN WANT TO SOFTEN US UP!
THESE LIZARDS DON'T KNOW WHAT THEY'RE UP AGAINST!
WE ARE KLINGONS!
FFFZZZZSSSHHHHHH!
MY CREW IS READY TO DO BATTLE.

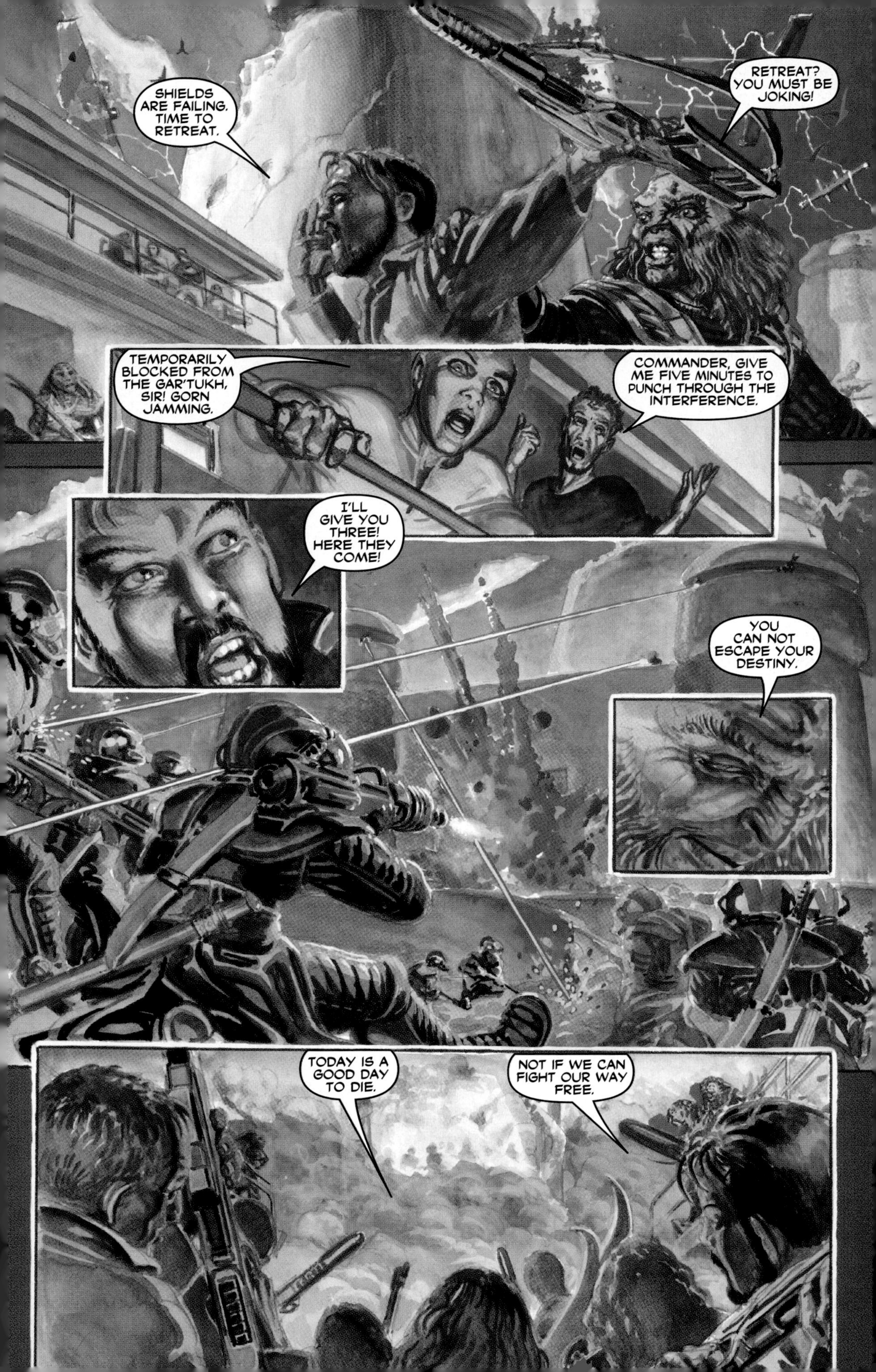
SHIELDS ARE FAILING. TIME TO RETREAT.
RETREAT? YOU MUST BE JOKING!
TEMPORARILY BLOCKED FROM THE GAR'TUKH, SIR! GORN JAMMING.
COMMANDER, GIVE ME FIVE MINUTES TO PUNCH THROUGH THE INTERFERENCE.
I'LL GIVE YOU THREE! HERE THEY COME!
YOU CAN NOT ESCAPE YOUR DESTINY.
TODAY IS A GOOD DAY TO DIE.
NOT IF WE CAN FIGHT OUR WAY FREE.

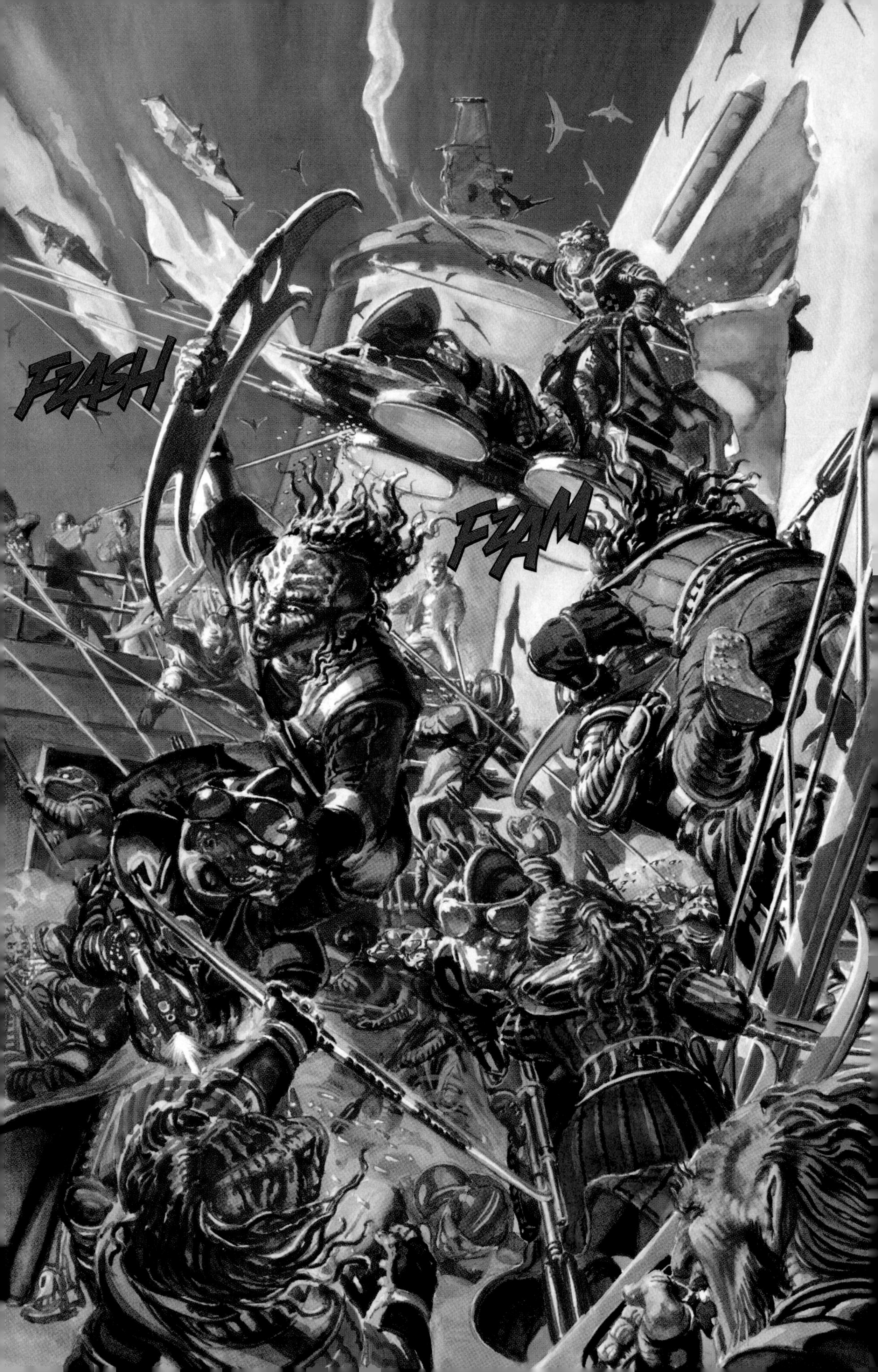
FZASH
FZAM

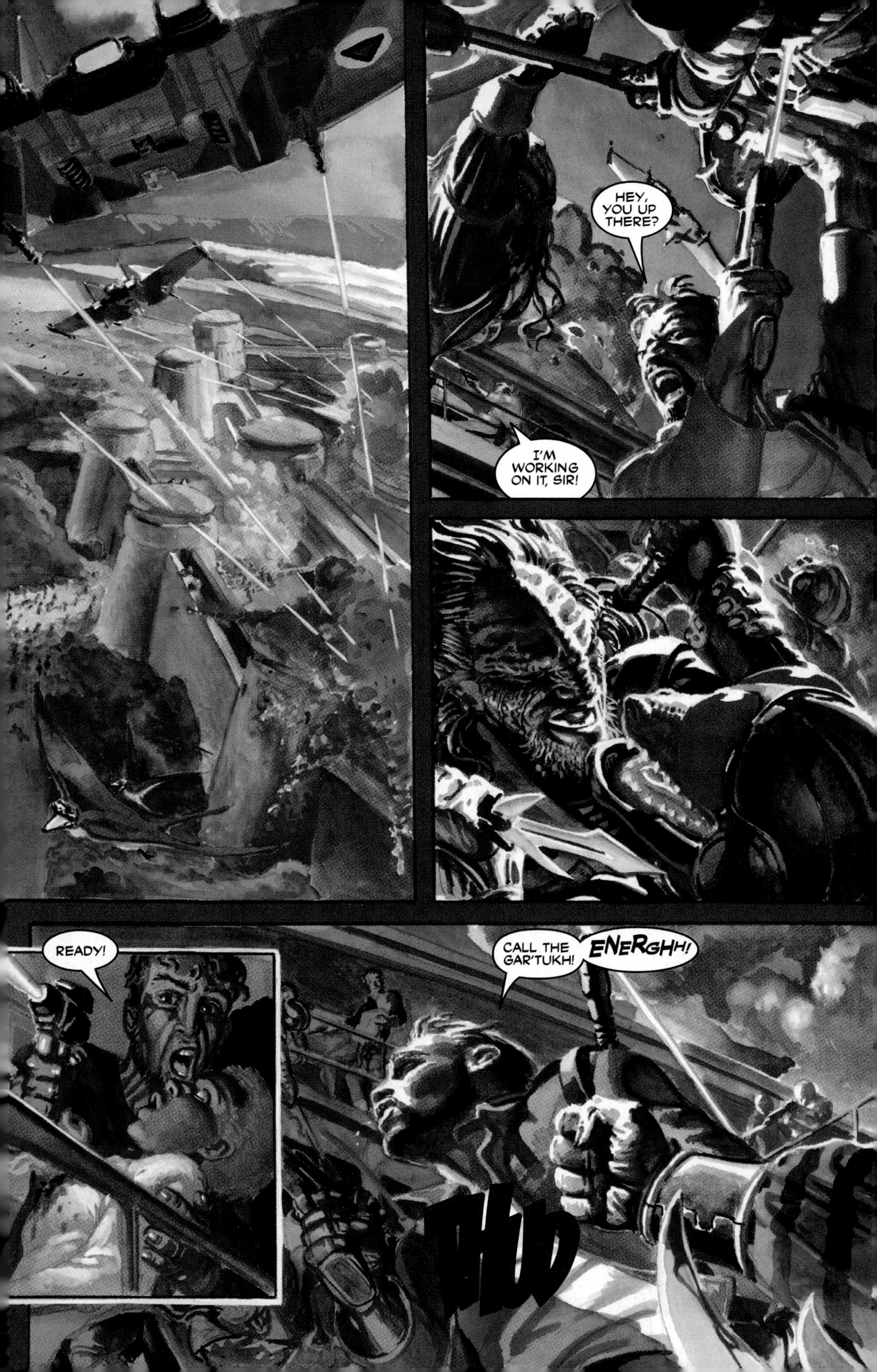
HEY, YOU UP THERE?
I'M WORKING ON IT, SIR!
READY!
CALL THE GAR'TUKH!
ENERGHH!
THUD

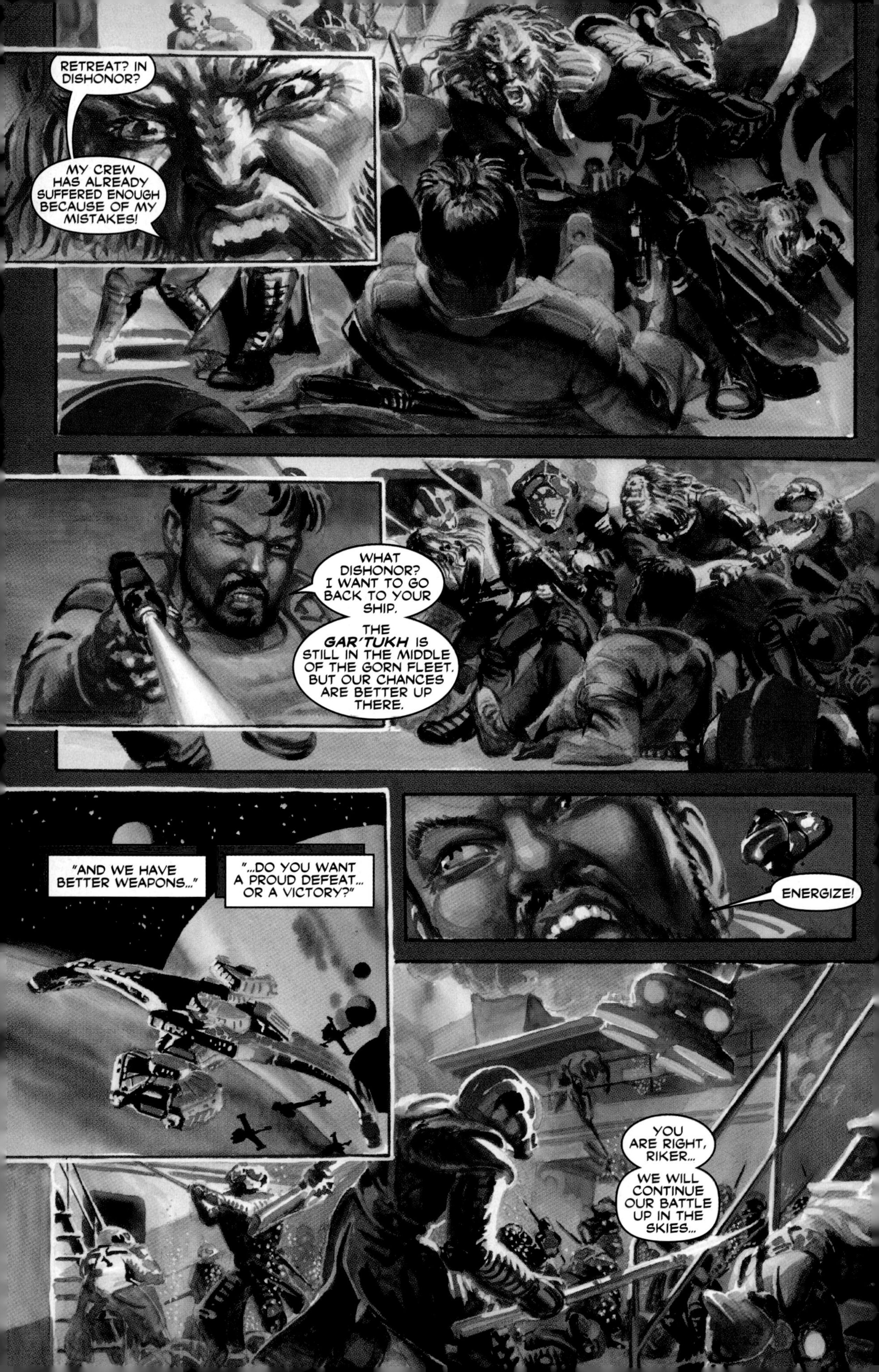
RETREAT? IN DISHONOR?
MY CREW HAS ALREADY SUFFERED ENOUGH BECAUSE OF MY MISTAKES!
WHAT DISHONOR? I WANT TO GO BACK TO YOUR SHIP.
THE GAR'TUKH IS STILL IN THE MIDDLE OF THE GORN FLEET. BUT OUR CHANCES ARE BETTER UP THERE.
"AND WE HAVE BETTER WEAPONS..."
"...DO YOU WANT A PROUD DEFEAT... OR A VICTORY?"
ENERGIZE!
YOU ARE RIGHT, RIKER...
WE WILL CONTINUE OUR BATTLE UP IN THE SKIES...

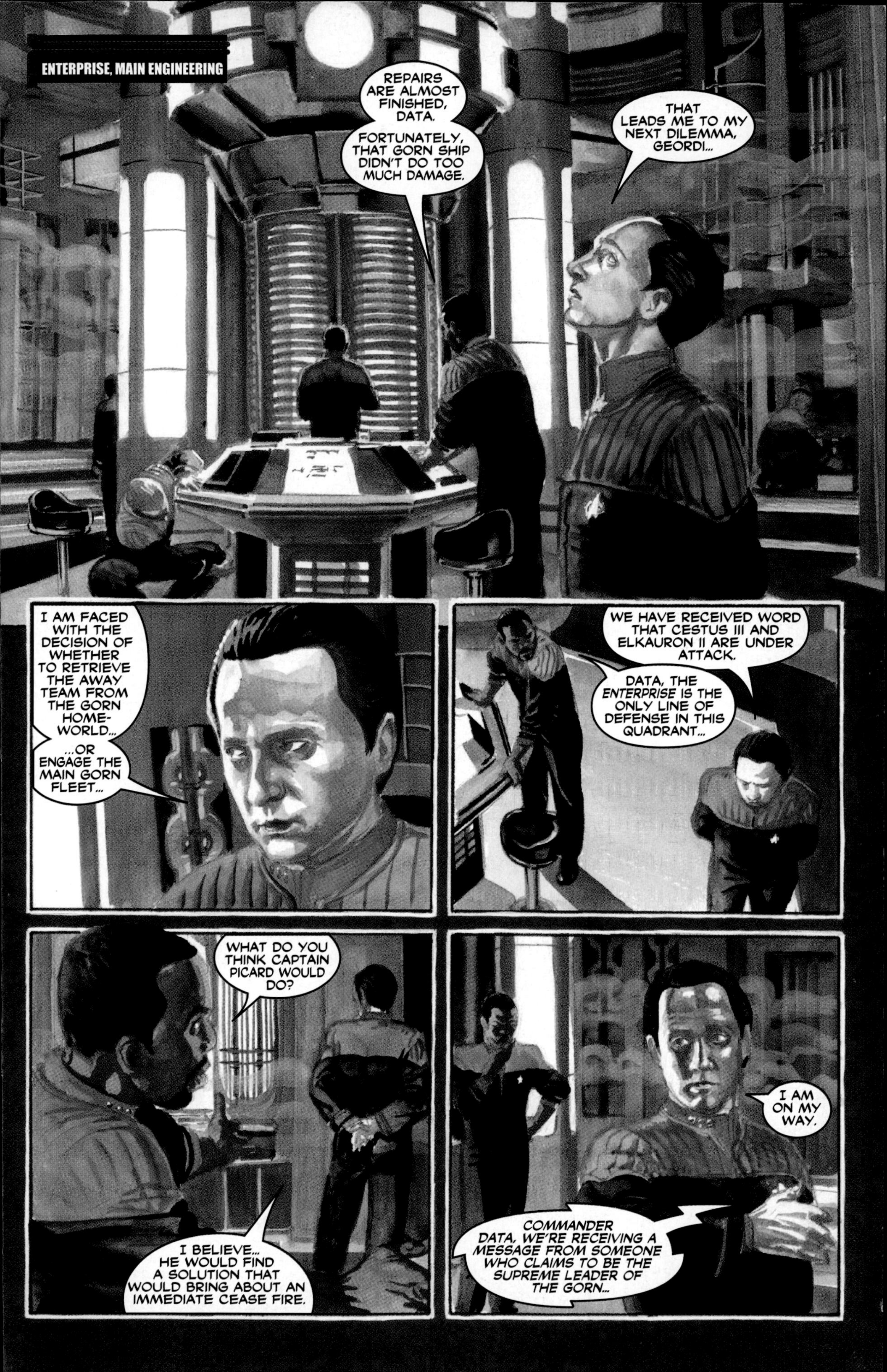
ENTERPRISE, MAIN ENGINEERING
REPAIRS ARE ALMOST FINISHED, DATA.
FORTUNATELY, THAT GORN SHIP DIDN'T DO TOO MUCH DAMAGE.
THAT LEADS ME TO MY NEXT DILEMMA, GEORDI...
I AM FACED WITH THE DECISION OF WHETHER TO RETRIEVE THE AWAY TEAM FROM THE GORN HOME-WORLD...
...OR ENGAGE THE MAIN GORN FLEET...
WE HAVE RECEIVED WORD THAT CESTUS III AND ELKAURON II ARE UNDER ATTACK.
DATA, THE ENTERPRISE IS THE ONLY LINE OF DEFENSE IN THIS QUADRANT...
WHAT DO YOU THINK CAPTAIN PICARD WOULD DO?
I BELIEVE... HE WOULD FIND A SOLUTION THAT WOULD BRING ABOUT AN IMMEDIATE CEASE FIRE.
COMMANDER DATA, WE'RE RECEIVING A MESSAGE FROM SOMEONE WHO CLAIMS TO BE THE SUPREME LEADER OF THE GORN...
I AM ON MY WAY.

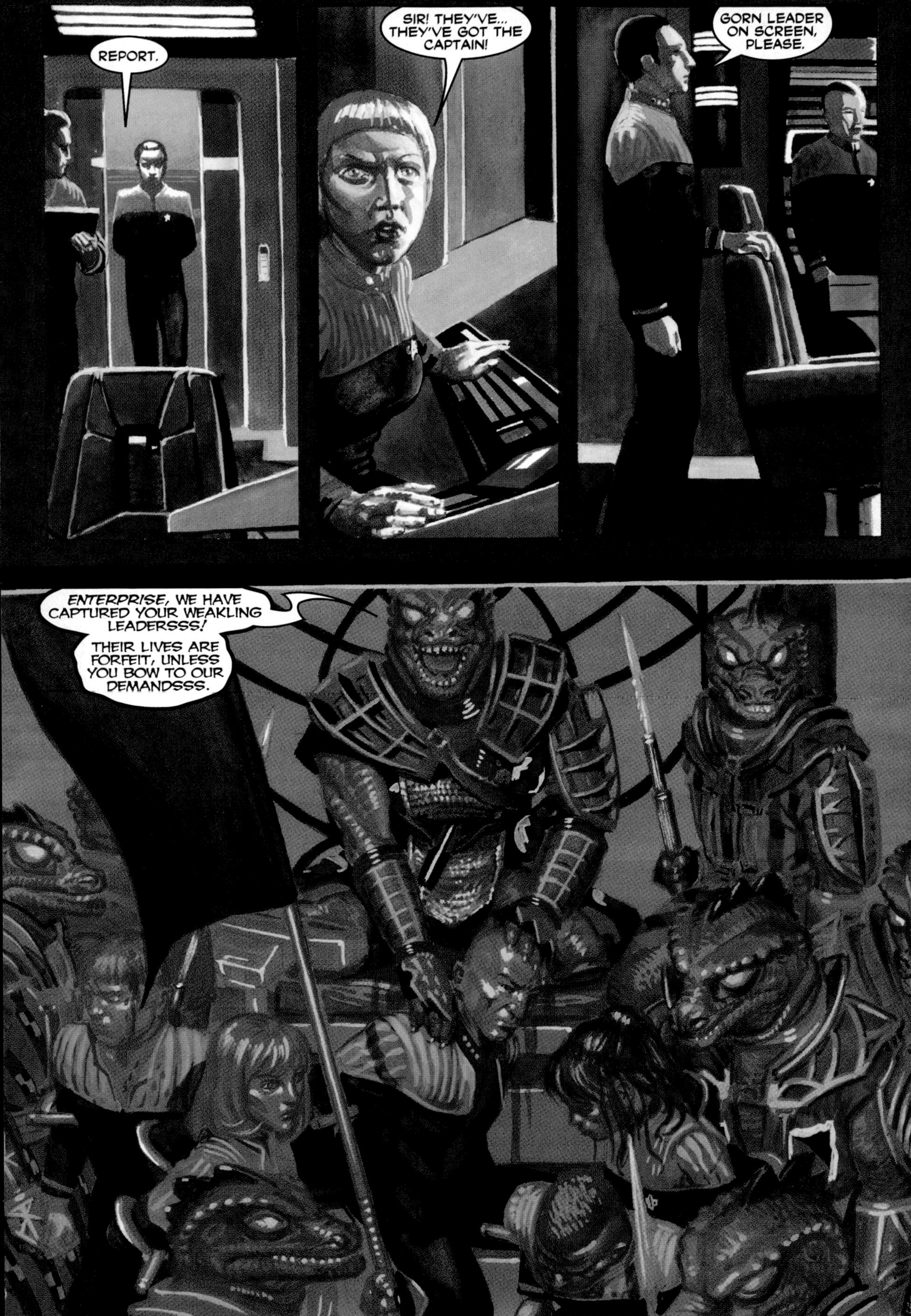
REPORT.
SIR! THEY'VE... THEY'VE GOT THE CAPTAIN!
GORN LEADER ON SCREEN, PLEASE.
ENTERPRISE, WE HAVE CAPTURED YOUR WEAKLING LEADERSSS!
THEIR LIVES ARE FORFEIT, UNLESS YOU BOW TO OUR DEMANDSSS.

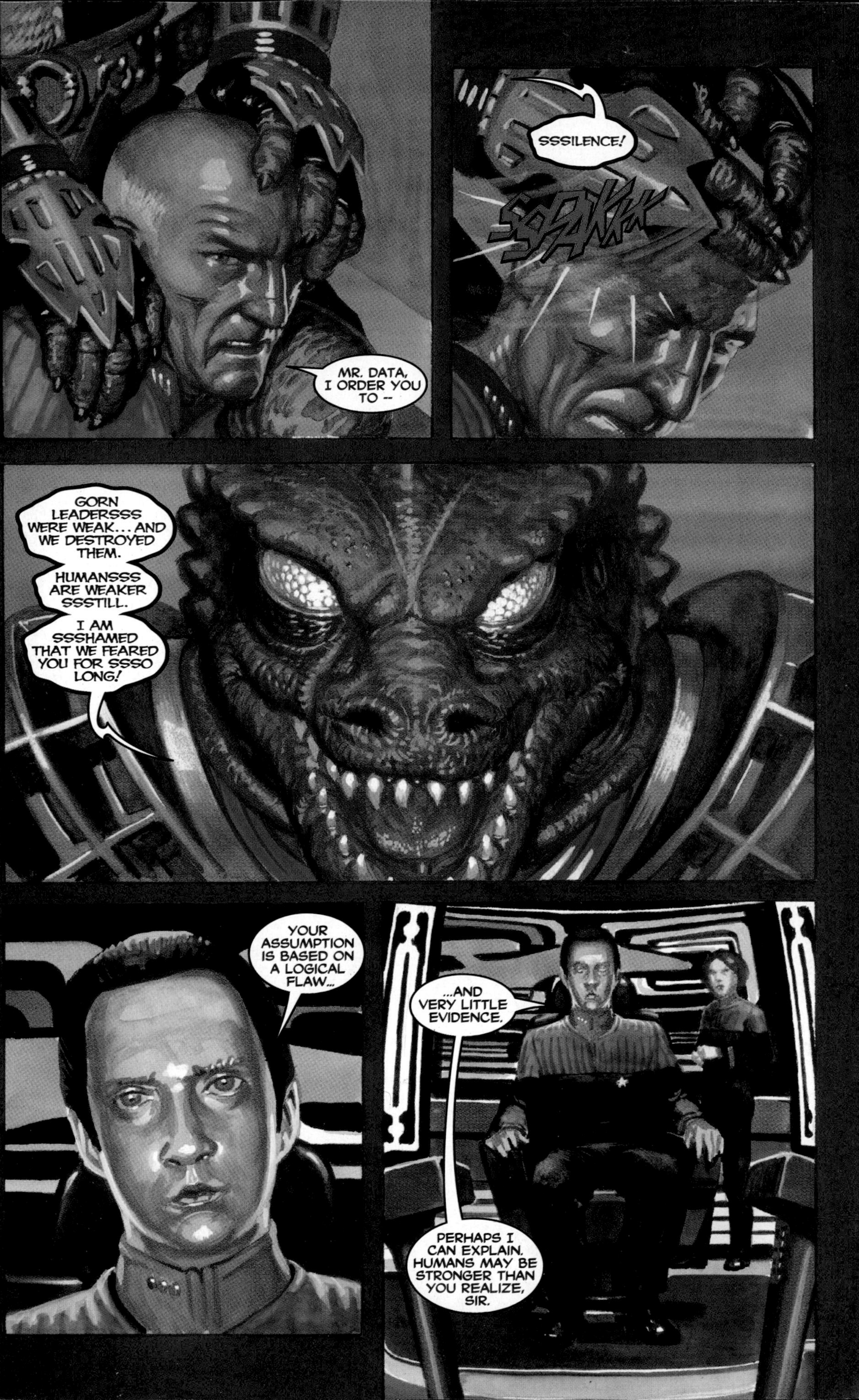
MR. DATA, I ORDER YOU TO --
SSSILENCE!
SSPAKKK
GORN LEADERSSS WERE WEAK... AND WE DESTROYED THEM.
HUMANSSS ARE WEAKER SSSTILL.
I AM SSSHAMED THAT WE FEARED YOU FOR SSSO LONG!
YOUR ASSUMPTION IS BASED ON A LOGICAL FLAW...
...AND VERY LITTLE EVIDENCE.
PERHAPS I CAN EXPLAIN. HUMANS MAY BE STRONGER THAN YOU REALIZE, SIR.

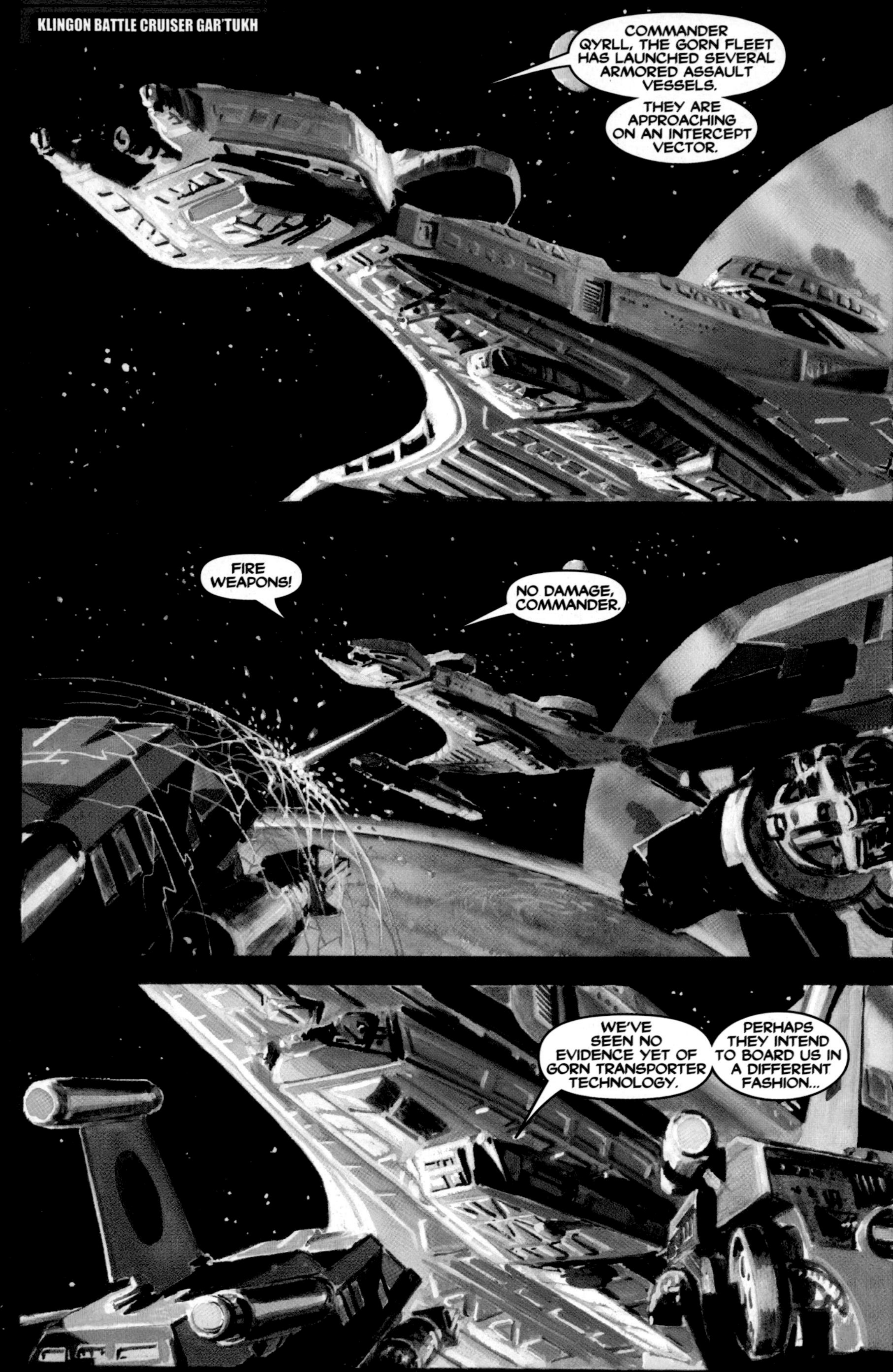
KLINGON BATTLE CRUISER GAR'TUKH
COMMANDER QYRLL, THE GORN FLEET HAS LAUNCHED SEVERAL ARMORED ASSAULT VESSELS.
THEY ARE APPROACHING ON AN INTERCEPT VECTOR.
FIRE WEAPONS!
NO DAMAGE, COMMANDER.
WE'VE SEEN NO EVIDENCE YET OF GORN TRANSPORTER TECHNOLOGY.
PERHAPS THEY INTEND TO BOARD US IN A DIFFERENT FASHION...

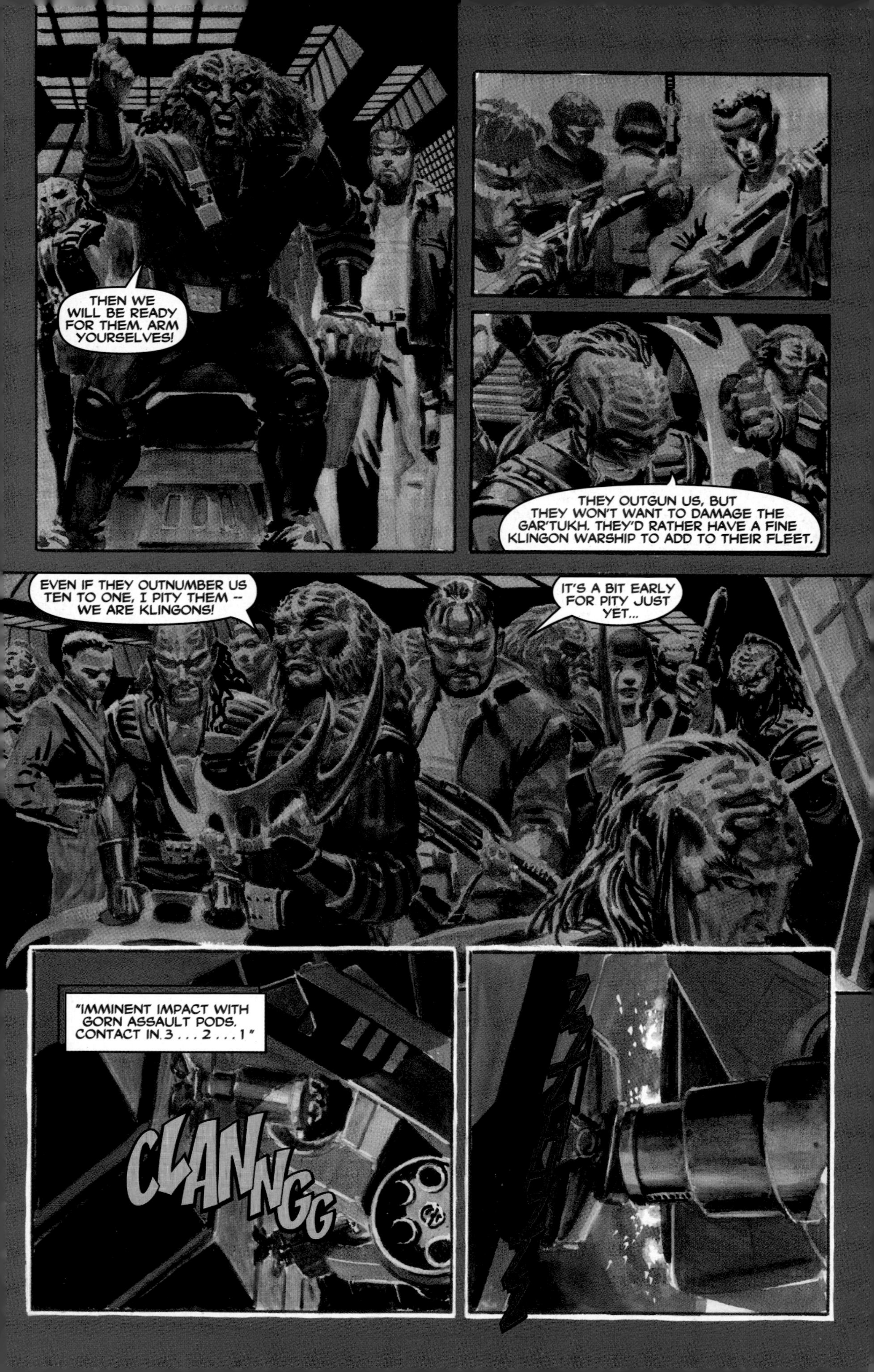
THEN WE WILL BE READY FOR THEM. ARM YOURSELVES!
THEY OUTGUN US, BUT THEY WON'T WANT TO DAMAGE THE GAR'TUKH. THEY'D RATHER HAVE A FINE KLINGON WARSHIP TO ADD TO THEIR FLEET.
EVEN IF THEY OUTNUMBER US TEN TO ONE, I PITY THEM -- WE ARE KLINGONS!
IT'S A BIT EARLY FOR PITY JUST YET...
"IMMINENT IMPACT WITH GORN ASSAULT PODS. CONTACT IN 3 . . . 2 . . . 1"
CLANNGG

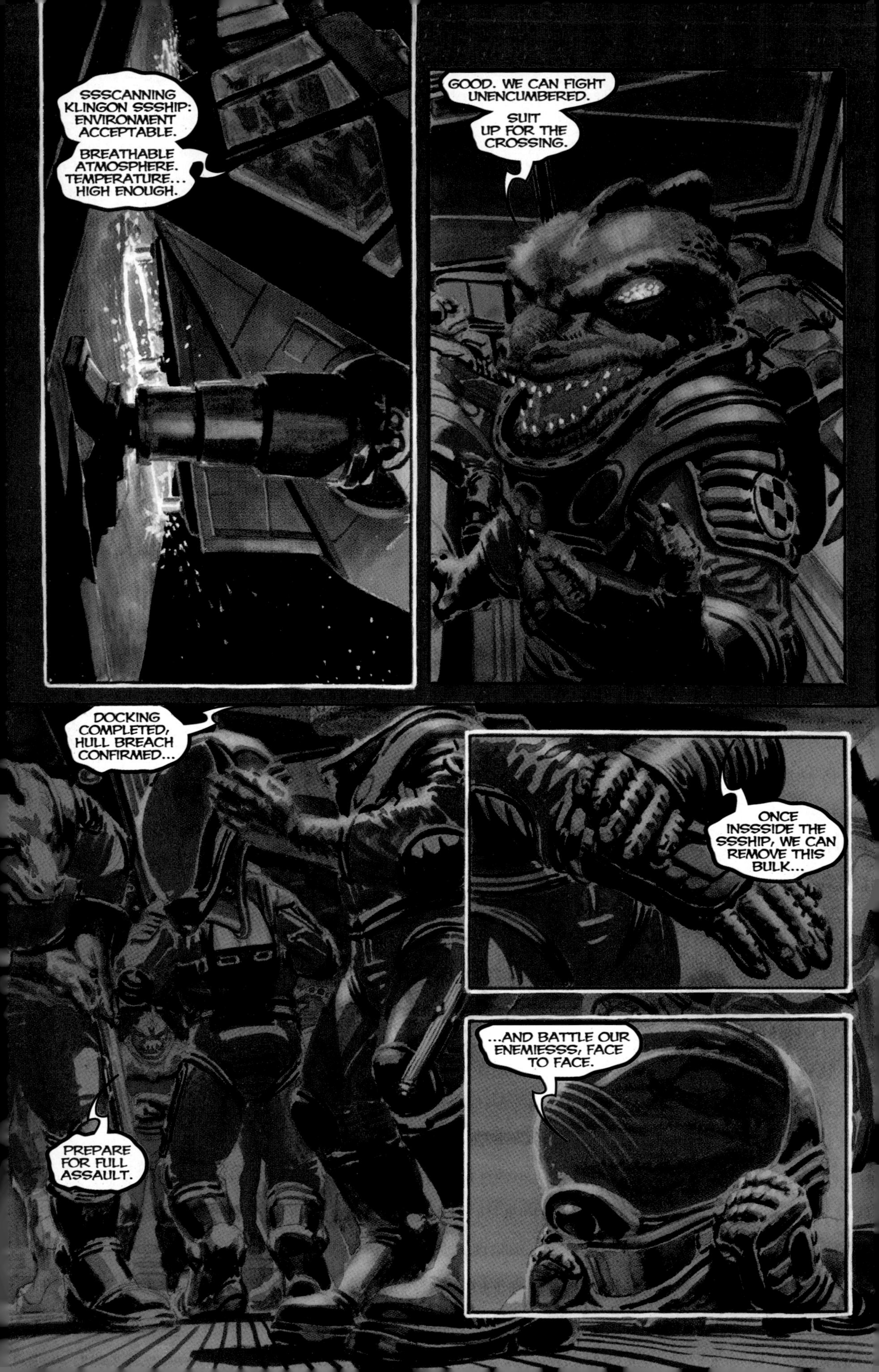
SSSCANNING KLINGON SSSHIP: ENVIRONMENT ACCEPTABLE.
BREATHABLE ATMOSPHERE. TEMPERATURE... HIGH ENOUGH.
GOOD. WE CAN FIGHT UNENCUMBERED.
SUIT UP FOR THE CROSSING.
DOCKING COMPLETED, HULL BREACH CONFIRMED...
PREPARE FOR FULL ASSAULT.
ONCE INSSSIDE THE SSSHIP, WE CAN REMOVE THIS BULK...
...AND BATTLE OUR ENEMIESSS, FACE TO FACE.

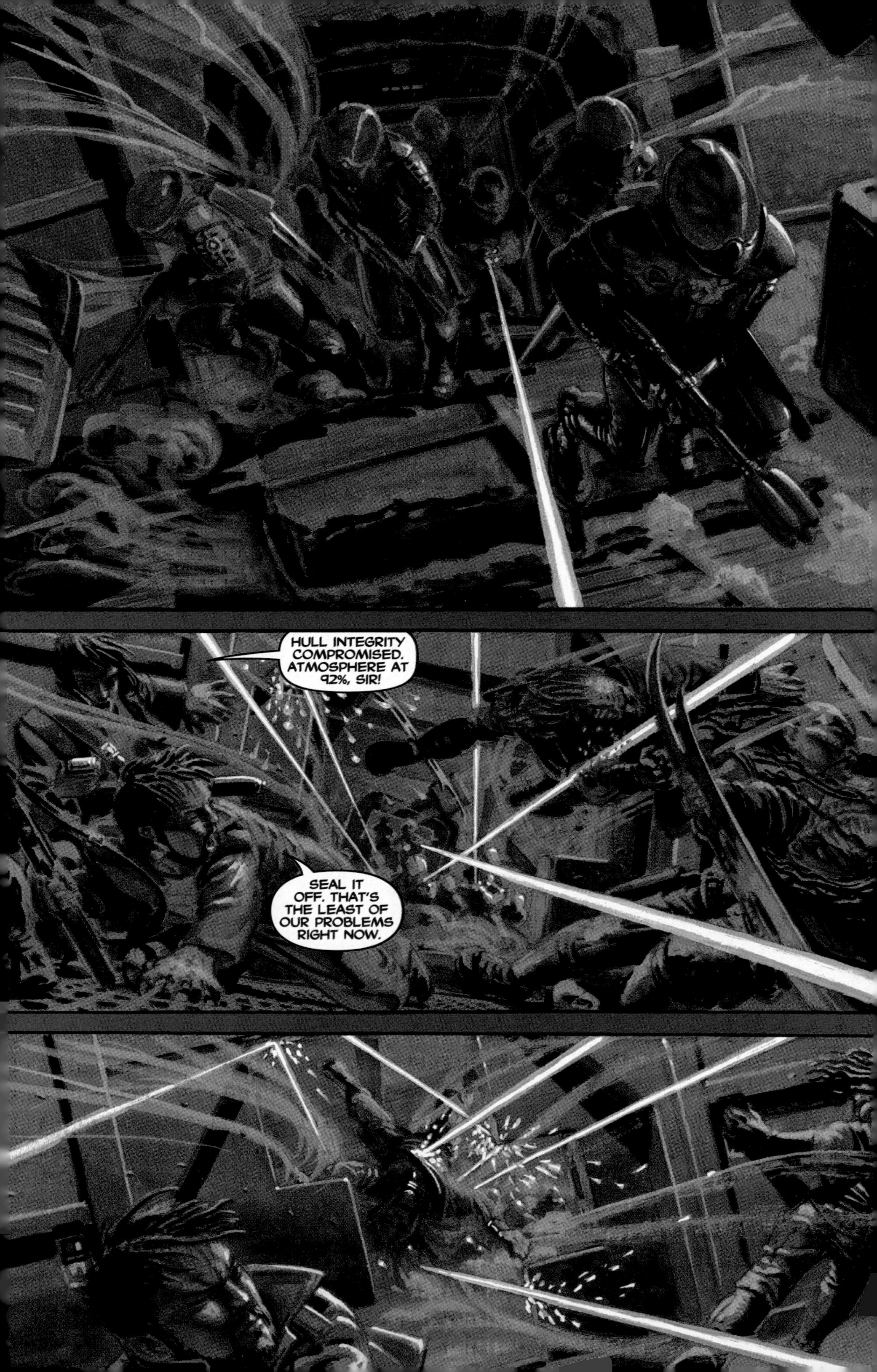
HULL INTEGRITY COMPROMISED. ATMOSPHERE AT 92%, SIR!
SEAL IT OFF. THAT'S THE LEAST OF OUR PROBLEMS RIGHT NOW.

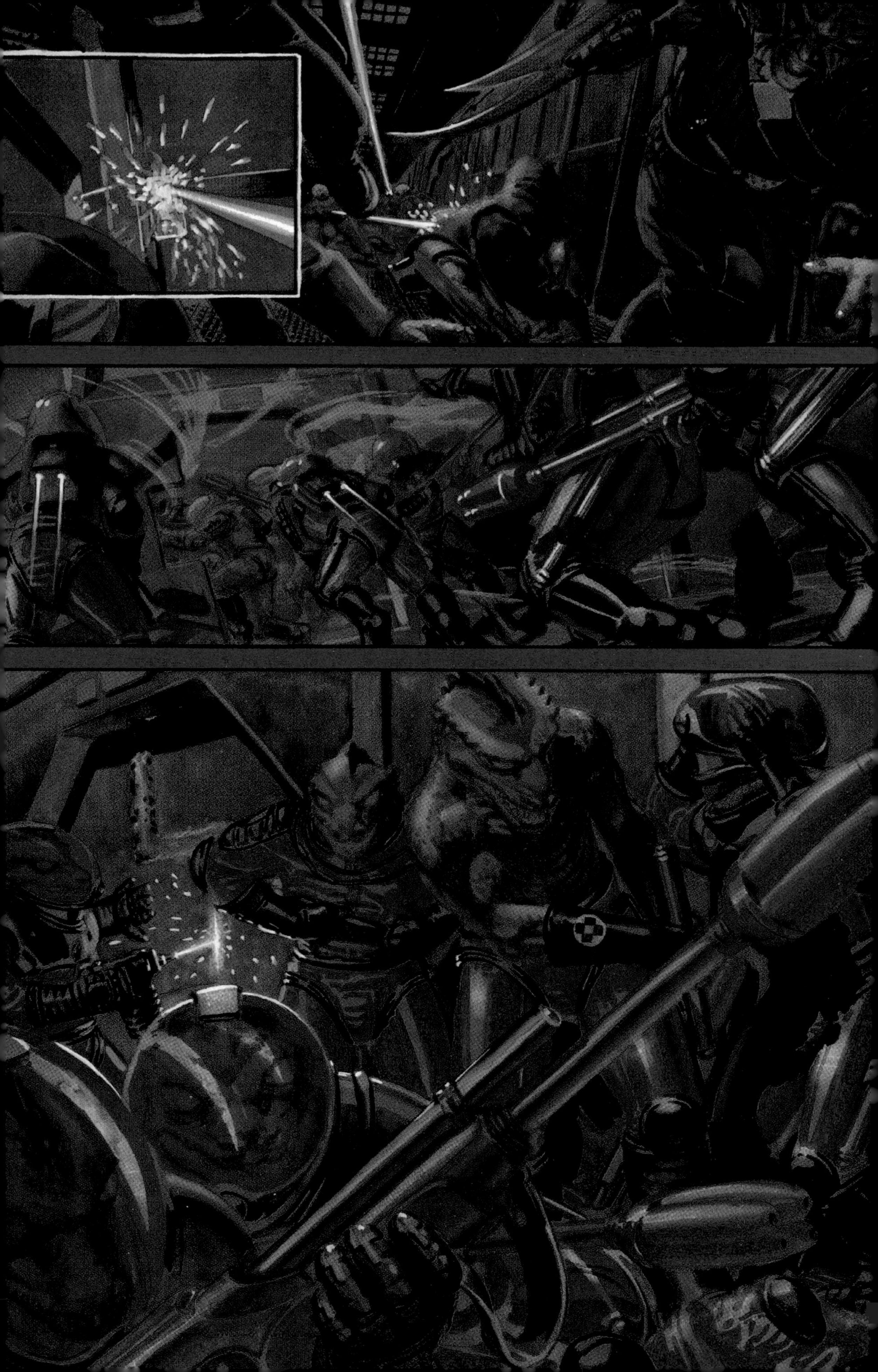

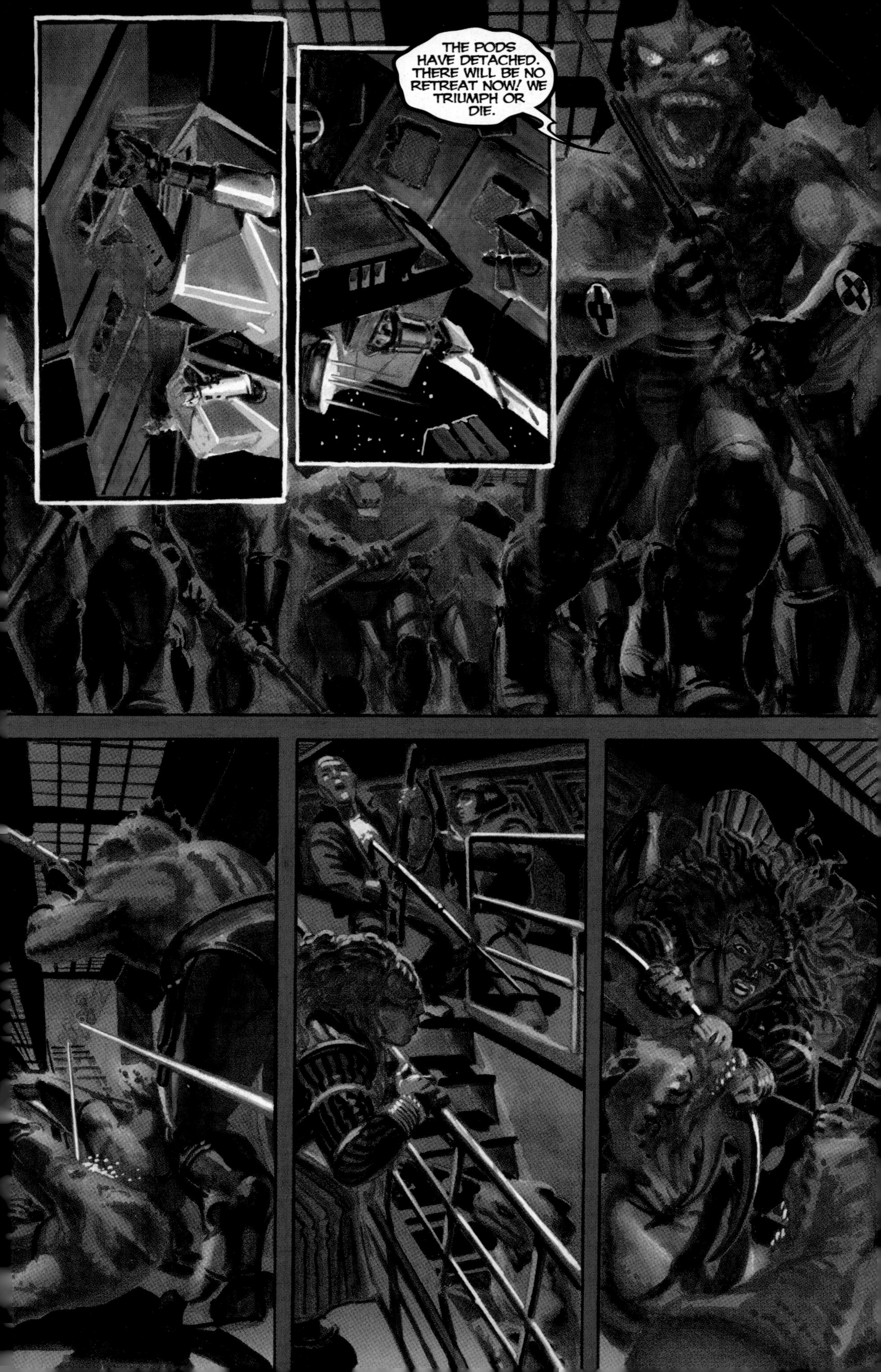
THE PODS HAVE DETACHED. THERE WILL BE NO RETREAT NOW! WE TRIUMPH OR DIE.

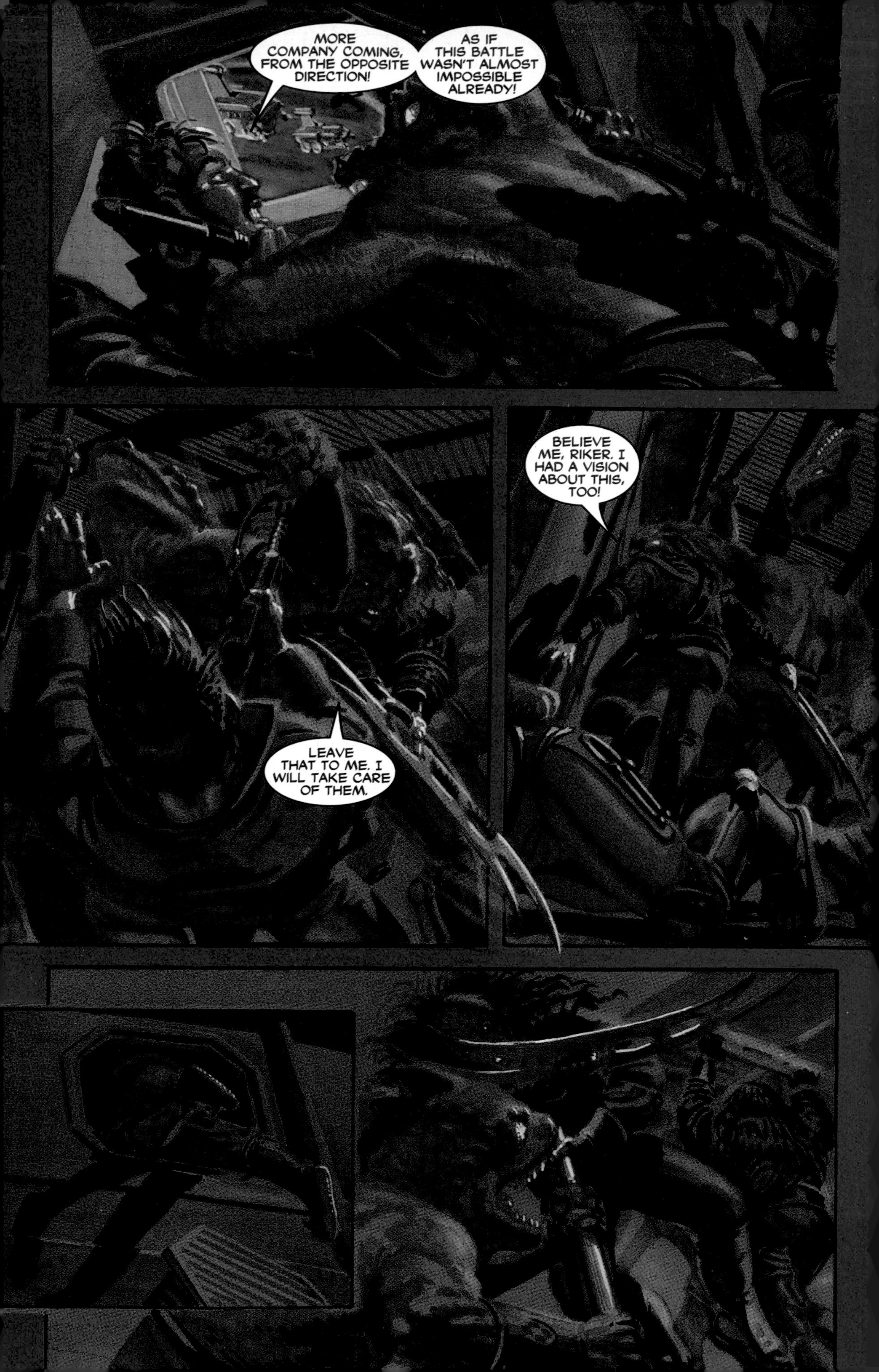
MORE COMPANY COMING, FROM THE OPPOSITE DIRECTION!
AS IF THIS BATTLE WASN'T ALMOST IMPOSSIBLE ALREADY!
LEAVE THAT TO ME. I WILL TAKE CARE OF THEM.
BELIEVE ME, RIKER. I HAD A VISION ABOUT THIS, TOO!

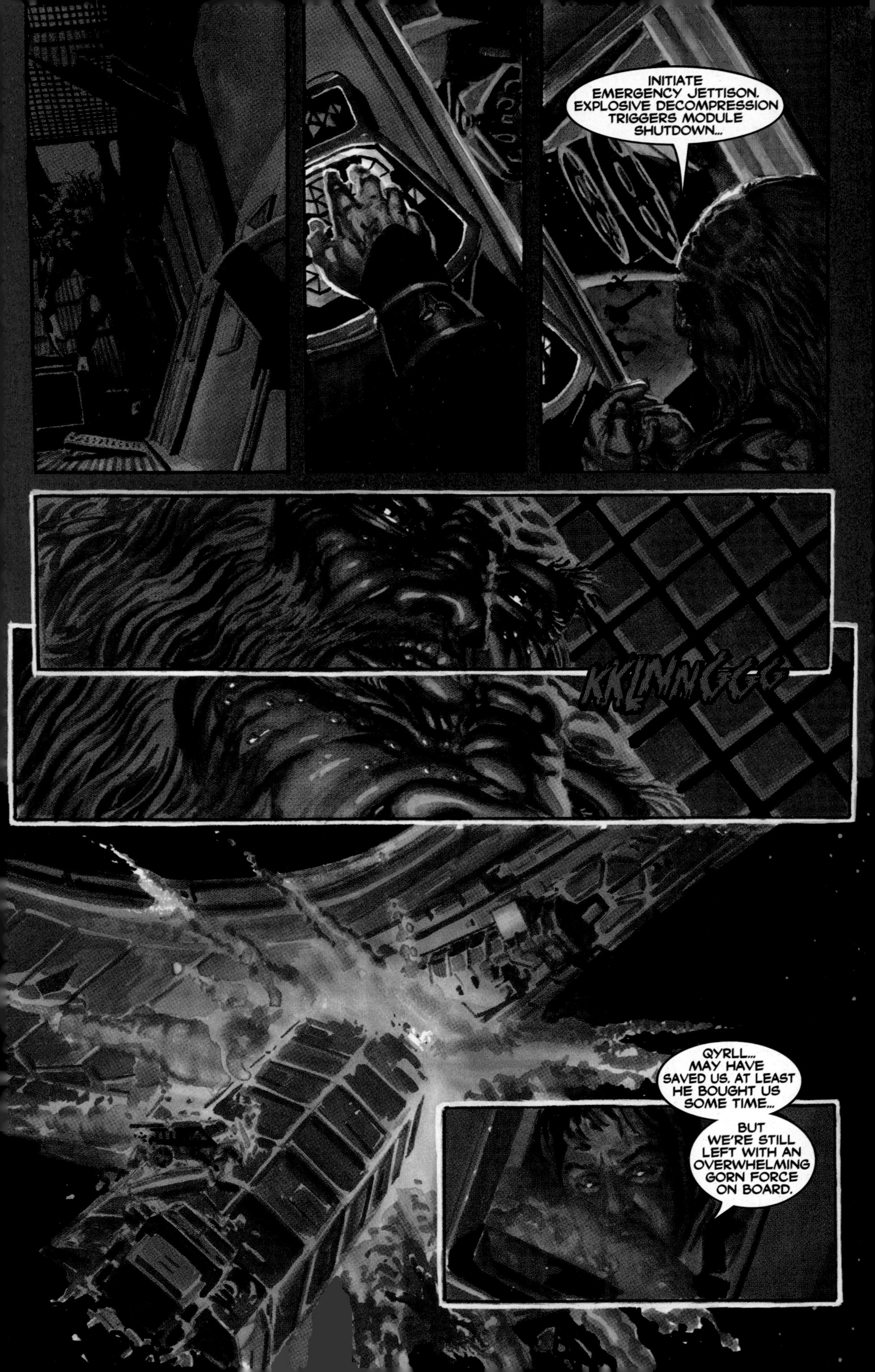
INITIATE EMERGENCY JETTISON. EXPLOSIVE DECOMPRESSION TRIGGERS MODULE SHUTDOWN...
KKLNNGGG
QYRLL... MAY HAVE SAVED US. AT LEAST HE BOUGHT US SOME TIME...
BUT WE'RE STILL LEFT WITH AN OVERWHELMING GORN FORCE ON BOARD.

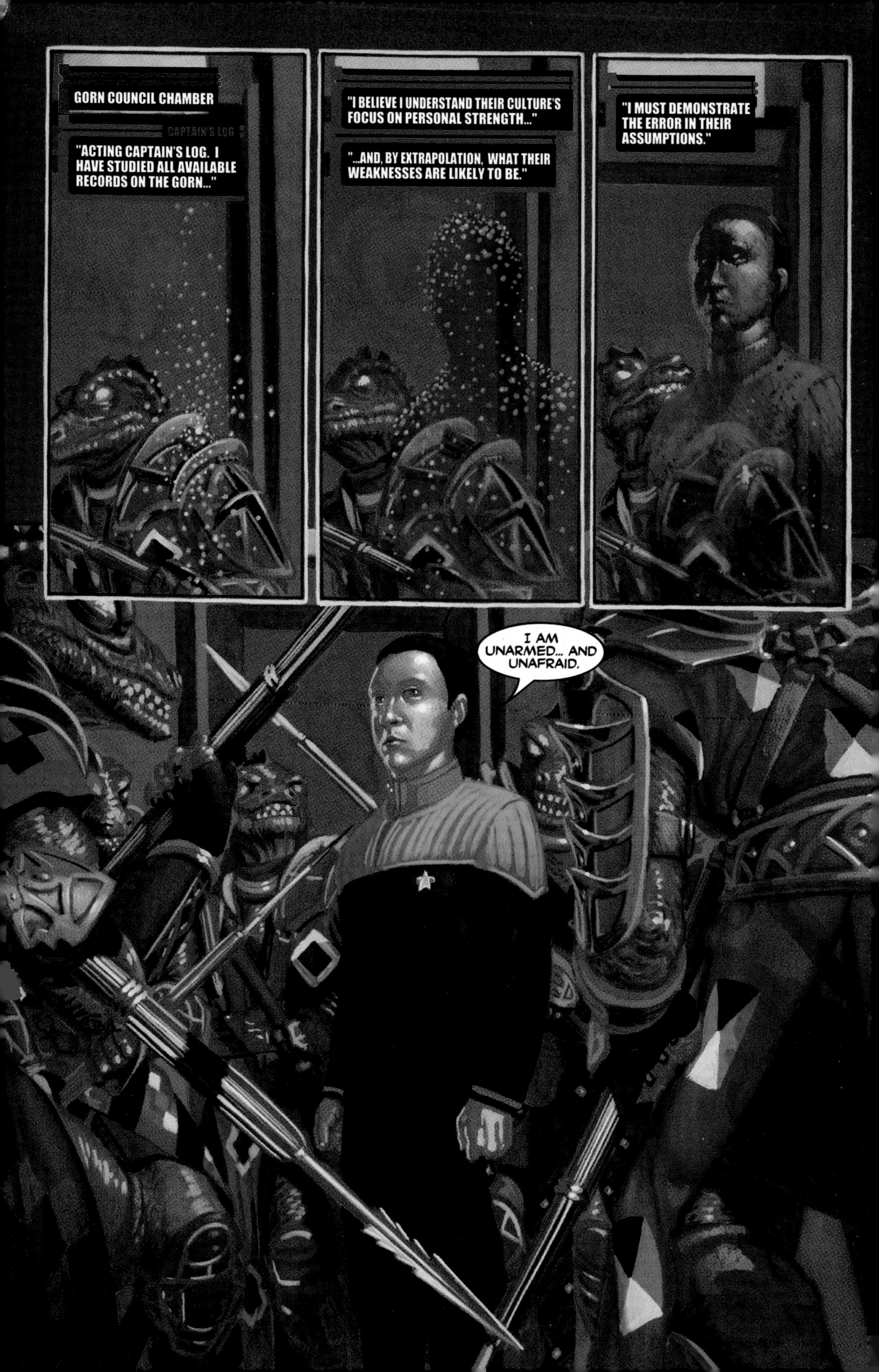
GORN COUNCIL CHAMBER
CAPTAIN'S LOG
"ACTING CAPTAIN'S LOG. I HAVE STUDIED ALL AVAILABLE RECORDS ON THE GORN..."
"I BELIEVE I UNDERSTAND THEIR CULTURE'S FOCUS ON PERSONAL STRENGTH..."
"...AND, BY EXTRAPOLATION, WHAT THEIR WEAKNESSES ARE LIKELY TO BE."
"I MUST DEMONSTRATE THE ERROR IN THEIR ASSUMPTIONS."
I AM UNARMED... AND UNAFRAID.

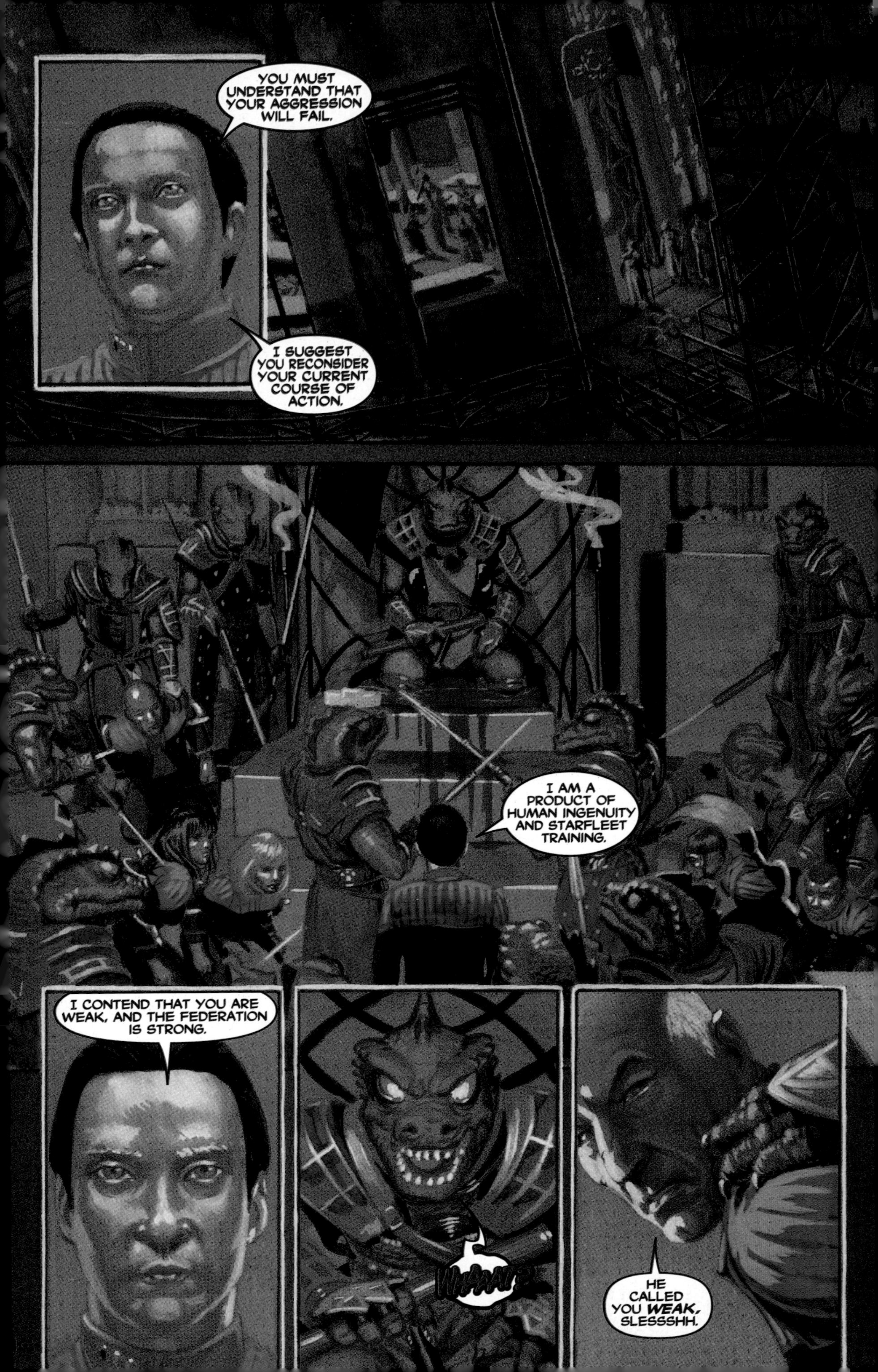
YOU MUST UNDERSTAND THAT YOUR AGGRESSION WILL FAIL.
I SUGGEST YOU RECONSIDER YOUR CURRENT COURSE OF ACTION.
I AM A PRODUCT OF HUMAN INGENUITY AND STARFLEET TRAINING.
I CONTEND THAT YOU ARE WEAK, AND THE FEDERATION IS STRONG.
WHAAT?!
HE CALLED YOU **WEAK,** SLESSSHH.

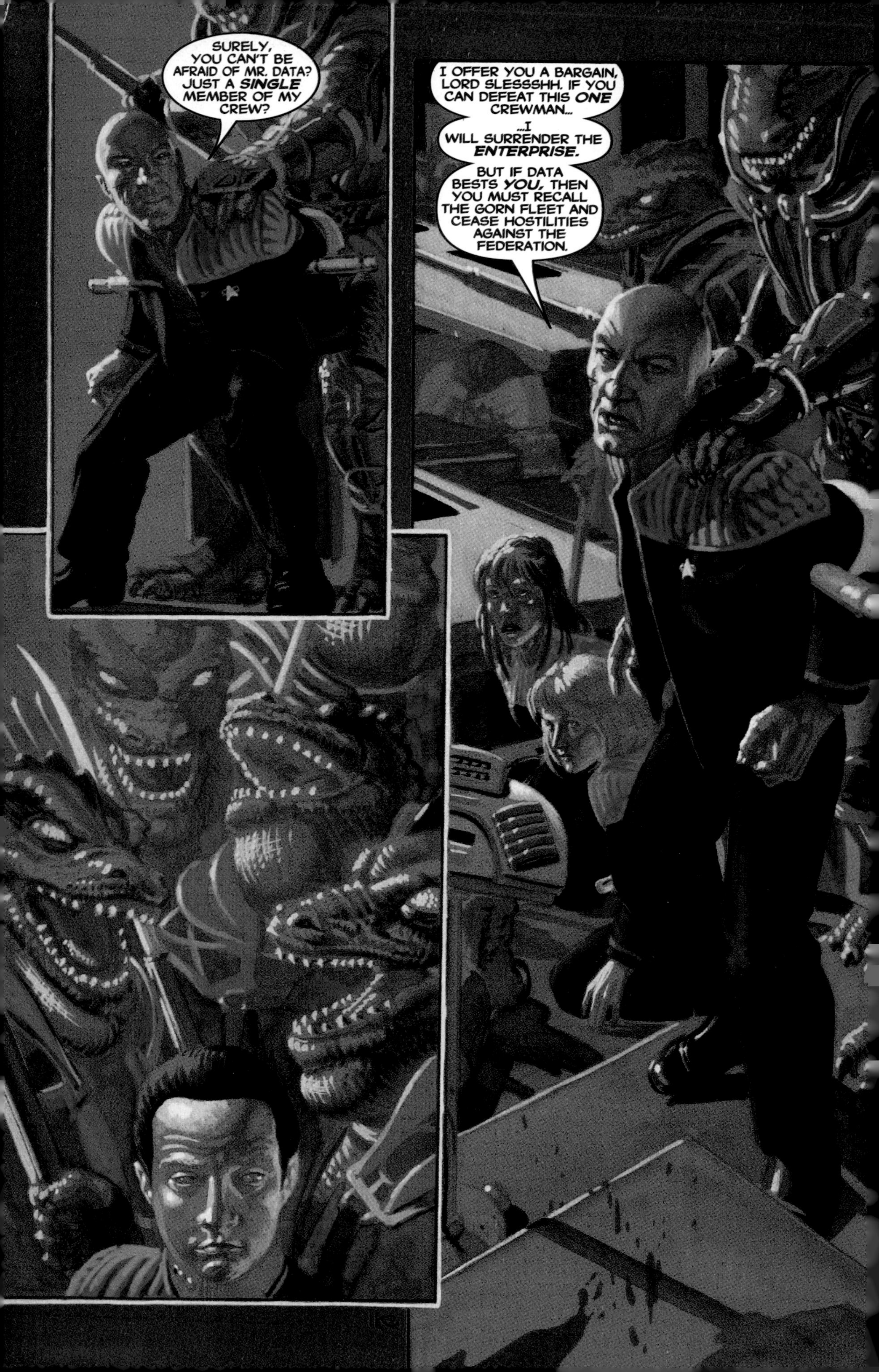
SURELY, YOU CAN'T BE AFRAID OF MR. DATA? JUST A SINGLE MEMBER OF MY CREW?
I OFFER YOU A BARGAIN, LORD SLESSSHH. IF YOU CAN DEFEAT THIS ONE CREWMAN...
...I WILL SURRENDER THE ENTERPRISE.
BUT IF DATA BESTS YOU, THEN YOU MUST RECALL THE GORN FLEET AND CEASE HOSTILITIES AGAINST THE FEDERATION.

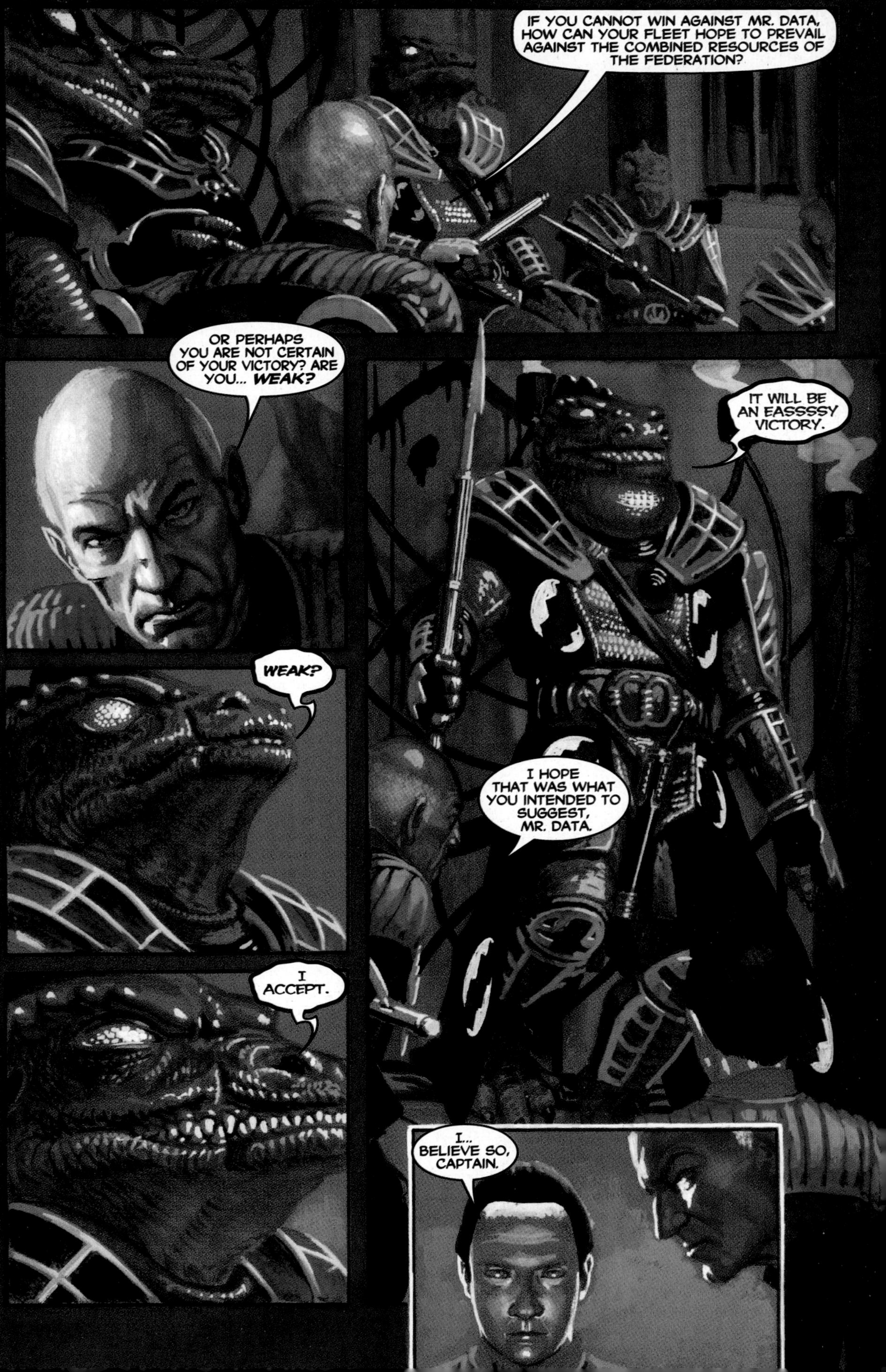
IF YOU CANNOT WIN AGAINST MR. DATA, HOW CAN YOUR FLEET HOPE TO PREVAIL AGAINST THE COMBINED RESOURCES OF THE FEDERATION?
OR PERHAPS YOU ARE NOT CERTAIN OF YOUR VICTORY? ARE YOU... WEAK?
WEAK?
I ACCEPT.
IT WILL BE AN EASSSSY VICTORY.
I HOPE THAT WAS WHAT YOU INTENDED TO SUGGEST, MR. DATA.
I... BELIEVE SO, CAPTAIN.

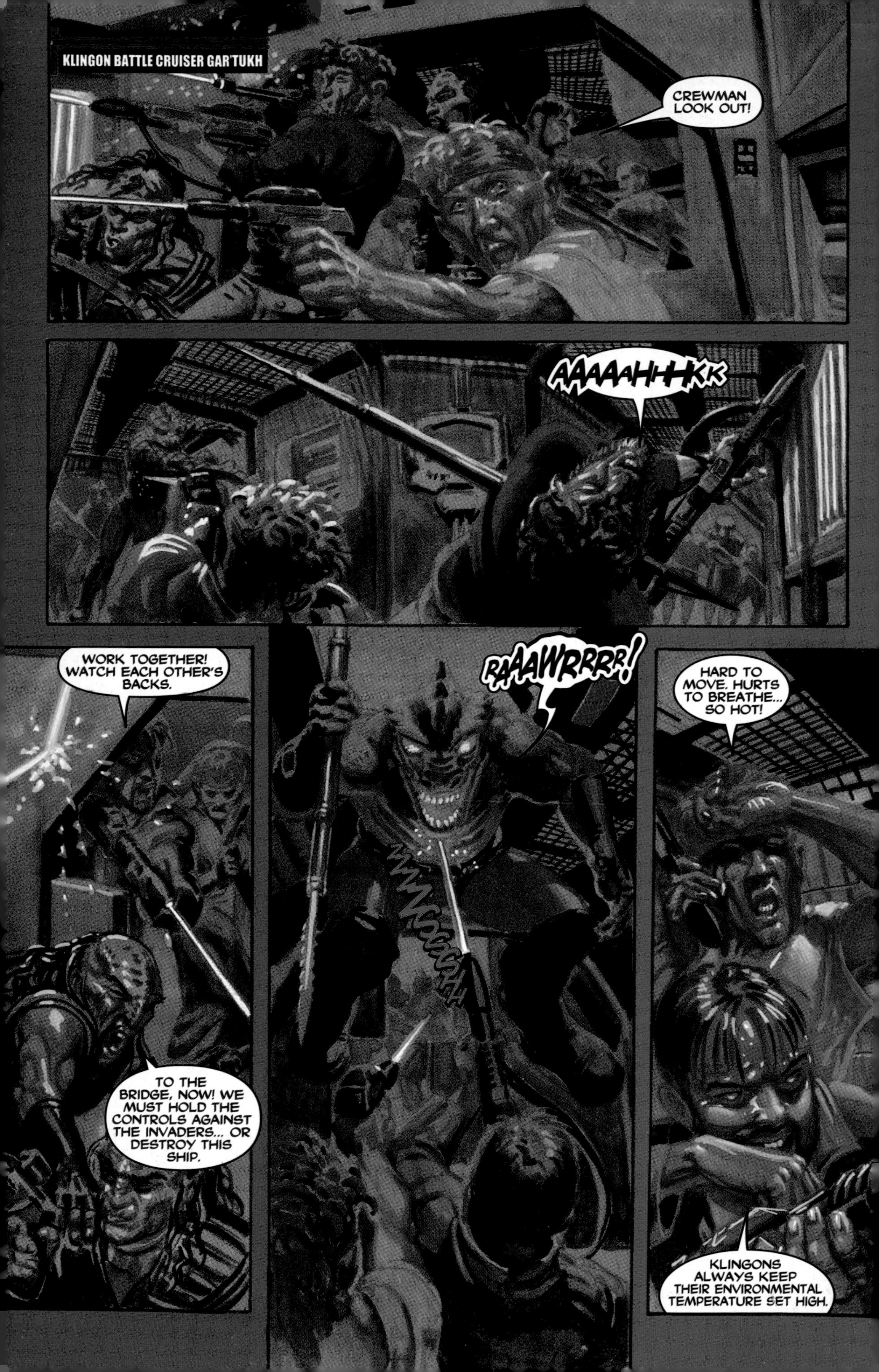
KLINGON BATTLE CRUISER GAR'TUKH
CREWMAN LOOK OUT!
AAAAAHHHKK
WORK TOGETHER! WATCH EACH OTHER'S BACKS.
TO THE BRIDGE, NOW! WE MUST HOLD THE CONTROLS AGAINST THE INVADERS... OR DESTROY THIS SHIP.
RAAAWRRRR!
HARD TO MOVE. HURTS TO BREATHE... SO HOT!
KLINGONS ALWAYS KEEP THEIR ENVIRONMENTAL TEMPERATURE SET HIGH.

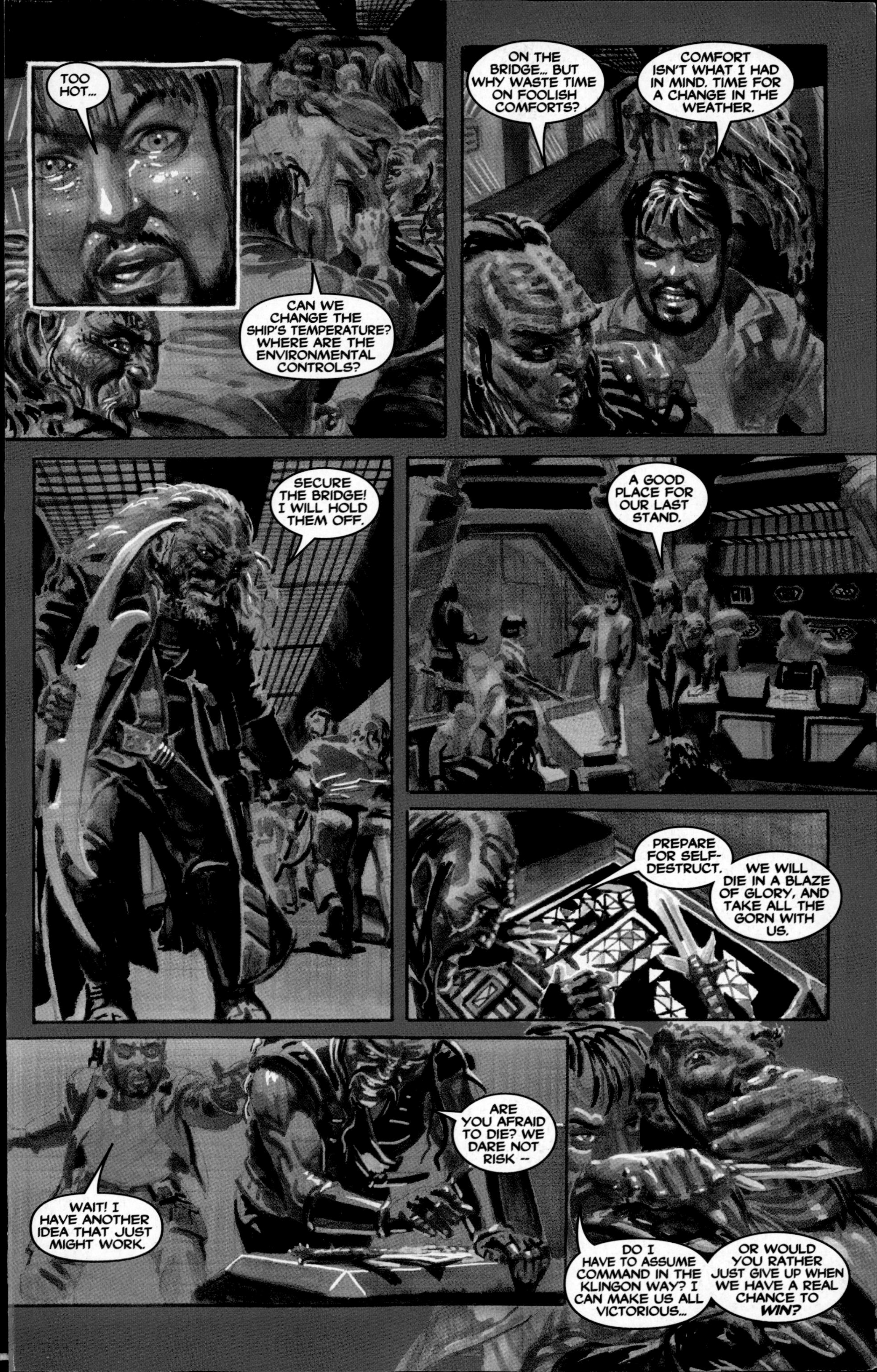
TOO HOT...
CAN WE CHANGE THE SHIP'S TEMPERATURE? WHERE ARE THE ENVIRONMENTAL CONTROLS?
ON THE BRIDGE... BUT WHY WASTE TIME ON FOOLISH COMFORTS?
COMFORT ISN'T WHAT I HAD IN MIND. TIME FOR A CHANGE IN THE WEATHER.
SECURE THE BRIDGE! I WILL HOLD THEM OFF.
A GOOD PLACE FOR OUR LAST STAND.
PREPARE FOR SELF-DESTRUCT.
WE WILL DIE IN A BLAZE OF GLORY, AND TAKE ALL THE GORN WITH US.
WAIT! I HAVE ANOTHER IDEA THAT JUST MIGHT WORK.
ARE YOU AFRAID TO DIE? WE DARE NOT RISK --
DO I HAVE TO ASSUME COMMAND IN THE KLINGON WAY? I CAN MAKE US ALL VICTORIOUS...
OR WOULD YOU RATHER JUST GIVE UP WHEN WE HAVE A REAL CHANCE TO *WIN*?

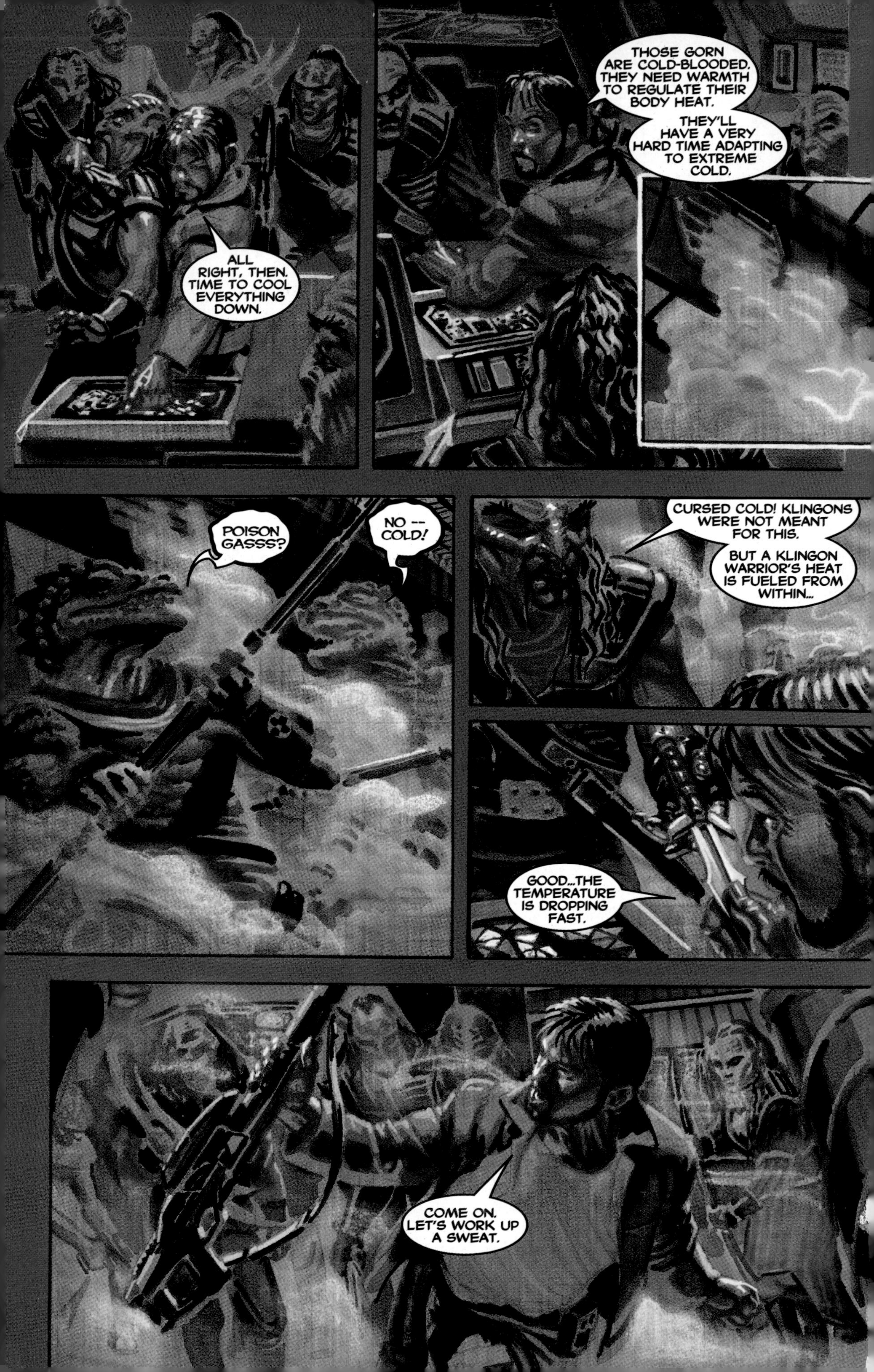
ALL RIGHT, THEN. TIME TO COOL EVERYTHING DOWN.
THOSE GORN ARE COLD-BLOODED. THEY NEED WARMTH TO REGULATE THEIR BODY HEAT.
THEY'LL HAVE A VERY HARD TIME ADAPTING TO EXTREME COLD.
POISON GASSS?
NO -- COLD!
CURSED COLD! KLINGONS WERE NOT MEANT FOR THIS.
BUT A KLINGON WARRIOR'S HEAT IS FUELED FROM WITHIN...
GOOD...THE TEMPERATURE IS DROPPING FAST.
COME ON. LET'S WORK UP A SWEAT.

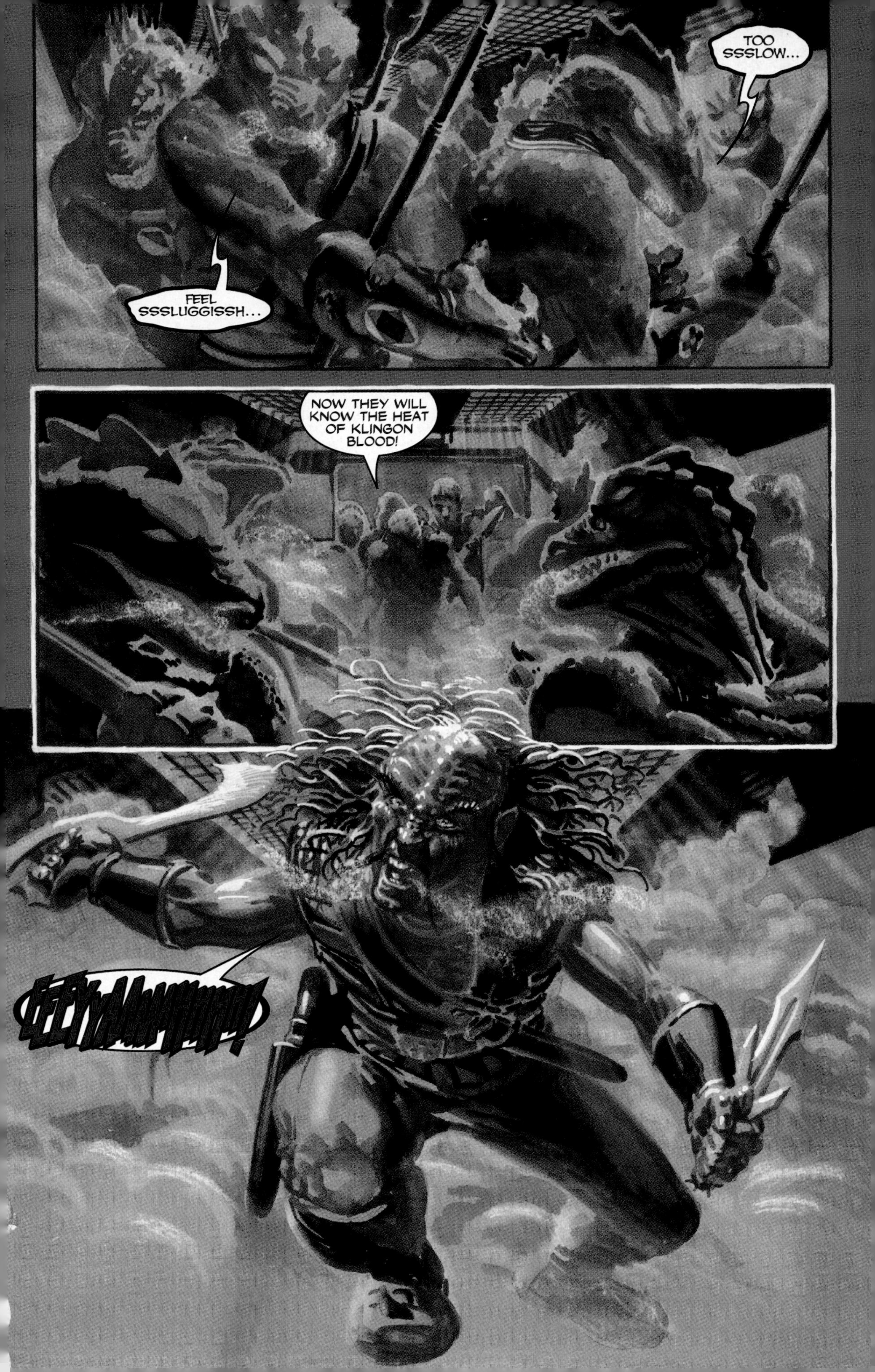
TOO SSSLOW...
FEEL SSSLUGGISSH...
NOW THEY WILL KNOW THE HEAT OF KLINGON BLOOD!

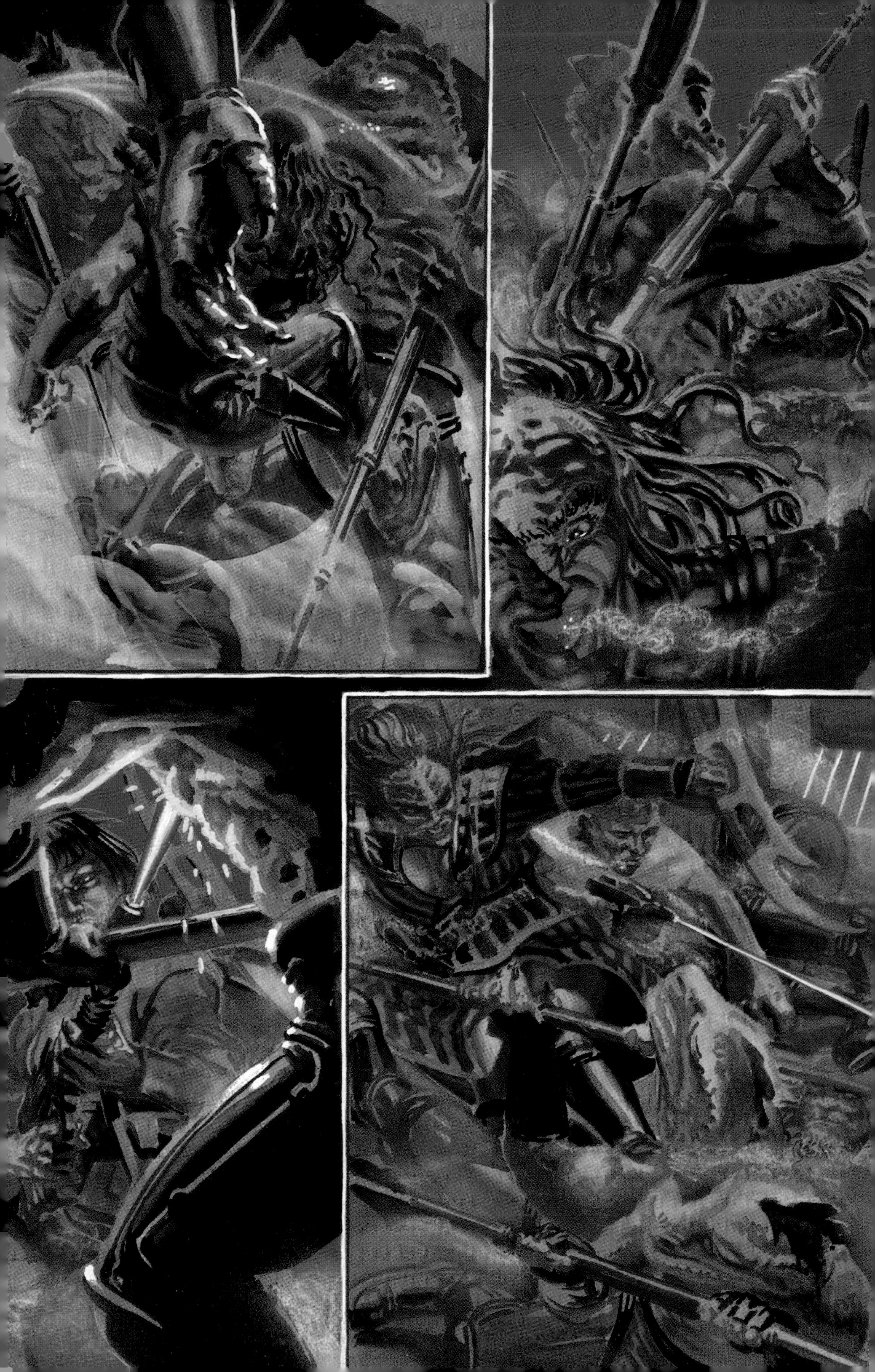

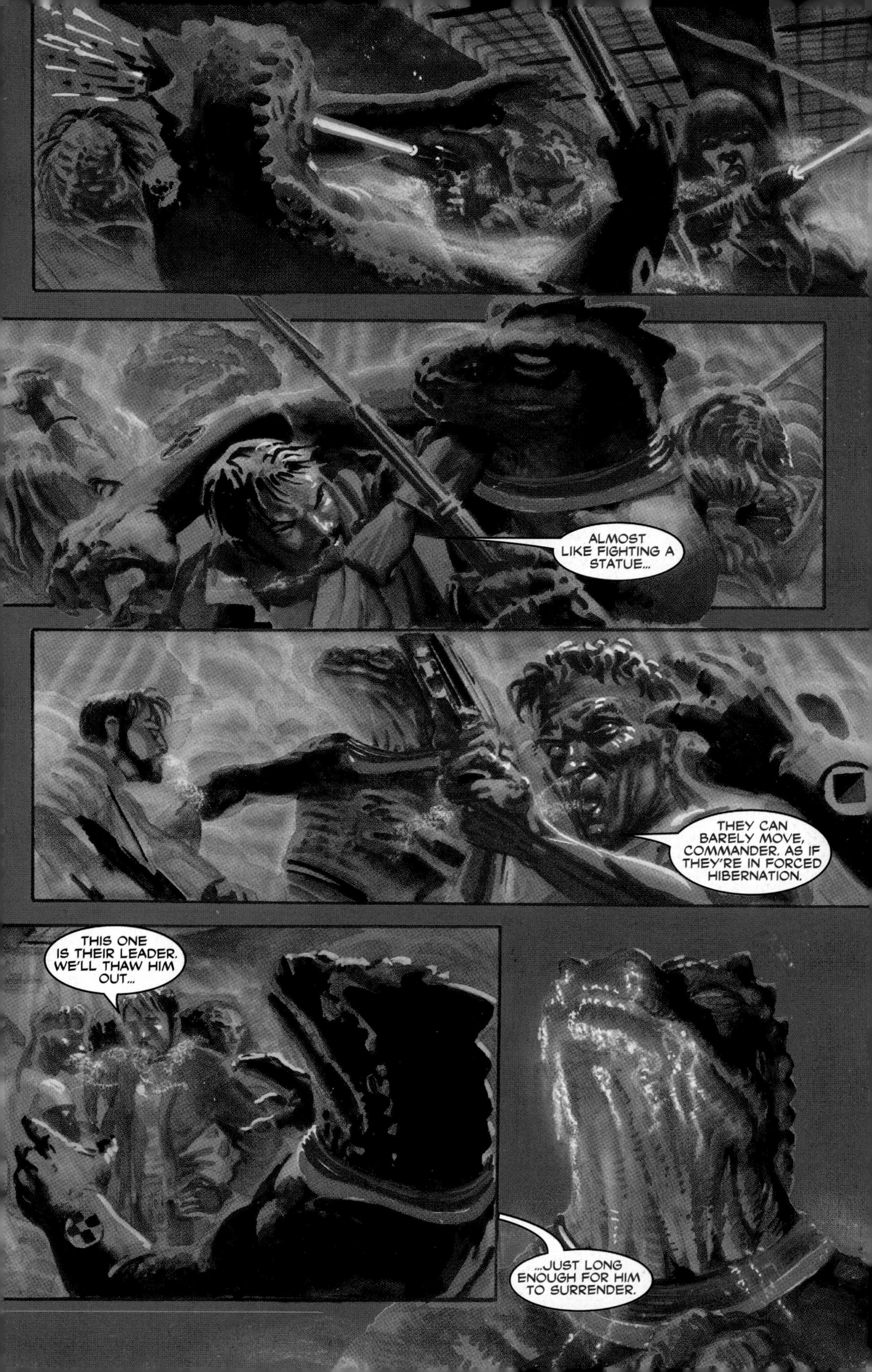
ALMOST LIKE FIGHTING A STATUE...
THEY CAN BARELY MOVE, COMMANDER. AS IF THEY'RE IN FORCED HIBERNATION.
THIS ONE IS THEIR LEADER. WE'LL THAW HIM OUT...
...JUST LONG ENOUGH FOR HIM TO SURRENDER.

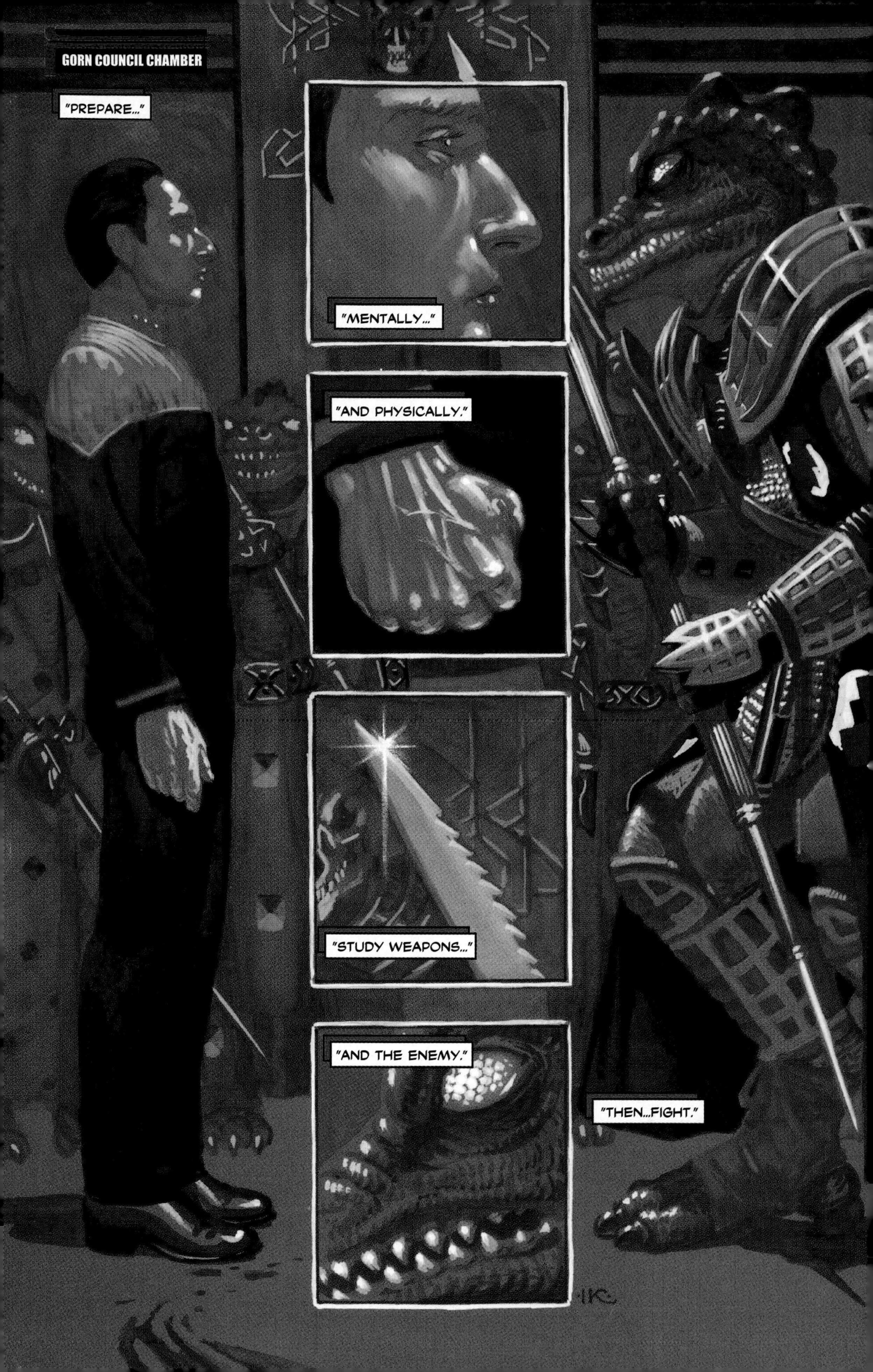
GORN COUNCIL CHAMBER
"PREPARE..."
"MENTALLY..."
"AND PHYSICALLY."
"STUDY WEAPONS..."
"AND THE ENEMY."
"THEN...FIGHT."

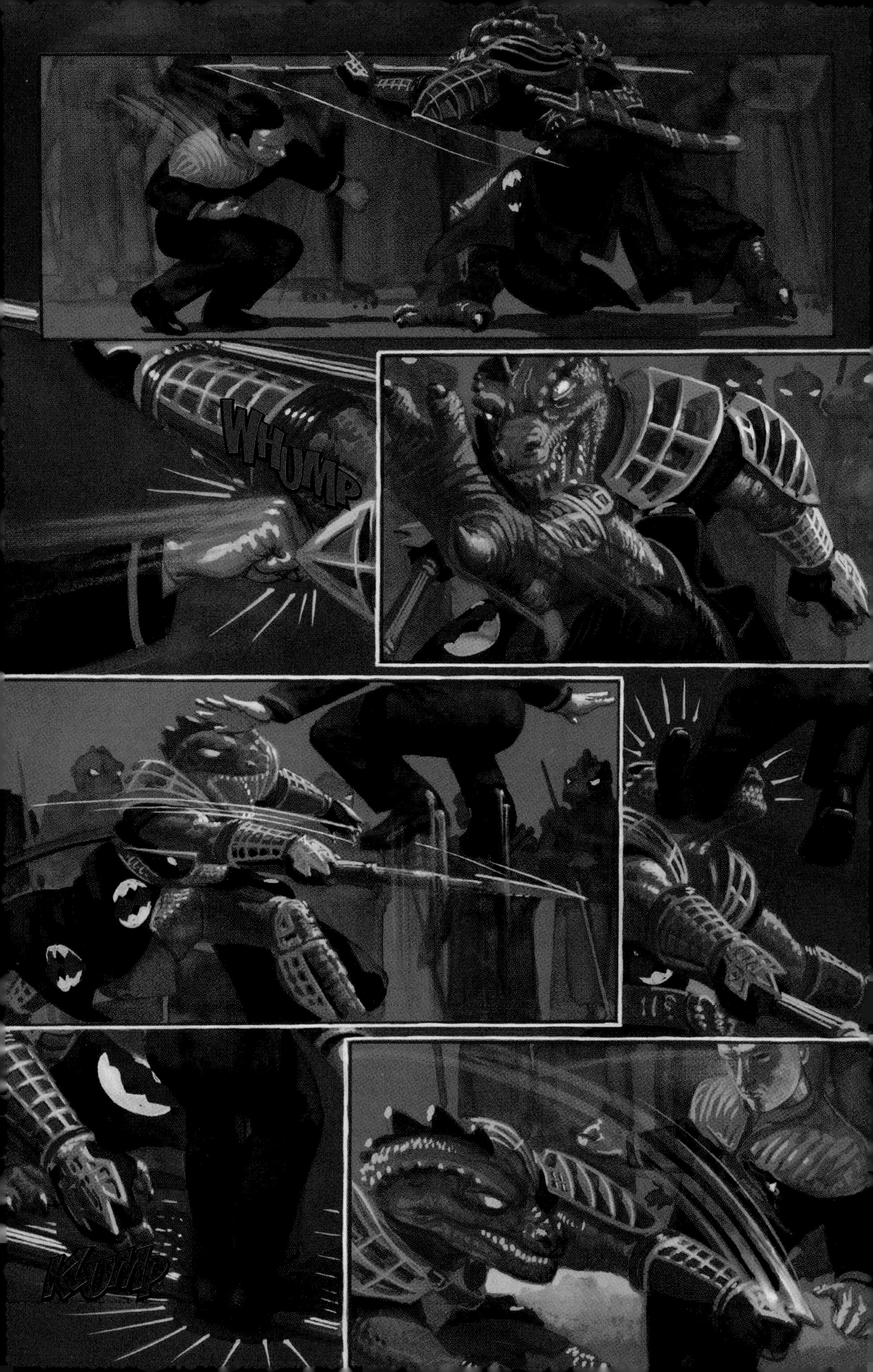
WHUMP
KLUMP

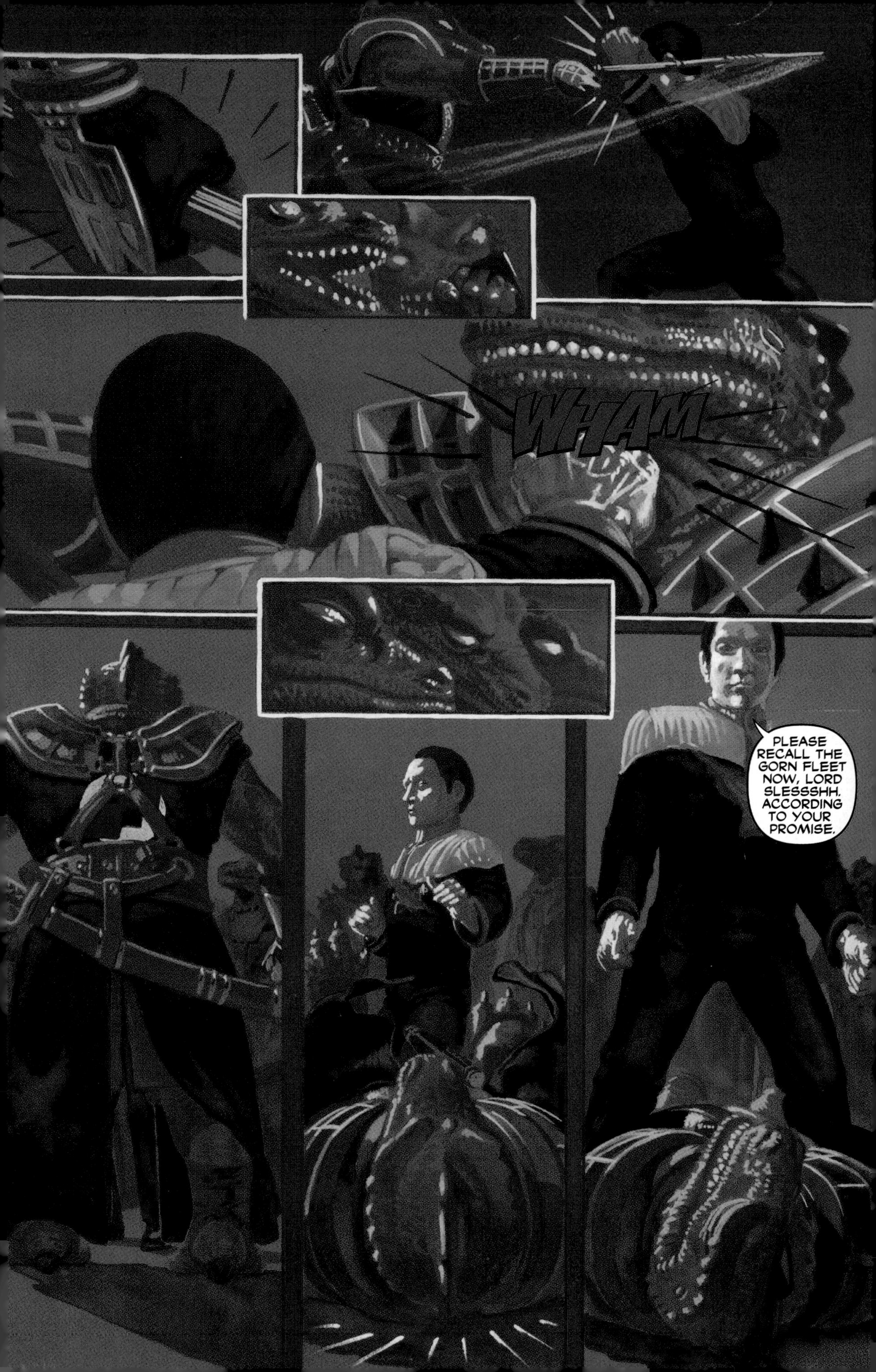
WHAM
PLEASE RECALL THE GORN FLEET NOW, LORD SLESSSHH. ACCORDING TO YOUR PROMISE.

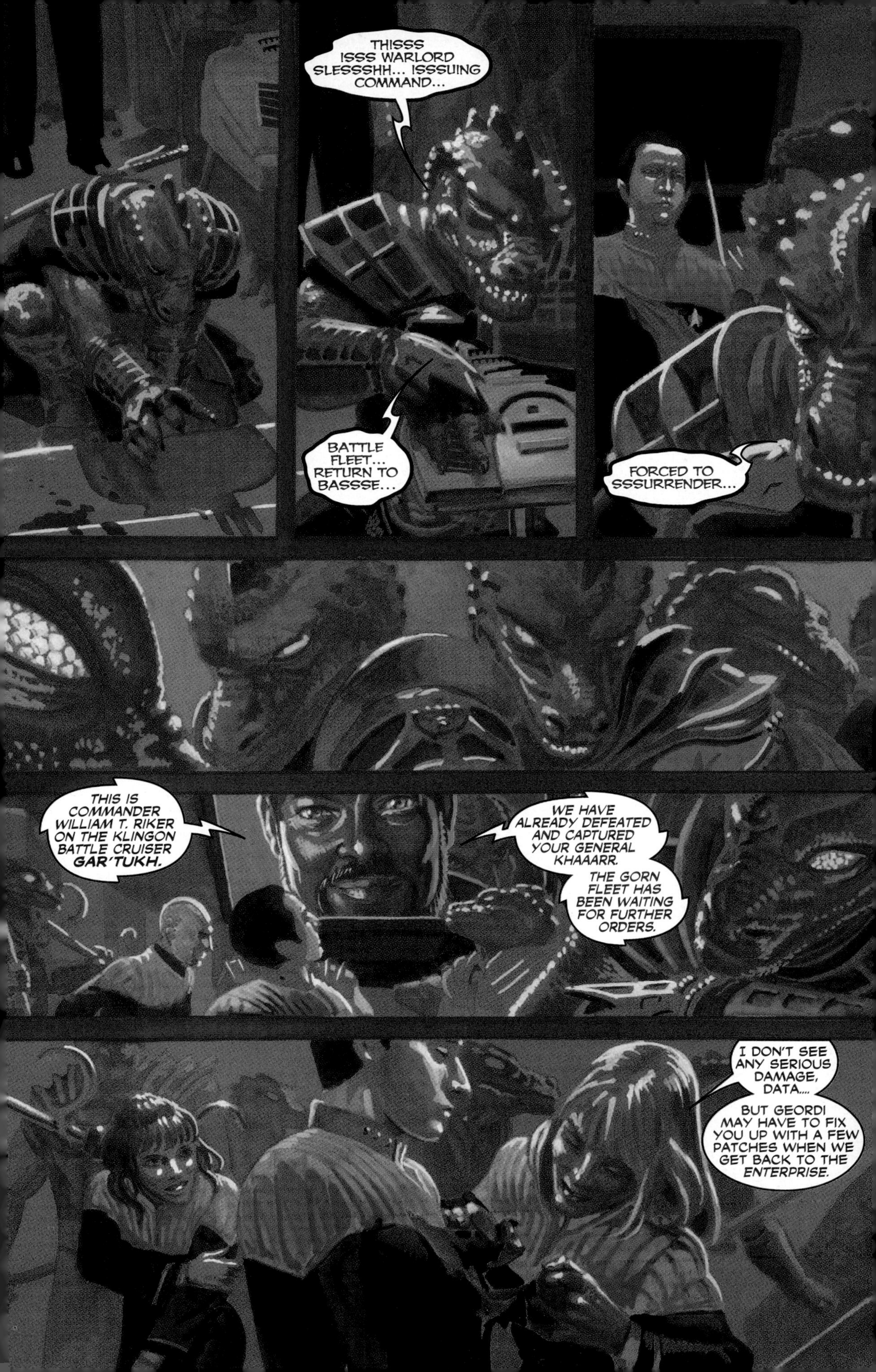
THISSS ISSS WARLORD SLESSSHH... ISSSUING COMMAND...
BATTLE FLEET... RETURN TO BASSSE...
FORCED TO SSSURRENDER...
THIS IS COMMANDER WILLIAM T. RIKER ON THE KLINGON BATTLE CRUISER *GAR'TUKH.*
WE HAVE ALREADY DEFEATED AND CAPTURED YOUR GENERAL KHAAARR.
THE GORN FLEET HAS BEEN WAITING FOR FURTHER ORDERS.
I DON'T SEE ANY SERIOUS DAMAGE, DATA....
BUT GEORDI MAY HAVE TO FIX YOU UP WITH A FEW PATCHES WHEN WE GET BACK TO THE *ENTERPRISE.*

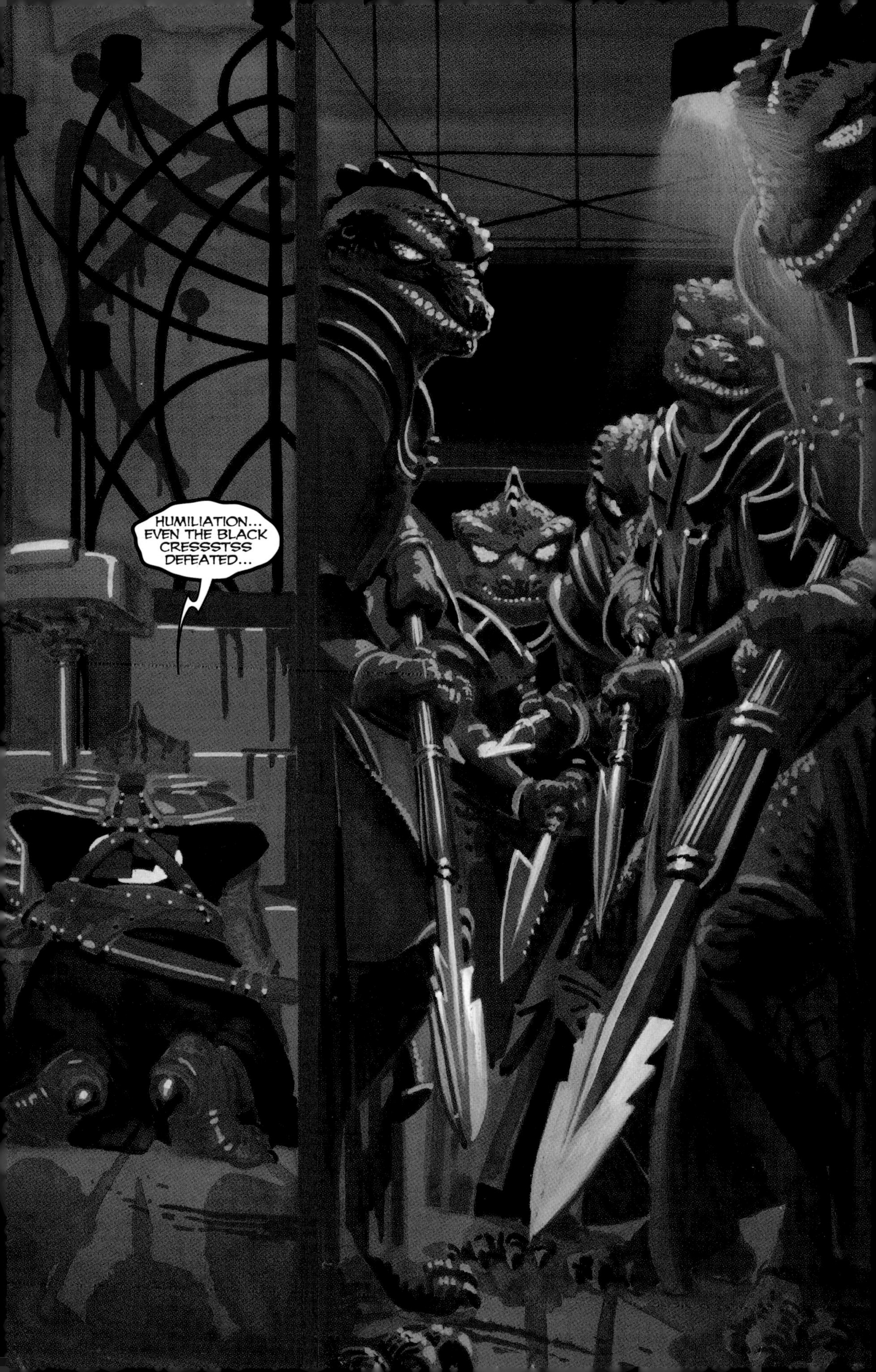
HUMILIATION... EVEN THE BLACK CRESSSTSS DEFEATED...

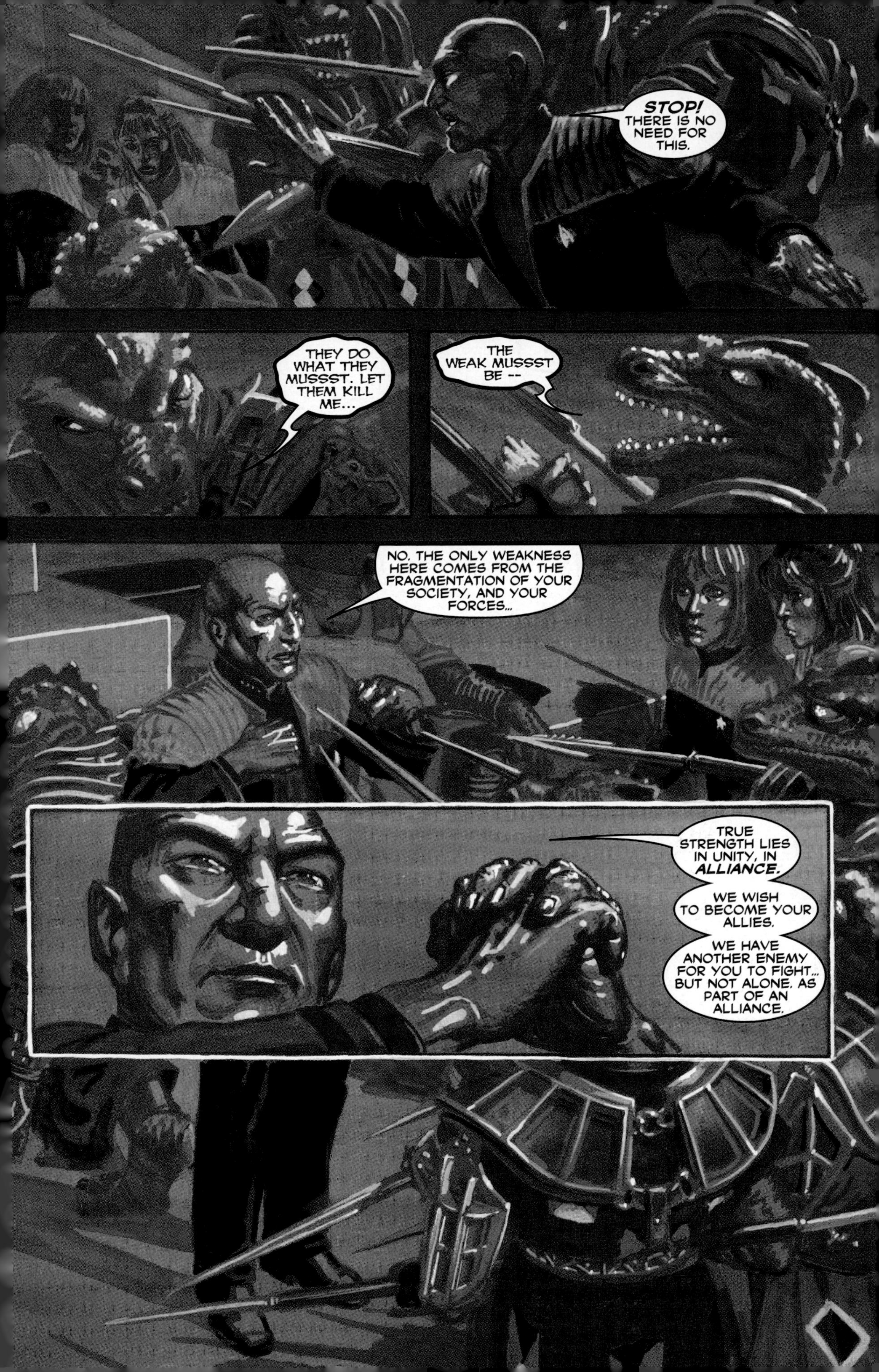
STOP! THERE IS NO NEED FOR THIS.
THEY DO WHAT THEY MUSSST. LET THEM KILL ME...
THE WEAK MUSSST BE --
NO. THE ONLY WEAKNESS HERE COMES FROM THE FRAGMENTATION OF YOUR SOCIETY, AND YOUR FORCES...
TRUE STRENGTH LIES IN UNITY, IN ALLIANCE.
WE WISH TO BECOME YOUR ALLIES.
WE HAVE ANOTHER ENEMY FOR YOU TO FIGHT... BUT NOT ALONE. AS PART OF AN ALLIANCE.

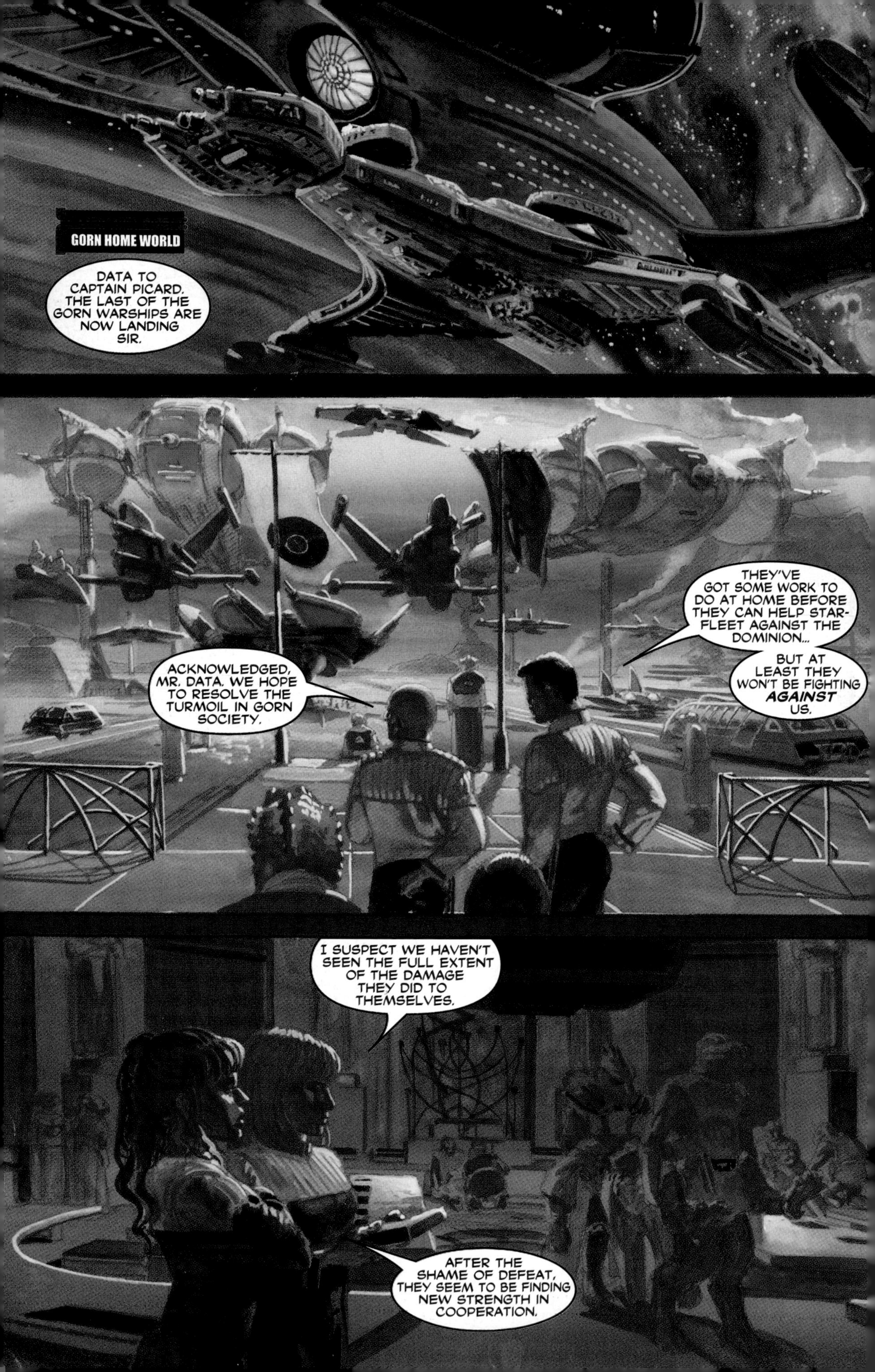
GORN HOME WORLD
DATA TO CAPTAIN PICARD. THE LAST OF THE GORN WARSHIPS ARE NOW LANDING SIR.
ACKNOWLEDGED, MR. DATA. WE HOPE TO RESOLVE THE TURMOIL IN GORN SOCIETY.
THEY'VE GOT SOME WORK TO DO AT HOME BEFORE THEY CAN HELP STAR-FLEET AGAINST THE DOMINION...
BUT AT LEAST THEY WON'T BE FIGHTING ***AGAINST*** US.
I SUSPECT WE HAVEN'T SEEN THE FULL EXTENT OF THE DAMAGE THEY DID TO THEMSELVES.
AFTER THE SHAME OF DEFEAT, THEY SEEM TO BE FINDING NEW STRENGTH IN COOPERATION.

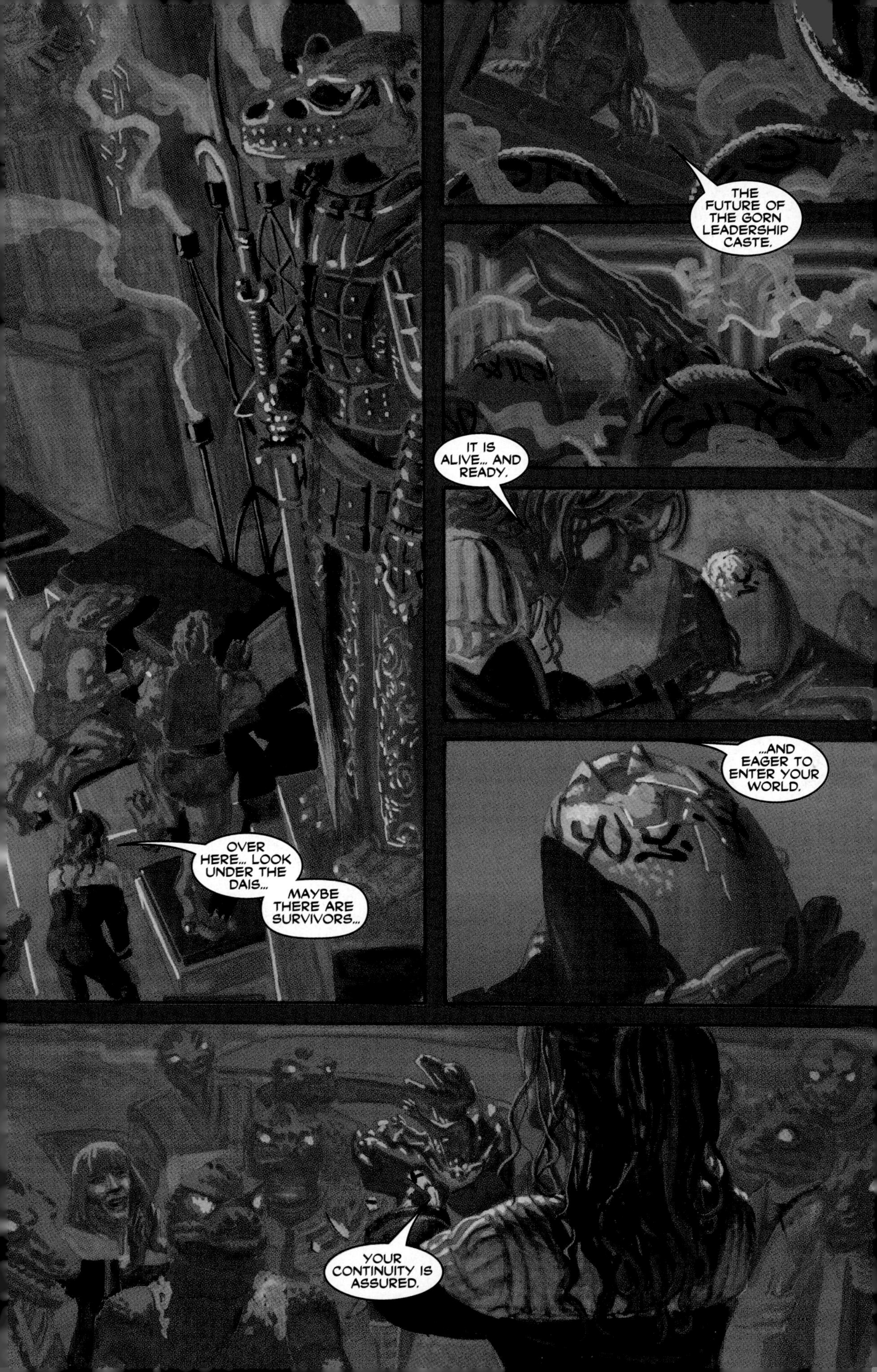
OVER HERE... LOOK UNDER THE DAIS...
MAYBE THERE ARE SURVIVORS...
THE FUTURE OF THE GORN LEADERSHIP CASTE.
IT IS ALIVE... AND READY.
...AND EAGER TO ENTER YOUR WORLD.
YOUR CONTINUITY IS ASSURED.

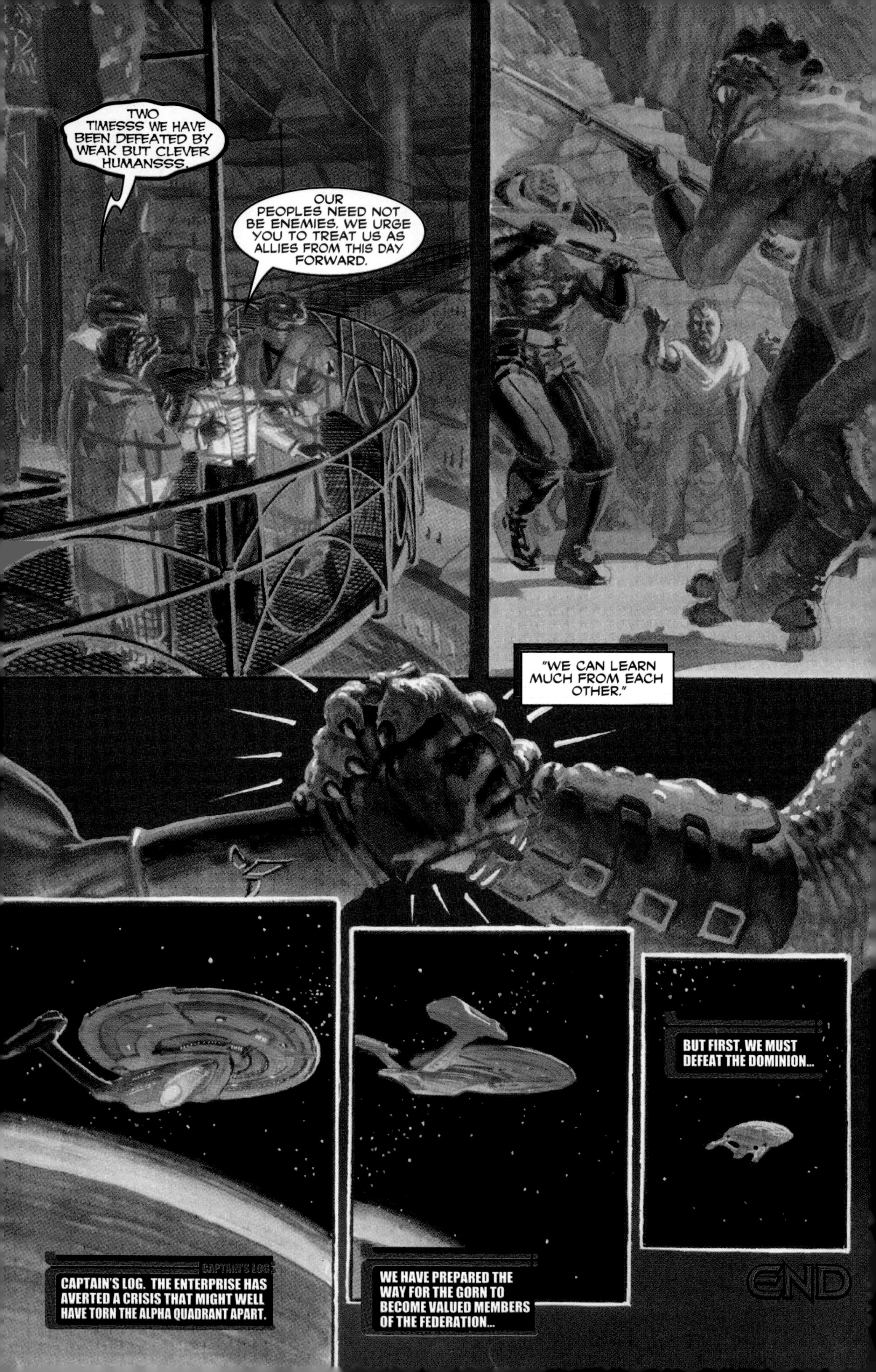
TWO TIMESSS WE HAVE BEEN DEFEATED BY WEAK BUT CLEVER HUMANSSS.
OUR PEOPLES NEED NOT BE ENEMIES. WE URGE YOU TO TREAT US AS ALLIES FROM THIS DAY FORWARD.
"WE CAN LEARN MUCH FROM EACH OTHER."
CAPTAIN'S LOG
CAPTAIN'S LOG. THE ENTERPRISE HAS AVERTED A CRISIS THAT MIGHT WELL HAVE TORN THE ALPHA QUADRANT APART.
WE HAVE PREPARED THE WAY FOR THE GORN TO BECOME VALUED MEMBERS OF THE FEDERATION...
BUT FIRST, WE MUST DEFEAT THE DOMINION...
END

THE GORN DOSSIER

By Igor Kordey: Federation Anthropologist

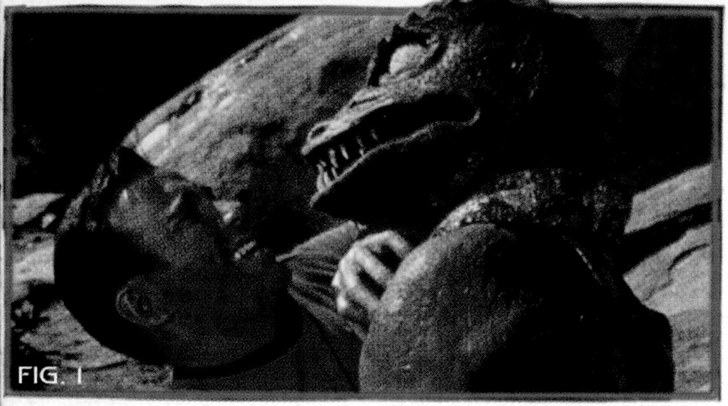

FIG. 1

Well, in the beginning it was this creature fighting Captain Kirk — Star Trek episode "Arena," 1967 (Fig.1). Extremely powerful but very slow, hard-breathing, dressed in a glitter miniskirt, looking like a human wearing a Mardi Gras mask. Okay, he's a lizard. Lizards are slow when their environment is too cold. Maybe he has a problem with air density. Maybe . . . hmm . . .

For this book, I wanted a really mean creature, a real opponent to the guys from the Enterprise, so when I got permission to redesign the Gorn, I started from the very infrastructure. (See Fig. 2)

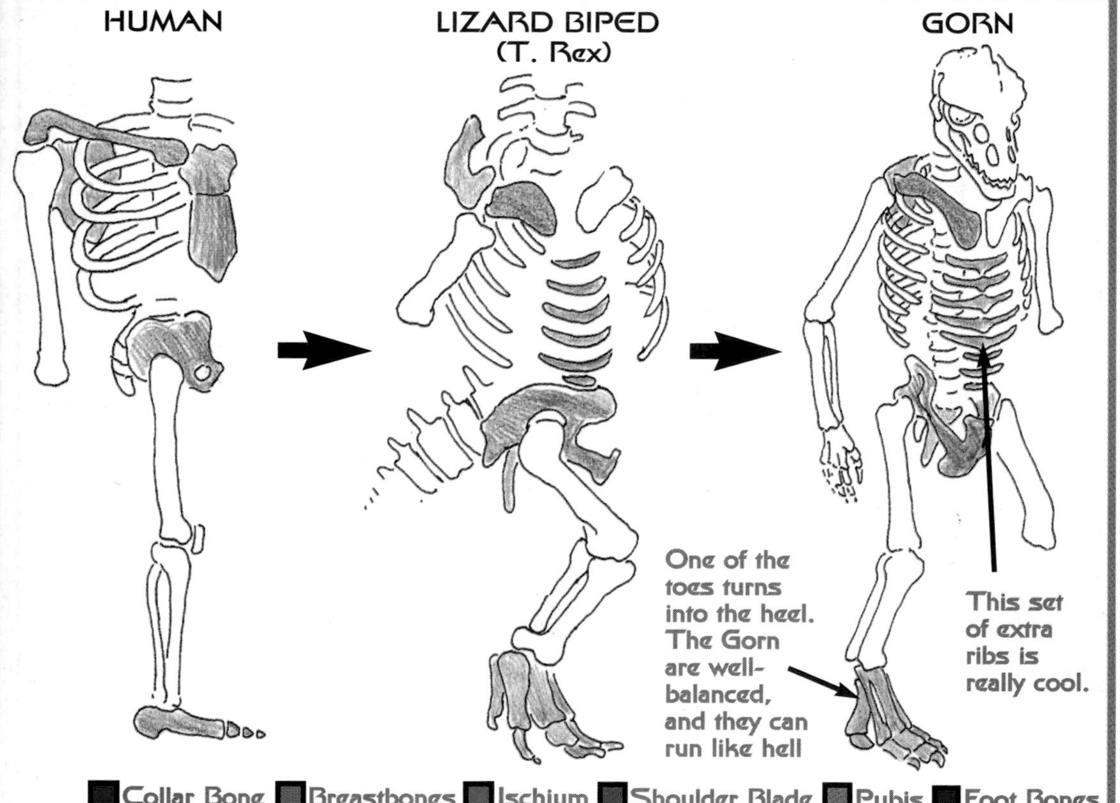
HUMAN
LIZARD BIPED (T. Rex)
GORN
One of the toes turns into the heel. The Gorn are well-balanced, and they can run like hell
This set of extra ribs is really cool.
Collar Bone
Breastbones
Ischium
Shoulder Blade
Pubis
Foot Bones

FIG. 2

Gorns breathe air, Gorns like it hot, so what is their ideal environment? Their planet is a big desert with huge mountains.

They prefer to live in big caves made by volcanoes (better if the volcanoes are still active). Volcanic heat and gases provide them with energy of all kinds. Their need for water is small — they use condensate moisture from the underground caves.

Because of their extra bones, Gorns have problems sitting. But they can kneel or squat or lie as long as necessary.

Gorn skull capacity leaves space for a large brain. The back (instinct) area is larger than in humans. (Fig. 3)

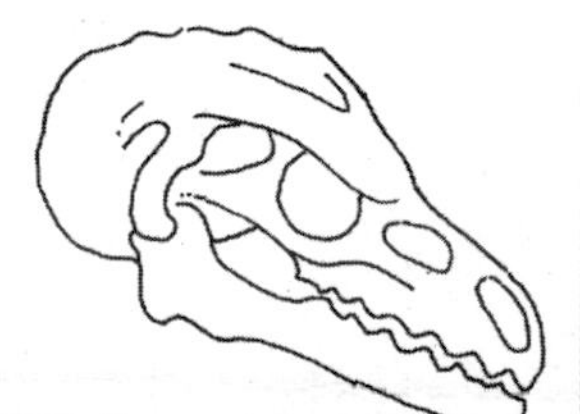

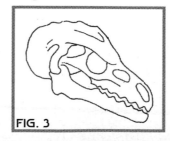

FIG. 3

Clan and status signs are a combination of sophisticated geometrical shapes and colors. There is no blue in the Gorn scale because they don't recognize blue.

More important clan = more perfect shape (Figs. 4 & 5). On the other hand, the older the clan, the simpler the sign.

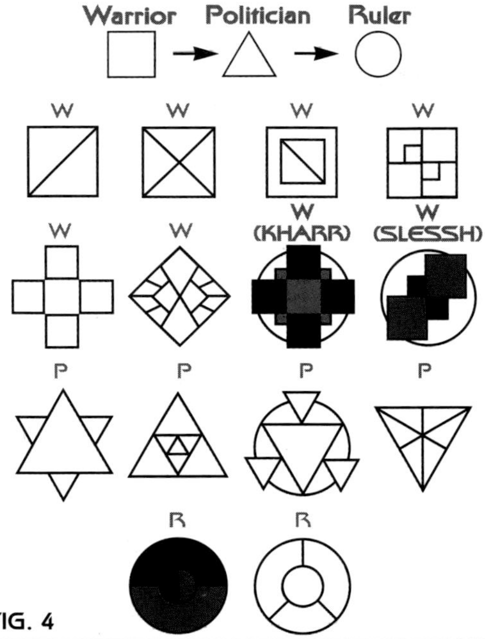
Warrior
Politician
Ruler
W
W
W
W
W
W
W
(KHARR)
W
(SLESSH)
P
P
P
P
R
R
FIG. 4

Now it's easy to reach the conclusion that both Khaar and Slessh came from ruling military families.

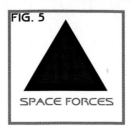

FIG. 5
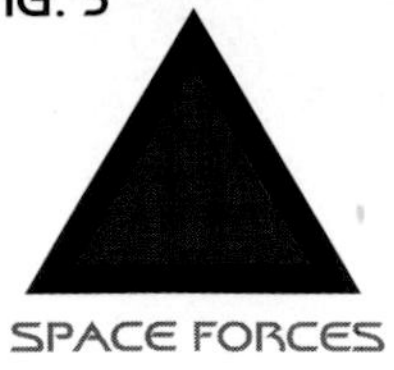
SPACE FORCES

FIG. 6
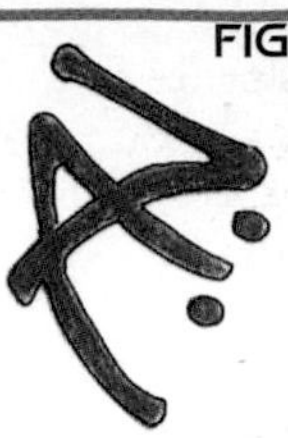

"Black Crests" sign is a pictograph (FIG. 6).

The Gorn walk around in clothes. They developed their fashions for practical reasons first and foremost. They are warriors. They need protection from weapons, and since they prefer combat at close range, their armor is designed to tangle or snag an opponent's sword or spear.

As you've seen in the book, they fancy bright colors. The reason for this is their vision. As with most lizards and frogs, they react to bright colors. Yes, they can smell each other, but this is kind of tricky because of the way their society is organized. They have enormous communes, divided by families (clans) and castes (1. warriors, 2. politicians and bureaucrats, 3. The rest). These are the three largest groups, divided again by a number of subcastes. So let's dress this guy up: (FIG.7)

The elite warriors like to keep it very traditional. Every piece of their uniform is handmade and unique. Mass production is for lower classes (see paratroopers on Cestus III).

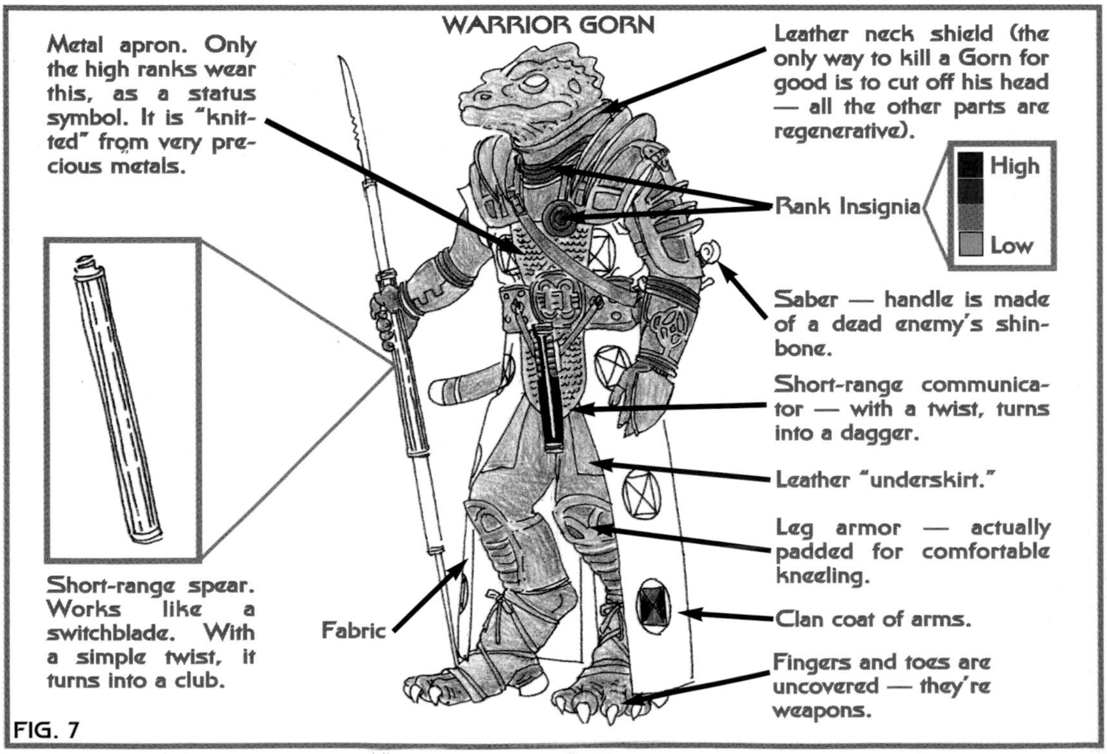
WARRIOR GORN
Metal apron. Only the high ranks wear this, as a status symbol. It is "knitted" from very precious metals.
Short-range spear. Works like a switchblade. With a simple twist, it turns into a club.
Fabric
Leather neck shield (the only way to kill a Gorn for good is to cut off his head — all the other parts are regenerative).
Rank Insignia
High
Low
Saber — handle is made of a dead enemy's shinbone.
Short-range communicator — with a twist, turns into a dagger.
Leather "underskirt."
Leg armor — actually padded for comfortable kneeling.
Clan coat of arms.
Fingers and toes are uncovered — they're weapons.
FIG. 7

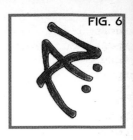

In the beginning of the book you'll notice similar pictographs on the eggs (protective spells). They developed from an ancient (the Gorn are a very ancient society) pictograph system shown in the Gorn Chamber Room (carved on the walls behind the skeletons*). The transition is shown on the big chandelier behind the throne and the chamber room doors. Each one represents a single sacred word with an egg symbol in the center. The egg represents the source of life and the center of the universe.(FIG. 8)

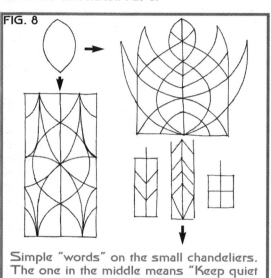

FIG. 8

Simple "words" on the small chandeliers. The one in the middle means "Keep quiet if you don't have anything smart to say."

These artifacts tell us about the highest level of cultural development of Gorn society, their industrial achievements, and their sophisticated art.

Gorn are top metallurgists, known all around the universe for their skills. The rank-rings around their arms and necks, for example, are made of a light, phosphorescent alloy — one more consequence of their weak eye-sight and gloomy environment. Metal plays a big part in their architecture as well. Their basic buildings were made generations ago, carved from rock and giant stalactites.

All later development is made of metal: bridges, roads, terraces, elevators, etc. Their main energy comes from electricity and gases (volcanic heat and lava give them endless sources of both). As you can see in the book, they use different systems of monorails (electric and based on magnets). To the casual viewer, their cities look like a 19th-century industrial nightmare, but closer examination reveals considerable thought and highly economical reasons for building the way they have.

The Gorn system of governing is evident in the Chamber Room: (FIG. 9)

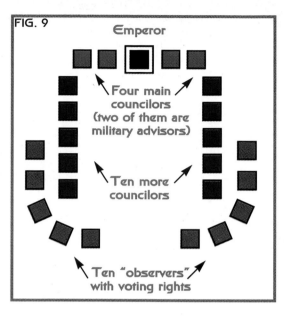

FIG. 9

Emperor

Four main councilors (two of them are military advisors)

Ten more councilors

Ten "observers" with voting rights

Altogether, twenty-five**. And, of course, the Emperor decides about everything, giving his vote to one side or the other.

The Gorn's favorite entertainment is theater, especially comedy. They can laugh, but their sense of humor is highly incompatible with ours. The sound laughing Gorns produce with their throatbag is a deafening roar. The Gorn also talk very loud.

FIG. 10

And of course, the Gorn are not the only intelligent race on their planet. In the North is a small, swampy area where we can find their relatives with telepathic abilities . . . But I'll tell you that story another time!

---

*These are actual preserved skeletons of important and heroic Gorns from Gorn history
**25 is the Gorn's sacred number.